Fiction by T. Allen Winn

Trudy Wagner Detective Thrillers

Road Rage

North of the Border

The Bully Series

Dark Thirty

Memoir by T. Allen Winn

The Caregiver's Son,
Outside the Window Looking In

*The oldest and strongest emotion of
mankind is fear,
and the oldest and strongest
kind of fear is
fear of the unknown.*

- H. P. Lovecraft

T. Allen Winn's

THE PERFECT SPOOK HOUSE

Pp

PROSEPRESS

www.prosepress.biz

The Perfect Spook House
Copyright © 2014
T. Allen Winn

Comments:
Contact T. Allen Winn
TALLENWINN@mail.com, and T. Allen Winn's Face Book

The perfect Spook House is a fictional novel. Any reference to real people or historical events or places is coincidental. All places are used fictitiously and the author's imagination has shaped them to fit the story.

ISBN: 978-1-941069-14-1

Published by ProsePress
75 Red Maple Drive,
Pawleys Island, South Carolina 29585

www.Prosepress.biz
proseNcons@live.com

ACKNOWLEDGEMENTS

Danny Singleton, always good to have a kicking, screaming and willing friend to see things through and keep you on the right track.

My home town used as a backdrop in this totally fictitious tale, provided me with the perfect nostalgic moments. Any similarities to actual incidences or people are purely accidental and I won't tell if you don't.

Thanks to the new friendships made at the beach, especially those sprouting from the Beach Author Network; authors promoting their goods and sharing their pain and gains along the way. Support means the world.

Halloween, perhaps my favorite holiday, building those spook houses with cousins and friends was a large part of my youthful bliss; Night of the Monsters, a Super 8 Classic does exist…I applaud those young budding stars.

*Heel to Toe...
Hold the Line*

1

The proceeds were tallied, and the Haunted House had brought in more cash than the school's other jamboree venues combined. All of our hard work had been rewarded. Now would come the fun part, dismantling our hard work. I had not built a Spook House in more than twenty years, not since that awful Halloween event had ruined my favorite holiday, but I hadn't lost my touch.

"Great job, Payne," greeted the jamboree chairman, an eye catching, hard bodied vice principal. "The committee can't thank you enough for volunteering this year. You succeeded in breaking last year's jamboree record for the school. You clearly doubled 1986's event"

She eyed me head to toe, as if sizing me up for something more than just being the best spook house builder around. Me, standing an even six feet tall and one hundred eighty pounds, jet black wavy hair, haunting brown eyes and an almost olive complexion underneath a thick beard, there was no mistaking her look. I was too old to stay after school and clean the chalk boards. I wondered what she had in mind. She knew me as the only photographer for the town's newspaper, but didn't realize how badly I actually aspired to be more; hungered to be a writer, a journalist. Thus far that opportunity had not arisen.

"Hey, glad I could do it," I tried to answer modestly,

while attempting to conceal my ever swelling ego, or that's what I called it.

"Nice touch with the fortune telling routine," added Madam Chairman. "The kids really got a kick out of those voices from beyond."

"Cassandra and I certainly enjoyed scaring the crap out of the paying customers. She's such a natural at it too." Did I just say, crap? I guess I could have said worse.

Cassandra Blake certainly looked the part of a gypsy. She wore a black wig that hung just below her shoulders. Her skin was as dark, very tanned, but smooth and unblemished. She wore a lot of eye shadow and bright red lipstick. She had the sex appeal and allure of Trish Gomez from the Adam's Family sitcom. Cassandra, in a long black gypsy style dress and sleek high heeled boots, hair in a red scarf, tons of bracelets and rings adorning her wrist and fingers, certainly pulled off her character perfectly.

After shutting down our little Spook House, located in one of two portable double wide buildings outside the main brick structure, I had stayed in costume and roamed the hallways, wrecking havoc with the kids still enjoying the jamboree. My homemade costume, a cross between the Frankenstein Monster and a mad scientist, worked its magic. No one had a clue of my identity.

Cassandra had been operating a fortune telling booth in one of the class rooms at the end of the hallway. I joined her, and I had hidden behind a curtain, providing various voices from the dead when she asked questions while gazing in her crystal ball. We definitely mesmerized the unsuspecting kiddies, and oh yes, we did scare the crap out of them.

"I should be able to restore your building to a class room before I leave, all except for the coffin," I informed the getting better looking by the minute chairman, now displaying duel head lights. Either she had become chilled, or she was mighty glad to see me. It didn't feel cold in here, and I do sort of grow on people.

"Where did you come up with that coffin?"

"My pal, Night Train has a friend who owns a funeral home. Train and DABO-DOO will pick it up Sunday. I'm sure you've heard them on the local radio station. Train has used it as a prop for one the Opera House plays. He's a little twisted like me. DABO-DOO is his radio sidekick and partner in crime on their program. They're on week nights, midnight to six."

"I have heard them a time or two, and I must say, they are a strange duo, and are very laid back, improvise a lot don't they?"

"That would be them, hams at heart, but friends that never let you down."

"How did you become friends?"

"I'm not sure I'm ready to share my dirty little secrets with you. They might not appreciate me airing the dirty laundry to strangers."

"I suppose I'll have to upgrade my status, won't I?"

"Uh, yeah, maybe one day I can share it with you. Anyway, they'll pick it up Sunday. You must admit it is quite an authentic looking old casket. It resembles one of those straight out of a Count Dracula flick. My old buddy Barry made a great blued eyed and blonde haired vampire, didn't he?"

"He sure had the timing and theatrics down, rising from the coffin on your cue, screaming and herding those kids for the exit. That was a nice touch," she said, now placing her hand on my arm, and giving it a little affectionate squeeze.

Yep, she was glad to see me all right. I was now convinced of that. She was definitely hitting on me. It looked like I might be getting a Halloween treat after all, no tricks tonight.

"I see you're still here Mister Evil Spirit."

Turning, I saw Cassandra standing behind me, more gorgeous than ever. My mind raced, leaving my lustful thoughts of the madam Chairman in its wake. Cassandra had removed her wig and now sported her short cropped reddish hair. She still looked lovely but not quite like the fortune teller from earlier. We had known each other from several years ago. I had met her while in high school. We had crossed paths on the town square at a fall festival in 1968. We didn't go to the same school but had both been juniors when we had become friends. She was from Due West, a few miles up the road, but in Abbeville County.

Back in the day I had thought about asking her out, but then Halloween arrived and changed everything. Cassandra was a friend of one of the organizers. I had been taken by surprise seeing her here. I thought back to better days, before that night that changed my life. I had seen her from time to time, a passing moment here or there over the years, but this felt different. Look at me! I'm such a dog, lusting left and right. It's late and I'm spooked out possibly, and not thinking too clearly.

"Let me go take care of some house keeping chores," advised Madam Chairman, rubbing her hand gently down my back. "Please come see me before you leave."

"Will do," I answered, seeing the obvious desire in her eyes, or maybe just wishful thinking on my part.

"I was concerned this might bring it all back up for you again," said Cassandra, in a genuine caring tone, after my treat had gotten out of hearing range. "You know I've always believed what you said happened, even when others didn't. I'd like to hear the entire story sometime, if you ever care to share it."

Everyone surely wanted to know my little secrets tonight. "I'm okay with it. Thank you for believing. I can't change it by dwelling on it. I'd love to make it end differently, but I know what's done is done. I certainly can't help it if others don't want to accept what happened. Sometimes that is hard for me to swallow. Many of the town folks were pretty harsh." I avoided the invite, not willing to dig too deeply and open fresh wounds.

"Do you ever ride by there?"

"I used to, but...well I guess I can tell you. Every time I drove by, I felt like something was beckoning me to return to that house. I don't know how to explain it, but it tugged at me. It gave me the impression that whatever it was, might be trying to take control of the wheel. I guess I still wanted answers, but not bad enough to pull in that drive. Sounds weird, doesn't it?"

"Stay away from there, Payne. Don't ever drive by there again. Pure evil thrives on that property, and it will devour your soul."

"You're serious, aren't you? This isn't that wild gipsy act, is it?"

"I can connect to my gipsy persona in ways. I sort of have this uncanny sense when it comes to the unknown and unexplained, almost a curse sometimes."

"And I always just thought you were superstitious." What did I really known about the real Cassandra Blake. We had only been friends briefly before that October night.

"I am indeed. I shouldn't be prying into your business."

"Don't worry, I didn't judge them and I'm not judging you now. We all have things that bother us. Look at me. I should know."

"Thanks for understanding," she said, melting me with those killer gypsy eyes. "Have you talked to any of the others lately, those that were with you that night?"

"I see Shorty every week. We bowl in a league in Greenwood. His brother Brody used to bowl with us, but he dropped out for personal reasons."

"Does Shorty ever talk about it?"

"None of us talk about it, if we can help it."

"I saw that Stan Bronson a couple of weeks ago," she continued relentlessly, determined to force this conversation down a path I was not willing to go. "He was three sheets in the wind, at least two twelve packs beyond oblivion, I think they call it. That poor guy has just about become the town drunk."

She could certainly talk my language. I nodded, "He's had a tough go of it."

"He never got over that night, is what I suspect," she diagnosed his problem dead on, but I didn't acknowledge she had been right. "Peter seems to have fared better. He has his own landscape business over in Hartwell, but he too has had a bumpy road to put the past where it belongs, so I hear."

I nodded, but really didn't need this. Before she had an opportunity to work her way down the whole list, I excused myself, saying I had to dismantle the spook house

"Sorry, I would help," she said and meant it, "but I have an early appointment in the morning. I still have to drive back to Due West. You need to drop by and let me give you a massage, on the house of course."

She operated her own spa and massages were on the menu. Boy, how I knew I would love that. "I'll hold you to it. Be careful driving home. Watch out for those deer." The drive on rural roads this time of night was prone to deer and automobile encounters. The automobiles seldom won the chance meetings.

She had really worked me up. I could hardly get my mind off that night. I regretted that I rarely ever saw or spoke to those once inseparable friends. A chill ran down my spine and I shivered. I had not felt like this in months. I didn't want to either.

If I left the school right now, all I would have to do is take one right turn and I could be there in less than fifteen, maybe twenty minutes. I visualized that drive, every curve, every landmark, including Parson's Mountain; Little Mountain is what we called it, our old swimming hole, and just like that, I would be at that old house. I tried to shake the urge to return. I occupied my mind with cleaning up the aftermath left by the spook house patrons. Why was this happening again now? I didn't invite the stroll down memory lane.

Just over an hour later, I leaned against my old Chevy pick-up truck, drinking a nightcap. Chasing it with a Pepsi, I sipped on a freshly opened fifth of Jim Beam, one that I had retrieved from behind the seat. The warm bourbon hit the spot. I wrestled with should I heed Cassandra's warning or should I say what the hell and face my demons? Before I could decide, I heard foot steps on the gravel behind me. For a fleeting second, I thought my demons had sought me out.

"I see you must have called it a night. What have you got there?"

It wasn't a demon and it wasn't Cassandra Blake this time. "Madam Chairman, you're still here?" Now looking like a devil in her short, slinky, red satin dress, one she had not been sporting during the jamboree, I suddenly felt like a bad boy in need of a paddling.

"You did ask me to see you before I left and I see you just fine." I tried to be as sexy as possible in my dripping wet, sweaty clothes, and then I took another quick pull from old Jim.

"Care to share?" She reached for the bottle and me at the same time. "And you may call me Francis."

Guess I wouldn't be making that right turn after all tonight. The demon hunting had been placed on hold. Things happen for a reason and for me, it was all good tonight. Francis, it seemed appropriate. It beat Madam Chairman, a mouthful to spit out.

2

Thank goodness, it was Sunday morning and not a work day. I could now cross one fantasy off my wish list. I had made wild, nasty love last night in my original first grade class room with an assistant principal. The Madam Chairman, Francis married and with four kids, had fulfilled quite a few fantasies of her own, I am pleased to say. Thank you Francis, I sighed, and then I propped up in my own bed, alone.

And to think, I had received a hand paddling with a ruler in that very same room, my very first day in the first grade, for kissing a girl on the lips while climbing on the monkey bars. Actually every boy in the first grade had gotten their hands whacked because the snitches wouldn't ID me, and I wouldn't confess. I wonder what punishment the class would get for me screwing the vice principle on the teacher's desk. Thank goodness there were no snitches last night, but we did monkey around.

Participating in the Halloween jamboree, guiding those kids through the various themed rooms, had certainly unleashed a flood of memories and fare share of emotions. The worst of times ran rampant in my little pea brain. I couldn't help but break into a grin, thinking of that very first Spook House we had built.

It was 1965 and our first year of being too old to participate as trick or treaters. Not to be outdone, my buddies and I schemed up a little plan to overcome our sweet tooth for the candy. We decided to build a spook house. I had the perfect place, our attic.

I hoped my folks would share my sentiments.

Using my patented puppy dog look and whining just a tad, I managed to con or should I say, convince my Mom into allowing us to have the spook house. She had to persuade dad. The dominos fell flawlessly. We were on our way. After recruiting my ghoulish crew, tapping in on my imagination and acquiring a few props, we were well on our way to creating the perfect spook house and our potential Halloween goldmine.

The attic, the full length of the house and floored fourteen feet wide, would serve as our stage for the ultimate haunted experience. As bad as I am trying, I can't keep my thoughts off the Cedar Springs road and that other Halloween night. There were no treats, but the night was loaded with plenty of dark tricks.

Focus on my trip down the good memory lane, I keep telling myself. My Mom used the attic as a place to hang freshly washed clothes when the weather didn't permit hanging them outdoors to dry. Dad had strung two wire lines the full length, perfect for hanging the tarps that would separate our ghoulish themed rooms.

I just remembered those eleven rooms in the Frazier-Pressley House, down on the Cedar Springs Road, and I received my second chill in less than eight hours. Too bad the wild woman in red, Francis and I had finished off that bottle of Jim Beam in the wee hours. I don't normally drink bourbon to kick start my mornings, but this particular morning doesn't feel very normal.

My three pals were up for the task of building the best spook house to ever have been built. Actually it would be the first to be constructed in the neighborhood. Our legacy awaited us.

"Charley, make sure that tarp is fastened real good," I barked orders, like a ring master. "And Stephen, how are you coming with that stuffed dummy?"

"Well it won't pass close inspection," he told me. "Those rags make it sort of lumpy in the arms and legs, but I suppose it will have to do."

"It'll be dark up here, and you'll keep them busy, mister werewolf, so they shouldn't notice." Stephen had selected the wolf man mask with matching hairy gloves.

"What about me?" asked Charley's little brother, Cody, five

years younger.

"Knuckle head, mama will be taking you trick or treating, remember?"

"But I want to be a monster with you, right here."

"No can do," replied Charley. "Enjoy while you can. That's what we would be doing if we hadn't gotten too big. Now you need to head to the house. It's about your bedtime."

"Shucks, ya'll get to do all the good stuff," fussed Cody, stepping backwards, ascending the pull down stairway, the only access to the attic from the narrow hallway below.

Fun stuff, I thought. Fun would wear out its welcome in just three short years from then. I just didn't know it. I wish I didn't know it now. Spook houses can be real. No one knows that more than me, or the rest of the gang.

Charley, a head and a half taller than Stephen and I, and sixty five pounds heavier, much bigger for his age, had dressed as a sword carrying Cyclops. The rubber mask covered his head. Stephen touched off his costume with a brown fur, zip out liner from his trench coat. Wearing it backwards with an open shirt gave it the look of one very hairy animal chest. We were so innovative back then.

We had other props, snakes, bats, a couple of costumed dummies and such. I stepped up to the plate, my best acting gig, and performed as the haunt's tour guide. I so relished my role. Being the tour guide offered me the opportunity to witness everyone's reactions.

Our attic spook-tacular didn't bring in nearly the amount of money or candy we had envisioned but, the twenty or so kids that did fork over their candy or a quarter for the admission price got their money's worth. Many climbed up those retractable stairs several times.

That would be our last event in that attic after mom found out her den had been transformed into a waiting room full of kids, many of them strangers to our neighborhood. She didn't take kindly to the aspect of strangers being left unattended in her household.

Before we tore down our spook house and returned the attic to normal, we used my super 8 mm movie camera to film our first major film production, entitled Night of the Monsters. It wasn't a Stephen Spielberg master piece, but I still have it, and show it to friends and family occasionally. It's cheesy and corny to say the least, but I like it.

I would have given anything to have had the super 8 along that night nearly twenty years ago. Capturing the events would have possibly made believers out of the many naysayers, especially those taking pot shots at me. Bad things happened that night. I, more than anyone, was blamed for them. Many town folks still hold me accountable. The phone rang, jolting me from my little stroll down memory lane. Answering it, I recognized the voice on the other end. "Good morning, Cassandra."

"I just felt this need to call and check on you Payne," she told me in a voice that sent a different kind of feeling through my bones. "You doing okay?"

"I'm just fine as frog hair. You're not having one of your premonitions, are you?"

"Just an uneasy feeling... you do know its Halloween next Friday."

She had a sexy phone voice. She could have made a fortune taking calls for one of those late night x-rated hot lines. I would never tell her that though, and I never use them personally. "Yep, it comes every year about this time," I answered in my typical sarcastic manner.

"What are you doing Halloween night?"

"Nothing special, I'm too old to go trick or treating. I'll probably be photographing the Boo-fest on the Square. The merchants always give out candy to the trick or treaters, starting about five o'clock. The newspaper expects me to take plenty of photos. It is my job after all. Why do you ask?"

The phone remained silent for several seconds before she answered. "I was going to invite you up for supper, if you weren't doing anything special."

I paused this time, unsure what to make of her invite. Her sixth sense kicked in, and she blurted out, "I've been divorced for over two years. I didn't know if you knew that or not. Sometimes things don't work out and you have to just move on, but I guess you've been there too, haven't you?"

The room swirled with that revelation. I didn't have one of my smartass come backs for once. "Can you give me a rain check? I really do have to work. Can we make it Saturday night instead?"

I interpreted the long pause meaning I had disappointed her. Before I could back peddle she said, "Saturday will be fine. I look forward to it. You take care until then. Call me if you need a shoulder. I mean it."

"It's a date. Thanks for the shoulder and the invite."

After she hung up the phone, I sat there dazed and excited. I was giddy like a school boy and that was just plain silly. I don't know what prompted me to go digging for my old high school annuals, but I did. I glanced at the clock; it was eleven, the morning almost gone.

I opened the closet in the hallway and began dragging out dilapidated cardboard boxes, bits and pieces of my past. I spotted the one marked high school stuff and began sliding it out, when another one caught my eye. It was my stash of old super 8 home movies. I grabbed it instead. Rummaging through the box, I found what I must have been looking for, a single 50 foot reel of film, marked *Night of the Monsters* on its blue plastic oval cover.

I held it in my hand, rotating it and still thinking. I had a lightening flashback of Stan's face. I saw clear as day the fear portrayed on it. I dropped the reel to the floor. The plush shag carpet cushioned the fall. I could relate to why Stan had turned into a lush. I certainly drank more than I should. Unlike him, I realized it didn't help me outrun the demons from that night, or did it?

I dug a little deeper in the closet until I found my still functional super 8 projector. I positioned the projector on the den's coffee table, opting to use the wall instead of the projector screen.

I decided to have a batch of Jiffy Pop to set the stage for my movie experience. Nothing beats having popcorn for breakfast or in this case, brunch. I so enjoyed shaking that ingenious all in one pan with a handle covered in foil, and watching the foil expand until the kernels were miraculously transformed into full blown crunching popcorn. Add a little salt, pepper and butter and I was at the movies. Well. Possibly movie goers don't use pepper.

Watching the antics of us portraying the likes of the mad

doctor, the werewolf, the ghoul and the Cyclops, caused wonderful goose bumps. Unfortunately our amateurish attempt at a horror flick couldn't divert my thoughts from real monsters. That night from so long ago had begun chipping away at my soul once again, and I didn't like it. Sadly, I couldn't stop it either. Hindsight, I should have probably taken up Cassandra on the Halloween supper invite.

Munching on popcorn, I remembered the next spook house we had built. Thinking about it helped force the Cedar Springs house from my thoughts. That second one was in our cinder block, one car garage. We had learned from our attic fiasco, and we had made creative changes. Improved staging of our old props and better use of our new ones, transformed it into a cash cow this time. It turned out we had established a reputation from last year's one.

We had curtained off the one car garage, making four uniquely themed rooms. Stepping into the entrance, our adventurers would first have to cross a bridge, actually an old sturdy wooden door supported by two levels of cinder blocks. In the pit below were a couple of dozen snakes, all rubber of course. Dry ice caused a floor hugging fog and dad's rotating multicolored light used for our silver Christmas tree, added a nice eerie touch.

Next, through a narrow passage way would be our best illusion. Using one of my dad's old army uniforms we had found in his duffle bag in the attic, we had made our best realistic dummy ever, Mister Cyclops. Dad would later be pissed when he discovered we had rummaged through his old army duffle bag from Korea. I had used them without his permission. Asking forgiveness is often easier than asking permission.

We strategically hung Mister Cyclops from the ceiling and wall using my bulldog's dog chains, to portray the creature as a captive one. Close quarters would ensure the haunt's tourist could barely slip pass him, while heading to the next room.

Knowing we were assured of having repeat visits from our horde of monster hunters, we staged a surprise for them on every other visit or so. Charley, wearing a matching army uniform substituted for the Cyclops dummy. He scarred many of our peers to the point of almost crapping in their britches. Each new visit, they weren't sure if the one eyed monster was Memorex or the real deal.

Following that theme, every other tour or so, I took my would-be victims around the back of the garage where the Cyclops would jump off the garage roof. Charlie would send them running for the hills. One rather robust big boned neighborhood kid nick named Beulah, fell to his knees, tears running down his cheeks, begging for mercy. It was priceless.

Closing out the other rooms was Stephen as the werewolf, me as a machete carrying doctor in the mad scientist lab. Our friend Darrel had been recruited to pose as a long, stringy, white, haired freaky and disfigured tour guide. I had opted to perform instead of being the guide.

We could have used a guide that night in that old house on Cedar Springs Road and an exorcist, a paranormal expert, a medium or even a super hero. We had been out of our element and knew it from the get go. There were no staged stuffed dummies lurking anywhere inside. The only dummies in that house had been us. What had we been thinking? Too young, damn near stupid and self proclaimed bullet proof, and undoubtedly unbelievers, we hadn't been thinking at all. We never did back then.

Enough of that other night, I tried to focus on the make-believe spook house instead. We had established a well deserved reputation for theatrics from last year's attic side show. Kids had assembled outside even before dark. Many had ventured from other side of town, just to check us out. Some of those same people avoid me like the plague now. That other Halloween night in the old Cedar Spring's house has forever changed my life and their opinion of me.

Back to good memories, needless to say, we cleaned house that night, relieving our little trick or treaters of most of their collected candy and cash to boot. We wound up with two paper grocery bags overflowing with an assortment of goodies and over twenty bucks in collected fees. Life was good.

The only blemish on our record had come at the hands of the monsters inside carrying things just a tad too far. A girl, a couple of years older than us and built like a 4th of July fire cracker, decided to take the tour. Monsters, real or make believe, have no scruples. We sort of took advantage of the situation and copped a few feels from our victim.

Boy was she furious with us. We claimed it was accidental, while secretly high fiving one another. She knew better. We held our breath, expecting her to tell her parents. She didn't. We avoided eye contact with her at school for weeks, but we sure did bask in the glory of our conquest. That was the first time we had ever felt real tits. It wouldn't be the last for most of us.

Fantasy and erotic dreams can carry kids just so far. Waking up in the middle of the night with those boyish erections would soon be replaced by night sweats and screams. There would be nothing satisfying about it. Terror would reach new heights in the mind of someone who thrived on horror movies. I would become a believer in the unknown and it would forever haunt my life and the lives of my partners in crime.

3

The flapping of the film's end against the projector jolted me back to the present. I threaded the reel and rewound Night of the Monsters, before taking a well deserved piss to relieve my aching bladder.

Standing in from of the toilet, I suddenly remembered that night, making that piss stop, just outside the old cabin, next to the main house. A shiver ran down my spine. I should have never gone back inside the house, but his screams beckoned me to his rescue. I had failed to accomplish my goal. I was no rescue ranger by a long shot.

I had a fleeting memory of my ex-wife. It seemed odd to think about her now. Depositing it back in my pants, I wondered why we had really gotten divorced. We had been so in love and sex had always been good. I had certainly enjoyed it. Maybe she felt differently. That night kept creeping back into our lives and hadn't helped. She finally had had enough of it I suppose, and moved on and never looked back, nor did I. I had not been in a serious relationship since we parted ways, almost a year ago. It's much easier, not getting attached to anyone.

I stood before the mirror, washing my hands and almost didn't recognize the haggard looking face staring back at me. I certainly hadn't looked this bad yesterday, had I? My usual boyish qualities appeared too mature for my liking. Where did I get those crows feet?

Black circles under my blood shot brown eyes set the stage

for an almost pale complexion. I never ever looked pale, even after puking my guts out after an all night drinking binge. My olive complexion had always given me a tanned look, an Indian quality, causing many people to try and guess my nationality. I was 100% home grown southerner and proud of it.

I rubbed my belly, sucking it in, and then letting it out. It appeared a little pudgy around the middle, but a long way from being a spare tire, more like love handles. I raked my hands through my thick black hair. It certainly felt oily and in need of a wash and trim.

That night had done this to me as surely as I stand here. It was gnawing at me, attempting to reclaim me again. I had worked vigorously to distance myself from it. Yet, it tugged at me, tormented me, and it had hooked me like a fish, trying to reel me in. I fought the pull. I really needed to talk to someone. I thought of Cassandra's offer, and then the phone rang.

"Shorty, your timing is impeccable," I said, my voice cracking up and feeling like the air going out of a balloon.

"What's up, Dude?" He paused, and then asked, "Its happening again isn't it? I can tell."

"You known me too well old buddy. Can you come over this afternoon?"

"It will have to be after five. The old lady has me lassoed into FFF with the in-laws, and you know how I hate forced family fun."

"Cocktail hour, perfect," I told him. "Try to act civil for your forced family fun activity. And if you tire of Kim, I'll be glad to take her off your hands, no questions asked."

"She would probably love that as much as you, Mister Stud Muffin. She always had the hots for you back in high school. She just settled for me, when you ignored her stalking."

"And me, with the hots for you," I egged him on. "Just get here as soon as you can sneak off, okay."

"It sounds like you need something a little more potent than a shot of bourbon. I have this dime bag, real good reefer. I'll bring it, and roll us a couple, and then we can reflect on what if. You might just get lucky."

"Once you've had me, you won't ever go back to her," I said in my sexiest put on gay voice. Straight guys make terrible queer impersonators. We tend to over do the stereotyping.

"Watch what you wish far, Dick Head," he rebutted, in a similar lisping voice. "Seriously, you hang loose and don't do anything stupid without me."

"Hey, you're the king of stupid. Why would I start without you?"

"You know all the right things to say, don't you big boy. I'll be there as soon as I can weasel a kitchen pass."

I hung up the phone, relieved to know the Calvary was on the way, even if I had five hours to fend off the onslaught, before he arrived. I returned to the closet. I dragged out the box marked High School Stuff. Apparently I had slipped firmly into the grasp of a nostalgic Sunday afternoon, ready or not.

I normally don't spend Sunday afternoons at home alone or even at home at all, if I can find something better to do. Today, the past had a strangle hold on me, so abnormal conditions ran rampant. A sunny October afternoon in my little hometown of Abbeville gave way to brewing storm clouds, the kind that don't register on the Weather Man's radar screen.

I picked through the half dozen high school annuals until I eyed the one that interested me, 1968, my junior year. That year so happened to coincide with the year it happened, the year my life came unraveled. I flipped through the pages, reliving the scenes as if they were just yesterday. They would have been joyous care free times, if not had it been for that day, Thursday, October 31st.

I had very few signings in the year book. Hardly anyone had wished me luck or told me what a joy I had been to know, except for my very closest friends. Real friends were few and far between, after the incident that night. Most gave me wide berth. I would have probably been a social outcast at a Leper colony. My senior year had so sucked. The class nerds had gotten more attention than me.

Flipping the pages, I gazed on pictures of happy students walking the hallways, cheering at various sports events, crowned kings and queens, mostly likely to be or do this and that. The photos looked nothing like the year I remembered. I appeared in none of them. My fellow classmates had scorned me, banished me to a desert island, all because of what had happened, and what couldn't have been prevented. Maybe it could have, if we would have stayed away from that damned old house.

I would have loved to have seen any one of them do any better, considering the circumstances. I needed a drink. After all, it was past noon. I checked the pantry and spotted a pint of rum, not my preferred drink, but what the hell. I poured an ample amount in a mug, added a couple of ice cubes, some Pepsi and a splattering of lime juice. I was off and running. After a couple of long swigs, all was good, or at least getting better. That catchy 1970's tune leaped into my head. I began singing while I danced around the room. It just seemed the right thing to do.

> *She put the lime in the coconut, and drank them both up*
> *She put the lime in the coconut, and drank them both up*
> *She put the lime in the coconut,*
> *Called the doctor, woke him up, and said,*
> *"Doctor, ain't there nothin' I can take,*
> *I say, Doctor, to relieve this belly ache?*
> *I say, Doctor, ain't there nothin' I can take,*
> *I say, Doctor, to relieve this belly ache?"*
> *She put the lime in the coconut, and drank them both up*
> *She put the lime in the coconut, and drank them both up*

"Ah hell, it goes something like that. Damn this stuff is good. But even rum can't help my pathetic singing."

We had all been pretty wasted that night and good thing, because I don't think I could have handled it sober. My life has certainly gone to hell in hand basket. I'm usually way too laid back to let this kind of crap get to me. I used to be a lot of things, before it happened. I've lost my happy place. I've fallen and I can't get up. That doesn't even make sense does it? Damn this rum is good.

My wrist watch says it's just two o'clock. Shorty won't be here for at least another three hours, if he can get away at all. I could be insane by then, or just passed out, if I'm lucky. The house on Cedar Springs Road probably wouldn't be so scary on a sunny day like today. I could drive down there. I could face it head on. I better stay put until he gets here. He'll be expecting me to be here, not there. I'm such a wimp.

I picked the 1968 edition back up and flipped to the photographs of the juniors. Alphabetically I began perusing the photos one by one, locating my cohorts in crime from that night. I just realized what a motley crew we were back then. Trouble was stamped on each and every forehead, or so would say the hometown people. There really wasn't a better bunch of guys, well, my opinion. I'm proud to have been part of that gang of misfits.

Stan Bronson was now our resident town drunk, round face, pudgy and squatty, chipmunk cheeks, always red flushed like he was on the verge of a heat stroke. With that contagious laugh, wild and high pitched; you couldn't help but like him, and feel sorry for him at the same time. His family struggled for everything they had, and the kids were relentless with their taunting of him. He started drinking at a very early age to escape the torment. It saved him from them and their constant bullying, and prepared him for now, I suppose.

Donnie Ray Clark, the bruiser and our high school quarterback, always wanted to fight once he had a couple of drinks. His opponents were usually us. A big boned six footer, short cropped black hair and an oddly bird shaped mouth, he had an almost *Alley Oop* comic strip appearance. He had one hell of a throwing arm and could zip that football to the team's speedy receivers. Why he hung out with a bunch of losers like us didn't make much sense.

Lester Coburn, mechanically inclined, had customized his 1966 Dodge Charger, a sweet ride. Lester, even at age seventeen, wore a five o'clock shadow. He looked much older than the rest of us. His hair was always oily and slicked back. He had those mechanic's hands, oil and grime under the fingernails and imbedded in his knuckles. You got a straight shooter with Lester. He told it like it was. I can picture him now, always wearing faded jeans and a white t-shirt, no frills.

Leroy Hanks, six four and almost four years older than any of us, had been held back three years in school for failing grades. A little slow witted, but he was not stupid by any stretch, a farm boy in the most traditional way. His father made sure he put his chores ahead of his schooling. I liked Leroy. He was our own personal *Jethro Bodine*, of Beverly Hillbillies fame. He inspired me to appreciate life.

Wayne Henderson, Shorty, my very best friend then and now. I could count on him back then, and I was counting on him this afternoon. Shorty fit him perfectly. At one hundred sixty five pounds, just a tad over five feet tall and solid as a rock, he was as genuine as they come. Not someone you could imagine on a high school football field, but pound for pound, that little running back could be a handful.

Give Shorty the football, and he would bulldoze through opponents three times his size. He could make our Sunday cow pasture football pick-up games a most agonizing and painful experience, and we played touch football. Donnie Ray Clark never joined us in pick-up football. He saved it for the Friday night games and a stadium full of fans.

Brody Henderson, Shorty's brother, one year younger and five inches taller, was not in our class, but I couldn't think about one without the other. He always tried to walk in his older brother's shadow. They were tough shoes for him to fill. He had turned his skills to basketball and envisioned himself being the next Pistol Pete Maravich, always wearing a number 44 jersey. He even wore his hair Pistol Pete style. That's about where the comparisons stopped. He could be a hot head if things didn't go his way, and more often than not they didn't.

There's Payne Lewis. That would be me. Boy what a difference the years can make, and the toll it can take on my thirty five year old body, more mentally than physically, I reckon. I had just barely turned seventeen when that picture had been taken. What a skinny looking character, almost six feet tall and tipping the scales at a whopping one hundred fifty pounds soaking wet. Some contrast with now, nearly forty pounds heavier, a full facial beard, hair to my collar. I was the class clown then, but now I tend to struggle with being or thinking funny.

Larry McCurry, the shy guy until you got a few drinks in him. A cheap show drunk, just step aside and allow him to provide the entertainment. Sober, he could blend in and become lost in almost any crowd, typically very low key and quiet, a virtual invisible man. As if by magic, he transformed from Jekyll to Hyde, once the Boone's Farm Apple Wine or Mad Dog 20-20 kicked in. Off came his clothes, He became the ultimate streaker.

Don't look Ethel. We saw him buck naked way too many times. There was nothing stand out about him, even naked as a jaybird.

Charley Moody, my next door neighbor, was one of my spook house building partners. He was always big for his age and some what of a truth stretcher. Looking back now, I believe he should have been diagnosed as a pathological liar. He could really spin some yarns, and that hadn't helped our cause, that night it had happened. He wore these huge, goofy, black rimed glasses that framed his thick, neatly trimmed sideburns.

Stephen Pool, our other partner in the haunting business, was Lon Chaney, the wolf man and groper of unsuspecting female spook house patrons. Stephen had a dark side, none of us knew about. He experimented with all sorts of drugs and reefer, while the rest of us were sucking down alcohol. I didn't know the full extent of his drug abuse until that night. To this day, I believe his addiction dramatically impacted and possibly altered the outcome of that night for him.

And lastly, Peter Woods, aka Woody the Pecker, a self proclaimed lady's man, who got in more girl's pants than the rest of us combined, or so he claimed. There had been no witnesses the gigolo's tales. The girls certainly wouldn't confess their involvement. Woody was hung like a horse. Mortal man stood no chance when he was their rival.

Peter, blonde haired and blue eyed, five ten with that monstrosity between his legs, caused us all to suffer from penis envy. His favorite stunt was to whip it out and effortlessly slide his foreskin over a door knob. Then he would open the door and flaunt it at us like a runaway fire hose. Trust me. You wouldn't want to be second, third or forth in line at a gang bang, especially after he had secured the number one spot. I still don't know how he didn't end up in the porn industry. He could have shamed the likes of John Holmes.

I closed the year book and my eyes, and slid into a deeper, darker funk, wishing Shorty was already here. The demons had me surrounded. Circling the wagons would not save me. I was a lost cause.

4

The annoying snoring woke me from merely resting my eyes. Damn, it's still only three o'clock. Am I in some sort of time warp today? Now I know why I don't stay home on Sundays. Welcome to my version of the Twilight Zone, Mister Serling. That Halloween night years ago could have definitely qualified for an episode.

Oh, how to kill time until Shorty gets here, that is the million dollar question. I think I'll click on the TV and see what Sunday has to offer on cable. I hate it when the remote battery goes out and I don't have extra batteries. Channel surfing while sitting on the floor a foot from the boob tube just isn't the same. It's best to just pick something and be done with it.

Oh boy, this is just what I need. It's a rerun of that 1979 classic, *The Amityville Horror*. What wonderful timing on my part. I feel like I've already walked a mile in *George Lutz's* shoes. Great, there goes *Father Mancuso* blessing the house. That demonical voice is about to demand for him to 'GET OUT.' I loved reading the book, and always enjoyed this movie; however, it's hitting just a little too close to home right now. I need another drink of something.

Let's just see what else we have in the old liquor cabinet. Ah ha, a full bottle of Mescal, compliments of Shorty about two birthdays ago. I think I was saving this for the next special occasion. Guess I just found it. I always hated to be the one that got the worm. Maybe I should wait until Shorty arrives, to cut my chances by fifty percent.

What else do we have in here? What's that way in the back? It's a half fifth of Gin from last year's Christmas party. I hate Gin. It smells and taste like paint thinner. I wonder what I can mix with it. I definitely don't do Gin and tonic. I don't even own any tonic water. Let's just check the frig. My choices are sweet tea, Pepsi, lime juice or dill pickle juice. Guess I'm doing nasty shooters instead unless I break the cap on that Mescal. What do you think worm? Sadly, I'm carrying on a conversation with a worm in a bottle, how pathetic is that?

Did I act like this before that night at the Frazier-Pressley House? A little, I suppose. Captain James W. Frazier, just why did you have to build that house in the first place, and who or what did you piss off? I wonder if that weird architectural design had anything to do with it. Older and wiser, I think about things.

After researching and reading about the house, possibly those three octagonal elements joined with connecting hallways could hold the key to this mystery. I need to see if I can dig up those old clippings I got from the library a few years ago. Now where did I stash them? I'm too much of a damn packrat to throw anything away, especially when it pertains to that old house and its history. Maybe this Gin will jolt the old memory cells. Oh, this is nasty crap all right! Shooters will never work unless I chase them with something. Gin and dill pickle juice, I don't know...maybe...yes.

I've got an idea. Why don't I look in that shoe box marked Frazier-Pressley House? I don't own a pair of Reebok sneakers, so where in the hell did I get that shoe box in the first place? Oh, size six; it belonged to the ex-wife, never mind.

Let's just see what we got here. I forgot what I had put in the box in the first place, or maybe I just didn't want to remember. Dill pickle juice and Gin isn't half bad after about the forth or fifth shooter. It makes me wish I had a hamburger though and more pickle juice.

I'm postponing the inevitable, so just open the damn box, stupid. The Frazier-Pressley House is on the United States National Register of historical places. I knew that. We certainly made some history back when. It was built by Captain Frazer in the 1850s. I knew that too. Okay, so it's an old historical house.

We loved exploring all houses, historical or not.

It appears that the captain turned over ownership of the house to his daughter, Tallulah, and her husband, a Doctor Joseph Lowry Pressley, in 1875. What a weird name...Tallulah...isn't there a gorge in Georgia named after her? This I suppose is where the Frazier-Pressley connection came about. I'm smarter than the average...whatever. The doc was a surgeon in good ole Dixie's Confederate Army. Hello Major Pressely, sir. I salute you.

After the war, the major-doctor Joe continued his practice in Cedar Springs, setting up an office in the center of the house on the third floor. The third floor, interesting, I had forgotten about reading this, or maybe I had just blocked it out too. The third floor, I hate that third floor. It says here that he also taught medicine and dentistry. Joe could remove your appendix and your teeth in the same visit on that third floor. I hate dentists and that third floor.

Damn this historical stuff is such a blur. I reckon I wasn't quite ready to digest it the last time. Of course it could be the affects of pickle juice and gin. There's something pertinent about the house's shape. It keeps coming up. That octagon structure was unique, or how did they put it...exceptional.

The house was built around those three central octagons and they all connect by a hallway, circumscribing the house's central octagonal core and by a massive three story portico. The three tiers of the portico can be reached by seven entrances. All the entrances have transoms and side lights. All this crap has got to mean something important, but what? I've been circumscribed too. I break me up.

The kicker, the house's composition and plan is believed to be unique in the United States. Why is it here in South Carolina? Why in Cedar Springs? There's a key to be unlocked for sure. I can just feel it. Maybe I'm clairvoyant like Cassandra Blake. I wish she was here.

There's another house over in Laurens with the same octagon style design, the Zelotes Holmes House. That's about thirty miles from Cedar Springs. I still can't believe I couldn't wrap my mind around this the first time I obtained copies of these clippings from the Abbeville Library. Yeah I can. People gave me hell after that night. Why would I want to remember anything about it?

Okay, here's something. It seems this guy Orson Squire Fowler was into the whole octagon thing and wrote a book entitled *A Home for all the Gravel and Octagon Mode of Building*. I need to find a copy of that book and dig up more dirt on Captain Joe, his daughter and that Doctor Pressely. Oh well, here goes my last shot of gin and pickle juice. What time is it? 4 PM, Shorty should be here in about an hour, if he gets that damn kitchen pass.

What's this piece of paper all folded up at the bottom? It's about the Cedar Springs ARP church. I certainly don't recall reading about a church, but I guess I was more interested in the house. These shooters must like... stimulate the brain cells. I've got to remember that. Note to myself, buy more dill pickles. The Gin is almost growing on me. Man, I'm just shy of being ripped or just plain brain dead. I can sure read better if I cover one eye. Maybe I just need to close both eyes for just a minute, and then I can follow up on the church thing later.

5

"Hey Payne, wake your sorry butt up, how about it?"

"Dang it Shorty, quit slapping me in the friggin face, how about it back? What time is it?"

"Quarter pass five," said my best buddy.

"When did you get here?"

"Fourteen pass five, and what the hell did you do, eat a jar of pickles? You really need a breath mint."

"Gin and dill pickle juice shooters, and you've just got to try them some time, but I'm fresh out of juice. I think I'm out of Gin too."

"I saw the projector set up over there. Have you been watching those wedding movies again?"

"Hell no," I laughed. "I was watching *Night of the Monsters*, the classic."

"Just like I figured. You have been watching your wedding video."

"I'm soooooo glad you're here, bud."

"So I take you've been digging up all bones."

"How'd you guess?"

"Dude, the clippings on your chest was a dead give away," he said, removing one, and holding it up in front of my face.

"It still bothers me too and probably always will. You can't just make it go away. I've tried."

"Well I guess we could bury ourselves in a bottle like Stan has done."

"Looks like you've already got a serious jump start," he said, pointing to the empty bottle of gin and totally empty bottle of pickle juice. "You're right. I won't be trying that concoction today. Thank you Lord."

"I saved the Mescal until you got here," I said, retrieving it from beside the sofa on wobbly legs.

"Well that answered my next question," he said, grabbing the bottle, breaking the seal and taking a long draw. "You're not planning on losing this buzz, are you?"

"Worked too hard to get it," I chuckled, winking and miraculously seeing only one of him when I closed an eye.

"All right then, where do you want to start?"

"I guess by figuring out where all the guys are now."

"I figured that out too. I spotted the annual on the table. Dude, after all this time, you really want to open up this ugly can of worms?"

I nodded. "I don't think it can be over until we know the truth. What do they say; the truth will set us free."

"And the truth means we're going back in that damn house doesn't it?"

"You and Cassandra need to form an act, and take the show on the road," I snickered like a little girl, absolutely snookered.

"Whoa, what's Cassandra Blake got to do with this?" He asked, knowing how I had always had a crush on her. What can I say? He's my best friend. I tell him every thing.

"I saw her at the Halloween jamboree last night. She invited me to supper next Saturday night."

"What about that husband of hers?"

"She didn't invite him," I slurred, then giggled.

Shorty just took another pull from the Mescal. I think he's trying to set me up for the worm. "She was so pretty dressed up like that little traveling gypsy,"

"Is she going back with us too, or is this just another one of your stupid ideas, Payne?"

"Well, that might not be a bad idea. She's a medium you know?"

"I don't want to know her dress size, Dude."

"No, I mean a real one with a crystal ball and everything."

"Since when..."

"Since last night in room number eleven at the jamboree," I

said as a matter of fact.

"Pickle juice indeed," he laughed, taking another pull, nearer to that worm in the bottom. Lucky for us it was only a pint bottle. "Hey, did you know I did the dirty last night with the assistant principle on the first grade desk in that same first grade room of ours?"

"What was she dressed as, a Kosher pickle?"

"No, a bottle of Sloe Gin," I one upped him.

"Okay, enough, where do we start? I can't stay here all night."

"You used too."

"I wasn't married then, and we partied like fools."

"No, we were fools when we entered that house in Cedar Springs," I answered, suddenly feeling almost as sober as judge, if a judge drank pickle-juiced-gin-shooters.

"Then we are damned fools for even thinking about going back."

"And we're just plain damned forever if we don't. I'm tired of worrying about that night."

"Here, you need another drink," he said, passing me the Mescal.

"I wonder how it would taste with pickle juice."

"The worm is already pickled, and you just swallowed it. I got you again, Payne."

I swallowed and felt that worm slid past the old guzzle. He had that knack for making sure I always got it. It must be a gift.

"Okay, let's go down your list," Shorty said.

"What list?"

"The one you've scribbled on that pad," he said, pointing to my lap.

"I told you man, it's the pickle juice. That dill weed is some bad bama-jama."

"Let me see that pad," he told me, snatching it from my lap.

"Well we know about Stan," I said, seeing his name was the first one I had written down. Funny how I was able to read upside down with one eye closed.

"Maybe we don't know everything. Why don't we ask him over?"

"We don't have enough booze for one thing."

"I've got a fifth of Jack in the trunk," he grinned like a

possum. "Something told me this could be a marathon."

"And did you bring your PJ's?"

"I'm wearing them," he smiled, pulling down his pants to below his navel and showing me his tidy whites.

"You're not going Larry on me, are you, and climb naked up a tree?"

"You don't have a tree in your yard big enough," he snickered, feeling a developing buzz too. "And I don't drink that Mad Dog 20-20 crap any more like our little buddy Larry used to do."

"You're only tall enough to climb shrubs anyway, and I have plenty of them, but just stay away from the holly bush."

"Just shut the hell up, how about it? Who's next on the list?"

"Since we're talking naked, what about Larry McCurry, where is he now?"

"I haven't really kept up with him. He's so forgettable. He always flew under the radar screen."

"Except when he was drunk, and then he got naked," I reminded him.

"Let me make a note beside his name to call his sister. It's probably been ten or twelve years since I last saw him. I could tell that night was still in his head though, but he refused to talk about it."

"Nobody's tried to block it out more than me and guess what, it's not going to let us. That's why we've got to figure it out, and go back there and face our worse nightmare."

"I've already faced it once. Why now?"

I shrugged. "I don't know, but it'll never be over for any of us until we do. It's like a curse hanging over our heads."

"Hey, we've been cursed for almost twenty years, every since our stupid asses stepped foot in that place. Payne, I'm not going to lie to you. It scares the crap out of me, just thinking about going back. I'm not even sure there's enough booze or reefer to help me muster up the courage to do it. You didn't see what I saw."

"I didn't see what you saw but I saw plenty. I relive it almost every stinking day, especially at night. That's when it's the worst."

"I didn't mean it that way. I know things happened to all of us that night, stuff none of us can explain. What if going back don't fix a damn thing? Maybe returning just makes things worse. Maybe this is what it wants. Have you not thought it might be laying a trap to take the rest of us?"

"Why do you keeping calling it, IT?"

"Because I don't know what else to call what we saw, what we experienced, what took our very souls from us. I tried far too long to brush it off, blaming it on all the booze we had consumed that night. You know...we were all pretty tanked. We could have imagined stuff."

"You really believe that, Shorty?"

"I want to believe it, but I know what happened to me was real. It sobered me up quicker than hell. My life has been a mess ever since, no matter how hard I've tried to pretend it normal."

I wrapped my arms around my best friend and held him tight. We both cried. We had never done that before, hugged or cried in front of one another. We had always been too macho; not any longer. We were two troubled souls looking for answers, for redemption, our sanity, and we both knew what we had to do to restore hope. We just didn't like our only option.

All right, let's get back to that list before you slip me one of those wet French tongues. I hate the taste of pickle juice," Shorty laughed out loud, but his laugh didn't feel authentic to me.

"Did you just grab my ass you damn old perverted whore?" I tried to one up him and make light of the serious moment too.

"Only you left cheek," he said with a wink. "I was saving the whole ass until later, asshole."

"Where's Leroy now?" I asked, returning to the list I had jotted down, but didn't remember writing.

"Dead," he said. That word slammed into me like a runaway freight train. "You haven't kept up with any of them have you?"

I took a deep breath and replied, "No, not really. I guess it was my way of trying to forget about it. I've pretty much avoided everybody but you. Don't look at me like that Shorty! We all dealt with this crap our own way and that was mine. Don't put the guilt trip on me."

"Dude, I haven't said a word. You're putting that trip on yourself without my help."

I gave him *the whatever look*. "That's why I asked you over. I figured you had kept up with them. You deal with stuff differently than me."

"I have kept up with them, but sort of wished I hadn't. I really haven't dealt with this any better than you. Keeping up with them just made it worse. You want to hear some really sad stories? Take another drink and let me bleed for awhile. I haven't been honest with you for a very long time."

Shorty saying those words hurt me like a yellow jacket sting, and those little bastards can nail you. I had always been honest with him; well mostly. "All right, spill your guts, Runt."

"First, Leroy," he said. "He was killed on his farm in a bush hog accident. He died from his injuries. It's been about eleven years ago when he met his maker."

"Eleven years and I didn't even know. Well, you read about them flipping over in ditches all the time and hurting or killing the driver. Leroy was one of the good guys."

"It didn't flip, and he was no where near a ditch. He was in the middle of his back forty on perfectly flat land. He was found underneath the bed of the bush hog by his niece, ground up like hamburger meat. He never did get married you know."

"No, I didn't know," I shrugged. "So was he working on it, and just got caught in the blades or something?"

Shorty let out his breath like he was releasing steam. "The tractor's ignition was in the off position and it was out of diesel. The key was later found by the coroner in Leroy's pulverized remains, in his pants pocket."

"How could I have not heard about this? I work for a local news paper for heaven's sake."

"Leroy's farm was over in Laurens, and as I recall, you were on one of those two week Caribbean cruises with your wife and her family."

"Why didn't you tell me?"

"You never showed any interest in any of the guys when I brought up their names, so I quit trying." Shorty sort of scolded me. "It was pretty damned obvious that you didn't care, or just didn't want to know. Like you said, I've been the only one you've clung to all these years, and you didn't talk about that night even to me."

"I'm such a dick head."

"You're way below dick head status, Dude," he reprimanded

me again as only he could and get away with it.

"So what happened? Did it go down as one of those unsolved mysteries?"

"I don't know. I've still got the news clipping. I guess I'm a little guilty too. I reckon I acted like you and buried my head in the sand. I took it no further. I guess we should follow up on it, and see where it takes us now."

"I made a note by his name to do just that. And now, back to you. It's time to spill your guts, confess your sins and cleanse your soul, my son."

"Don't go Catholic on me. You grew up Pentecostal. If you start rolling your eyes and speaking in tongue like your grandmother, I'm out of here."

"Trust me. I'm so far from receiving the Holy Ghost it isn't funny. I haven't attended church since the divorce and probably long before the break-up. She and I did the Methodist thing and it does have Catholic roots. So there, I can Hail Mary you, guilt free."

"Dude, don't even joke around with religion with what we've been through. It so ain't right."

"Sorry, I guess I lost most of my old time religion at that house."

"You should have gotten religion, but instead you escaped with that smart ass mouth of yours."

"Enough of that; now let's discuss your troubled and tormented soul."

"Well, just like the rest of the crowd, I received my share of ragging and ridicule. I was shunned by most, but then again you know that, because you were too."

"Yeah, our senior year couldn't pass fast enough for me. I thought those kids would have forgotten about it over the summer, but no, they blamed us. They didn't believe a word we told the authorities."

"They didn't cut us any breaks. And of course, Susan, my one and only back then, broke up with me and never spoke to me again."

"Dispense with all that stuff. That I already know. Tell me something you kept from me or as you put it, you lied to me about."

"You didn't hear me say I lied to you, Dude. I said I just haven't been completely honest with you. There is a difference."

"Whatever." I rolled my eyes and mocked his blabbering. "And don't be looking for another hug. Tell me what's really on your mind."

"I know we are best friends, and we always have been since we were old enough to swipe each others pacifier, but we did go about two years after graduation without hardly ever speaking, or staying in contact. We weren't pissed off at one another, and we lived here in Abbeville County, just eleven miles apart. That was so wrong, Dude."

I penciled eleven on my note pad. It somehow seemed significant, but I didn't know why. "Go on," I encouraged him to continue, then passed him the bottle and motioned for him to take a swig of our latest bottle, bourbon. "It's your dime."

"It was probably as much my fault as it was yours. Go figure. Best friends usually stay in touch, even if they are hundreds of miles apart and we weren't."

"Are you trying to get me to cry again or something? Where is this going?"

"I started seeing a shrink in Greenwood about a month after we graduated." He dropped the first shocker on me. "I had to do something. The nightmares were getting unbearable. My folks actually made me go."

"You never told me you were having nightmares. I was having them too, but I didn't go to a head doctor."

"I knew you weren't going to make this easy with that unsympathetic attitude of yours," he snapped at me, serious as a heart attack.

"You should have let me know. We could have probably gotten a group rate."

"I went once a week for about a month, and then it increased to twice, and then three times a week."

I could tell this wasn't easy for him to confess. "Did it help?"

"For a while it did. I only go twice a month now and I have been doing that for about eleven years."

There's that eleven number again. I made another note.

"And you've been seeing the shrink now for sixteen years." I said this with my mouth open like a carp. "Does anyone else know?"

"Just the old lady. It's tough to hide something like that from your wife of six years."

"Much easier to hide it from your best friend, huh?" I lashed back without thinking.

"At least she didn't weather the worst of it with me, because we hadn't met until I had reduced the frequency dramatically. I had gotten my shit together a little."

And I didn't weather any of it with you, I thought, but this time I kept my feet out of my mouth. "You said for awhile," I inquired. "So how are you now?"

"They're back," he paused and almost teared up. "The nightmares are back with vengeance."

"When did they start?"

"First of October and they've been getting worse and worse every day since. It's just that night over and over and crazier and crazier." He really struggled to share this with me.

"What does the shrink say?"

"She's trying to decipher the trigger," he told me, now mentioning the doctor was female.

"That hurts. You can't tell me this crap, but can share it with a quack, a female one at that."

"Get off of that high and mighty horse of yours right now," he said, in a highly pissed off tone. "You weren't around. I did what I had to do. She came highly recommended."

"By who..."

"Lester..."

"Not our Lester Coburn?" I asked, shaking my head and waving my hands in disbelief. "He would never go to a shrink! He's not the type!"

"And you think I am."

"That's not what I meant, Shorty, and you know it!" I seemed to be doing a lot of back peddling today, another good reason to not be home on Sundays.

"You don't know shit do you, buddy boy!" he said, in even a higher pitched un-Shorty like voice.

He never called me buddy boy. I've heard him call other people buddy boy, but he didn't like them. He's supposed to like me.

"Brody sees her, and so did Leroy." He dropped another one on me.

"Well look how much good that has done," I tried to reclaim territory. "Leroy is dead."

"Brody isn't," he came back at me like I had never witnessed him to do before.

"How is Brody doing?" I tried to tone it down a tad.

"Not too damn good," he replied, not ready to tone it down a tad. "Thank you for finally asking about him."

I grabbed the back of my neck with both hands, and I started rubbing one hell of a pain, closed my eyes, and could say nothing.

"He's been back on Bull Street down in Columbia for almost a month now," he told me, his voice cracking up.

With both feet in my mouth and knee deep down my throat, I have no idea how I managed to spit out my next comment. "He's in the Looney Bin?" I asked quite stupidly.

"It's the third time since it happened," he said calmly. "And thank you for being so damn compassionate."

"You never told me any of this before, you inconsiderate bastard." I had never called him inconsiderate before or a bastard.

"You were dealing with it your way and we were dealing with it our way. I knew you weren't going to like hearing about it."

"You better get that bottle of Jack out of the car." I advised him. "We're going to need it."

"You're already drinking it, Dude."

"Oh..."

"I have some other stuff I'll bring in, so don't drink it all while I'm gone."

"Wonderful," I exclaimed. "More friggin surprises, I'm sure. I can hardly wait."

"You're the one that called me, remember? You wanted to know about the others."

"I know. I'm such a dumbass. Watch what you ask for...if my foot would reach my ass, I'd bury it ankle deep."

"What are buddies for," he mocked me. "Allow me."

6

Man oh man, I certainly never expected this. I felt like we had been going at it for hours, but my watch just said 6:11. That specific time should have clicked with me. The eleven phenomena kept surfacing, but unfortunately I hadn't connected the dots yet.

I can sure pick them. I have one friend, the town drunk, two living in the land of straight jackets and shock treatments, and one John Deere dead. Me, I'm just totally not right and lucky to be here almost mentally in tack. I still say the house and that night is to blame for all of this.

"Let's burn this joint and give the Jack a little rest." Shorty had clarified the pecking order, assured we would become further wasted.

"I really don't do this anymore," I said, while fondling the joint between my fingers.

"Me either," replied Shorty, flicking his Bic and lighting the joint I now held firmly between my lips. "Who's next on your list?"

"What about Lester? What pushed him over the edge?"

"You mean besides Halloween, 1968?"

"You know what I mean." I inhaled, frying both lungs. "Good shit." My voice sounded like I had inhaled helium instead.

"He just lost it. He could no longer focus on his passion, fixing up those old automobiles. By 1979, he confessed he had reached his breaking point. He started verbally, then physically abusing his wife, Norma. She filed for divorce later that year and has since then moved to Seattle with all three kids. She had to get as far away from him as she could. She didn't ask for any alimony, just full custody of the kids. He gave in to her without a fight."

"So that's when he started seeing her, the shrink."

"You need to hang with me, Dude" he said taking a toke. "I told you, he recommended I see his doctor. His folks sent him to her our senior year."

"Lester never said a thing about that to any of us."

"He was too embarrassed."

"But he told you," I choked out the words, still hurt I had been left out of the loop.

"Not until about six years later, I was at his house. He was working on my carburetor, and we just sort of eased into the subject. Once the floodgates were opened, we let it all rush out. He told me about Doctor Shirley Blanchard, and after a couple of months of soul searching, I finally scheduled an appointment. The rest is history. I dropped my other shrink for her."

"How's Lester now?"

"Lost his job, his house, his passion to live, and in 1982 he packed up what little he had, and then he caught a bus to Seattle to find Norma and his children."

"How did that work out for him?"

"I'm not sure," answered Shorty, lowering his head to stare at the floor, joint still smoldering between his fingers. "No one ever heard from him again. I talked to Norma about a month after he left. She said he never showed up there."

"And now..."

"Neither hide nor hair of him has ever been found. It's like he just dropped off the face of the earth, almost like he never existed."

"I'm so not liking this. I'm not liking this one damn bit. Pass me that bottle of Jack. What about Charley? Didn't he move out of town?"

"Close but no cigar. I'm impressed. You sort of know something after all. He actually joined the marines that winter after we graduated."

I didn't have a come back. I just listened.

"He went MIA in Nam. Charley was one of eleven brave men that went down with a chopper, far behind enemy lines in 71."

"Sorry to hear, and I don't know how I didn't know."

"You were off finding yourself in the Australian outback, if I remember correctly. You had won that trip for those pictures of southern covered bridges you had printed in the Times. I still have a copy. See, I even kept up with your worthless ass, even when you didn't know it."

"Maybe I should be working from the short list? Is there anyone else not dead or not totally insane?"

"Stephen and Peter are on neither list. We still have to follow up on Larry to confirm his where-abouts."

"This Jack is hitting the spot," I told him, as I gulped directly from the bottle. "Let's start with Stephen. Cassandra told me Peter has his own landscape business over in Hartwell."

"Stephen it is. Pass me the Jack, please."

I took another quick pull and gave him the bottle, no worm in this one. This wasn't going like I had imagined. I'm not sure what I had expected.

"He certainly answered his calling," smiled Shorty.

"Is he a drug dealer with the cartel?"

"Close...he's a pharmacist, somewhere near Spartanburg."

"Well it sounds like he did all right." I was relieved to hear that. Shorty told me, not exactly, and then burst my inflated bubble.

"Okay, so he prescribed drugs to Elvis and is responsible for the King's untimely death. That's a career stopper." I was proud of that little come back. "Do you reckon Elvis was kin to Doctor Joseph Lowry Pressley of Frazier-Pressley House fame? I smell motive for that night."

"Payne, he has Aids. He was diagnosed in 83."

That one hurt. I did the math. "He's still alive after three years. That's a good thing, isn't it? He's made it longer than most. Maybe he's licked it."

"I talked to him last night on the phone," said Shorty, in the most solemn tone. "He called me about 11:30, and told me his doctor said he would be lucky to see the New Year."

"All that drug abuse I suspect," was my best guess. "I heard dirty needles can cause Aids."

"His life style caught up with him all right," explained Shorty, as if expecting me to catch his drift. When I didn't, he said, "You didn't know he was gay, did you?"

"A queer?" I was stunned. "Not Stephen. He never pulled anything funny with me. Did you and he have something going on that I didn't know about?"

"You're pathetic, you know it," he ridiculed me. "Just because he's gay, it doesn't mean he's going to jump every guy's bones, especially his friends."

"Hey, I'm straight, and I would screw a snake, if I wasn't afraid it would sink its fangs in my pecker. When we all went out partying, we didn't turn down any opportunity to get a little, except if Peter got to it first. We all did that."

"You weren't his type nor were any of us," he kicked into scolding mode again. "We were friends."

"Now that I think about it, I don't ever remember seeing him actually date a girl. He did streak with Larry a couple of times though. You don't reckon..."

"Payne, stop it. He's our friend, and he's dying. It doesn't matter who he dated or didn't. He needs our full support."

"And he'll get it. He helped me with those spook houses. He's the wolf man. Only a silver bullet can take him down."

"What are you grinning about?"

"Stephen copped a feel from my neighbor in our garage spook house and she was a girl. Boy was she pissed. He sure made a good wolf man. I guess that character suited his life to a tee."

"What the hell are you mumbling about now, Dude?"

"Think about it. The wolf man lived two lives, the one everyone knew about and the one he lived under the influence of the full moon. I bet Lon Chaney was really a closet dweller."

"Great analogy, Dude, but just promise me you won't mention it in front of Stephen, all right? It's sort of freaky, even for you."

"That leaves us with Woody the Pecker, old loggerhead himself," I quickly moved on.

"Peter Woods," clarified Shorty. "Cassandra was dead on. He did move to Hartwell, Georgia in 1972, working at the Country Club over there. Eventually he opened a nursery, then a landscaping company by 1975."

"Well, that all sounds good."

"Things are a little sketchy, I'm afraid," said Shorty, rubbing his chin. "I knew his business folded in 1979 from some mysterious circumstances, but I didn't know the whole story. He sort of dropped off the radar screen for the past seven years, until about a week ago."

"What happened a week ago?" I asked, but this felt like another one of those times when I probably shouldn't have asked.

"Let's have another drink first."

Now I was certain I wasn't going to like this story. I decided then and there, that I would never spend another Sunday at home.

Leroy is dead under mysterious circumstances. Lester and Charley are both missing. Stephen is dying. Stan is a hopeless drunk. Brody has gone Looney Tunes. Larry's status is to be determined. Peter is the untold story. Shorty is seeing a shrink and has been withholding the truth from me. Me, I'm in some stage of denial, and Donnie Ray Clark...

"I still can't believe you knew about them and never uttered a word to me." It was my turn to dish out a little scolding.

"Like I said, you were into you and your life. You had put it all behind you after we graduated, or so I thought. The guys went their separate ways. You can be a selfish, self centered son of a bitch so effortlessly Payne."

"Hey where's that guy who was group hugging and crying with me earlier?"

"Did I forget, wise ass, who never takes anything seriously, making life one big joke." He had me pegged all right.

"Shorty, we have an unsolved mystery on our hands that's going Stephen King by the minute. We need to put the name calling behind us and focus."

"Kiss my butt, Payne."

"Later," I puckered up. "What's the scoop on Peter?"

"Well, like I said, he called me out of the blue, and said he needed to talk. He said I was always the best listener."

"Since when were you the best listener? I was a damned good listener. Hell, I'm doing it right now."

Snorting like a cow in heat, he continued, "Larry's business was going gang busters. He had several huge landscaping contracts and still operated the nursery for the public. To cut expenses, he had gotten greedy and hired a hand full of illegal Hispanics."

"Cheap labor," I asserted. "He was a smart businessman, using Mexicans."

"All was going well until our friend spotted a too ripe for the picking young brown eyed and dark skinned little senorita. She was one of the illegal worker's daughters. You know how he can't keep that thing in his pants."

"So he nailed her and pissed off Papa, right..."

"Not exactly," he continued. "Drunk one night, he did have his way with her, but unfortunately that thing ruined her and did some sort of internal damage to a sexually immature eleven year old. The girl died."

"He screwed an eleven year old. Peter is no better than a child molester or one of those sexual predators," I said in my best pissed off tone, and there was that number eleven again.

"Cut him a break, Payne. He said she had the body of an eighteen year old. She was an Amazon compared to others in her family. Good old Papa even encouraged it. He offered up his daughter to secure his job and the jobs of the nine additional family members."

"This is so wrong. How could he have done that to a child?" I threw up my hands in dismay. If I had done the math, I would have recognized papa plus daughter plus nine others, equaled eleven.

"Alcohol has a mind of its own. He was drinking when it happened. The girl's mama took matters into her own hands. Her brother was a gang member. She unleashed him, and he turned up the heat on Peter, threatening to kill him if he didn't sign over his business and leave the Peach State. Still blaming himself, he did. Peter just walked away from all that work, leaving this past September."

"It serves him right. He needs to learn how to control that damn snake in his britches. She was a kid, Shorty. He killed a kid."

"He's struggling with what he did. He told me he has asked a doctor to perform surgery on his appendage, and hack off two thirds of it to make sure this will never happen again."

"Couldn't he just practice celibacy?"

"He's serious about the surgery. He's a real basket case."

"Hell, even with two thirds removed he would still be above average and run circles around most."

Shorty couldn't believe how I could still be cutting wise cracks. I should have restrained myself. I have difficulty restraining.

"He's been back."

"Been back?" I required clarification.

"He has been back to the house. He said it was to blame for all his misfortunes."

"Did he go inside?" I attempted to swallow, but found I couldn't, experiencing one bad case of dry mouth.

"No, he just parked out front, on the road, but even there he said the evil pulled on him. He said he saw something."

I reached for the Jack but the bottle was empty. I didn't remember us finishing it. Even more frightening, I wasn't drunk. Hell I didn't even have a buzz. How could I have drank so much gin, mescal and bourbon, not to mention smoking that joint, and not be declared legally dead. It must be the dill pickle juice. I didn't want to ask the next obvious question, so I didn't.

"He saw movement in a third story window." Shorty just had to tell me anyway. "The shadowy figure beckoned him to come inside. He said he could almost make out a face, and then it was gone."

I said nothing. I just took the deer in the head lights approach and stared at him. Sundays really do suck.

"He hauled ass and then called me."

"So where is he now?"

"He's at my place, and he's been having nightmares too."

"So when were you going to tell me, and why didn't you bring him with you?"

"I had to feel you out first. I wasn't sure you were ready to hear any of this or even cared."

"You lied to me a-damn-gan. We're supposed to be best friends. I tell you stuff, and you don't tell me crap. Now what's wrong with this picture?"

He didn't have the balls to address that little tidbit, but did answer with another revelation. "Payne, the old lady and I are separated. She's with her folks. We agreed to the separation to allow this thing to run its course. She couldn't take me being like this, consumed by that event and sinking deeper every day. She saw the therapy wasn't helping. She has been supportive longer that I would have been, if I was in her place."

"You didn't hit her or anything like Lester hit his wife, did you? Because if you tell me you did, I am going to kick your ass."

"No, I didn't go down the Lester path. I just pushed her away and fell deeper into my dark and lonely abyss. I've taken time off from work to sort through it."

"So we're bachelor buddies again."

"Not hardly, Dude... when this is over, I want my marriage back. I need it. I love her."

"So what now?"

"Like you've already said, I guess we've got to go back to the scene of the crime."

"Do any of the others want to go back?"

"I suppose we should ask them."

"Do it then. Contact everyone. Have them meet us here Wednesday night and we'll decide." I was sounding way too serious.

"Brody can't make it due to his... situation, and I still have to locate Larry, but I believe the others will come. I know Peter is in."

"There aren't many others left are there?" I had mentally tallied the count. We were down to five, not counting Larry.

"We can still lick this thing with who we've got left. We have too. We don't have another option."

"Why don't you stay here tonight?"

"Better go back to the house since Peter is there."

"And you're such a damn good listener, right." I winked, giving him my second hug of the night. He hugged me back. At that moment, I felt recharged and optimistic. Would I feel the same way when we parked in that drive? Dread crept back in, even though I knew we were doing the right and only thing.

My dearest friend ever, departed for home just after midnight. I wondered how many more secrets he was keeping from me. Sleep evaded me, so I removed the article from her Reebok shoe box, entitled Cedar Springs ARP Church. I stared at the print. I drank a Pepsi, straight up. I still had that pickle juice after taste wrecking havoc in my mouth. Cassandra Blake popped in my head, but she was soon rooted out by the ever ominous Frazier-Pressley House.

I thought about Donnie Ray Clark and how he loved to pick a fight, mostly to his advantage, and typically with one of us who were guaranteed not to fight back. He sure picked the wrong opponent back in 68. He bit off more than he had expected. His new found opponent didn't back down, nor had been impressed by the challenger.

Donnie had been the concoctor of the ultimate slayer of brain cells. We depended on him mixing up his patented PJ juice for any of our social activities. PJ, aka Purple Jesus, was aptly named for the color produced by adding a bottle of grape juice to every gallon. It would kick your butt in a sneaky sort of way.

A typical gallon of PJ juice included the grape juice, one large can each of pineapple and orange juices, an assortment of sliced fruit like apples, oranges, lemons, and cherries, and then the main ingredient, a pint bottle of 190 grain alcohol. Donnie added a half pint of sloe gin, which made it sneak up on you. One minute you were sitting and feeling fine, the next you stood up, and then fell flat on your can. He made some good stuff.

I often wondered why we didn't bottle and market it. We could have made a fortune, pending any potential law suits of course by people who found themselves in very stupid situations. Oh yeah, and we were underage. I haven't drunk PJ since that night. Donnie wasn't around to make it.

Halloween night, 1968 had been one of those special occasions. Even though Thursday night was a school night, most of us had our asses covered by telling our parents we were sleeping over with various other members of our little clan. We had successfully pulled this stunt numerous times in the past. As long as no parent called another parent's house, we were free and clear. So far that had never happened. Trusting teenagers, what were they thinking?

We planned to lay out of school on Friday. Donnie's girl friend, Candy Kane, had written each one of us an excuse. Isn't that a great name? She was quite the forger back then. She was convicted on embezzlement charges at a local law firm in 1972. I have some great photos of her being served the arrest warrant and cuffed. She even autographed my personal copies, in her original hand writing for a change.

After her incarceration and release, she ran for city council in an adjacent county. She won by a landslide vote. I developed her campaign slogan. *Vote for Candy Kane. No one has licked me yet, but everyone has tried.* I often wondered if my slogan had been instrumental in her being elected, or if she had simply forged the votes. She's a congresswoman now. If memory serves me, her slogan had been the same for that run too.

My little exposé of her arrest had made the front page of our weekly news paper, the Wednesday Weekly. It was instrumental in me being hired there too. I've since been promoted to the position of the paper's head photographer. I relieved the owner of his part time duties as former head photographer. It certainly beat the hell out of delivering papers and soliciting the town's folks for advertisement, my previous position.

My mind keeps jumping from one subject to another. I can't seem to control its directional preferences. I'm sitting here still clutching the Cedar Springs ARP church clipping, but I haven't been able to focus on the article. I keep this up and I could be Brody's next room mate on Bull Street. I can be silently sarcastic too.

My thoughts shift to Halloween night 1968, yet again. I recall how we gathered at our local hang out, The Bantam Chef, about an hour before dark, priming up for our Halloween extravaganza. We arrived in my 1959 grey VW bug. Shorty and Brody had hitched a ride with me after school. We had visited Five Points Wednesday night, where we had purchased two six packs of Hoppin Gators, a new fruity malt liquor. This dude working at Five Points catered to underage drinkers like us. Sure we had to slip him a couple of extra bucks but it was a win-win situation. He did this behind the owner's back.

The Five Points grocery had gotten its name because five streets intersected at that spot. It provided excellent escape options for our convert operations. We had only to worry if an adult would happen to show up in the middle of one of our purchases.

Donnie and Peter soon arrived in Peter's 1961 two door red Chevy Impala convertible. They each had a gallon of PJ on ice in the trunk. That was enough of the Kool-Aid looking beverage to ensure a small army became wasted. Donnie, very passive for the moment, would transform into Jack Dempsey in his rendition of Requiem for a Heavyweight, once the PJ kicked in.

Peter, on the other hand, was the ultimate exhibitionist. The more intoxicated he became, the more he would expose his gargantuan manhood to any automobiles carrying prowling high school females. The girls giggled with delight, many thinking it couldn't possibly be real. What did they know? Most had never actually seen a real one of any size. We claimed all dicks were that size just to hedge our chances of getting lucky. I think it worked against us and scared most of them away.

Speaking of freaks...not to be out done and after consuming his fare share of wine, Larry had mastered the art of mooning. He thought he was good at it. He had one ugly butt. I also remember the time he was trying to piss in the Coke bottle and got his pecker caught in it. That was funny stuff. He claimed it made him look as large as Peter. The expression in his face was priceless when we claimed we would smash the bottle with a hammer to set him free.

Lester, riding solo, just pulled up in his 1965 Custom Dodge Charger. Revving the engine, the entire parking lot took note. Lester didn't bring any adult beverages and rarely drank. When he did decide to, he would just bum something off one of us. Lester, our *Arthur "The Fonz" Fonzarelli*, Mister Cool under pressure, would be tested tonight; we just didn't know it yet.

Here comes the rambling wreck, Stan, driving his folk's 1963 Rambler Classic Cross Country station wagon. It actually suited him to a tee. Stan had brought this week's beverage of choice, Orange Tommys, another little malt liquor with a kick. Before the night was over, Stan would usually end up drinking a little bit of what everyone brought. He would be stumbling down, wasted, memory wiped out completely. Some things haven't changed.

I really felt sorry for old Stan the time Donnie pissed in a beer bottle, and then staged it, knowing Stan would take the bait when he observed an ownerless beer, just sitting there for the taking. Too predictable, Stan confiscated it inconspicuously, and then he turned it up. He had gotten several good swallows down before the taste and warmth alerted him he had been snookered.

Realizing Donnie was the culprit, he instigated a fight. The fight consisted of several wild swings by Stan, and two push downs by Donnie, and Donnie offering Stan a cup of PJ. Friendships mended, all was forgotten, if ever to even be remembered by Stan.

Leroy rode with Charley in his 1966 Toyota Pick-up. Those two big old boys could fill up that small truck cab. Neither Leroy nor Charley were drinkers at all. Charley entertained Leroy with an assortment of lies, and Leroy never questioned a one, just smiled and nodded. Leroy did bring plenty of eggs for covert ambushes later. It was his contribution for living on a farm. Charley provided the TNT's. You had to be careful. You could lose a finger or two if you didn't time your toss. Miniature dynamite, they were indeed.

Stephen had snuck his folks Cadillac from the garage. Both parents worked the second shift in the local textile mill. He would take advantage, and drive the Caddy while they were at work. We would have to follow him back later, so he could park it safe and sound. Apparently his Dad never checked the odometer and Stephen always replenished the gas tank. Sometimes he would cut it a tad close to midnight, and the engine would still be pinging in cool down mode, just minutes before they arrived home. Fortunately they didn't park their second vehicle near the Caddy. Now I know luck wasn't on Stephen's side.

Larry had earlier sputtered up on his 1967 Yamaha 50, baby blue scooter. We called it the sewing machine or sometimes the Larooter. It was cheap on gas, but definitely not a chick magnet; not that old Larry would attract a horde of females. He carried several bottles of Boone's Farm Apple Wine in his cute little matching saddle bags. One bottle and he would be silly and giddy. After the second, you could count on him being naked somewhere. We always had to gather up his clothes and help him get dressed. We usually ended up hauling him and his scooter home.

The wild bunch was all here. We would wing an agenda as

we go. Mass quantities of alcohol always make us think better. We had quite the smorgasbord tonight with PJ juice, Hoppin Gators, Orange Tommys and Boone's Farm Apple Wine. We didn't know Steven was a pill popping, closet reefer smoker. Destiny waited for us on the Cedar Springs Road. We just didn't know it yet.

7

I finally focused in on the news clipping. The Cedar Springs ARP church congregation of 1791 had once been the Cedar Creek congregation of 1779 to 1780. It moved two miles northwest to its present location, where a frame building was constructed. The brick church we had seen had been built in 1853.

The article indicated that small farms apparently sprung up around the church in the eighteen hundreds. By the nineteenth century, the smaller farms that couldn't make it, folded and settlers moved on, leaving those left, fat and happy, taking possession of the vacated land. The Fraser-Pressely Home survived when all others went belly up. It alone ensured the existence of the Cedar Springs ARP church.

Interesting, a log cabin with a gabled roof was built next to the Fraser-Pressely House. I've been inside that cabin. It says here that it was a stage coach stop and inn. It was a routine stop for the stage coach's passengers between Augusta Georgia to my good old home town of Abbeville, and then on to Edgefield, South Carolina. Cedar Springs, an established community, had apparently contributed to this cabin's location being a popular stop.

Okay, what did I learn from reading this historical and factual information? I learned not a damn thing. I don't known anymore than I knew before we decided to journey down that road, into that community, and venture inside that house in 1968. All I know as fact is we should have never done it. We were young and bullet proof. What the hell did we know? We had no reason to fear the unknown. We were genuine dumbasses back then. That's my story and I'm sticking to it.

Hey, I'm dealing in the real world right now. I still can't decipher how I drank that gin and pickle juice, the mescal, the bourbon, and then burned one, and sit here way too sober. I should be comatose. I bet if I blew a breathalyzer they would be loading me in a body bag.

My watch says it is 3:15 AM, a significant time in the Amity Horror book, but not so in my world. I'm not sleepy at all. I can hardly wait until Wednesday to see who shows up for our little reunion. What if it is only me, Shorty and Peter? Do we dare return? I always thought there was supposed to be safety in numbers. It didn't work in 68, so why would I think it mattered now? Eleven of us entered that house, stupid juniors, looking for a rush.

We're screwed. I know it for a fact, but it won't stop me from returning. It can't. I can't. I'm ready for this to be over. I still can't believe the carnage caused by our little invasive and somewhat harmless visit. People dead and missing, others with a totally messed up life, and just how can a damn old house have that much influence over our lives? I am determined to solve that mystery and end this damn curse. I just hope the entity or whatever is down there, cooperates with me, with all of us.

I know I need to go to bed, but my brain just won't shut down. I don't do this often, but I guess I better pop a couple of sleeping pills. Monday is just a few short blinks away and I do have to report to work. Halloween looms ahead. It used to be my most favorite holiday just behind Christmas. Right now, I am not in much of a festive mode. Trick or treat, I think I know the final answer.

Halloween has taken on a new meaning and I don't like it. I know we must return, and we will Halloween night but my heart lacks enthusiasm. I just don't want anymore of us to pay the ultimate price of admission with our lives. Oh, we're so screwed, but I can't stop this runaway train. It must run its course for good or bad. I'm leaning towards bad, big time.

8

Please stop my aching head from ringing. Turning off the alarm clock at least halted the ringing part. If I finally dosed off sober as a judge, how come I have a spiteful hangover this morning? It has to be that damn pickle juice.

I'm just a shit, shave and a shower away from reporting to the Wednesday Weekly to see what assignments await me in the bustling metropolis of Abbeville. Well, actually I can discount the shave part, since I have a full beard.

I have lived here all my life and still find it hard to believe that the town is such a hot bed for tourist. The Chamber did a good job in promoting our confederate roots, I suppose. The Abbeville Opera House is a big draw with its plays of Broadway quality. I remember when the Opera House was a walk-in movie theater. I paid a quarter to watch a movie matinee on the big screen. I still remember seeing the movie *Around the World in Eight Days* on the big screen there. It's funny how you remember weird crap.

The year 1968 marked the resurrection of the opera house, after a restoration project returned it as a legitimate theater, showcasing Thornton Wilder's *Our Town* that May. For us, 1968 would signify an event of epic proportions. Ours would not have the supportive fanfare. Funny how the Opera House is notorious for having haunts of its own. Locals accept this, but couldn't accept our experience.

The Opera House dates back to 1908, much newer than our mansion down on the Cedars Springs Road. A ghost is supposed to haunt the upper balcony. It was once reserved for the colored, as they were politely called back then. Sad but true, segregation was a part of that era. It is rumored that this one particular colored feller had apparently pissed off the locals by having a fondness for one of the community's white woman, taboo back then. Vigilantes reconciled this indiscretion by murdering the man. Part of my job is doing research so yes, it did happen.

His spirit supposedly haunts that balcony. A lone chair sits up there in his honor. There have been all sorts of reports of strange lights in that abandoned balcony. Some folks have even heard someone humming. Creaking boards have been reported, caused by some unseen entity pacing back and forth. Others have heard applauds from an audience of one from that balcony during play rehearsals. For the record, I've never experienced unexplained happenings there, so that should prove that I'm not a lightening rod for that sort of thing.

Why was it so difficult for people to believe what we saw, and experienced, if they can so easily embrace those stories and claims? Maybe some of his ancestors had already found the Fraser-Pressely House to their liking. We just deserved our fair shake. Was that so hard to ask? We were just kids for heaven's sake. We were not convicted felons.

Yep, good ole Abbeville, the birthplace of the Confederacy, made its historical foot print on the succession of the south from the United States. They even named a hill and street after the blessed event. Locals called it Secession Hill, but it is known as Session Street. November 22, 1860, local patrons voted to adopt the ordinance of South Carolina secession from the Union. The Fraser-Pressely House built in the 1850's was almost brand-spanking new back then.

Historical buildings are everywhere. North Main is home to the Burke Stark House. The Belmont Hotel, just next door to the opera house, is another historical landmark. Then there's that mystery concerning missing confederate gold. It is rumored to be buried in or around town somewhere. We made our mark in the history records when we invaded one of the south's grand historical markers that night, but no one paid homage to us.

I wonder if Leroy haunts his back forty. I still wonder about Donnie. And Lester, just what happened to him? Surely he couldn't have just disappeared off the face of the earth, like Shorty insinuated. Five nights from now, I hoped we would solve some of our unsolved mysteries, but I feared we may instead reopen Pandora's Box. I don't like surprises, never have. Would the town's folks be more tolerable of us a second time around, going there, where we had no business going? Honestly, I don't really care. We're not doing it for them or against them. We're doing it for us. I'm just a psycho babbling fool; after affects of that damned pickle juice and gin, I'm convinced.

After two BC Powders, my head has almost stopped throbbing. A couple of swigs of Scope removed the lingering after taste of the various adult beverages I consumed last night. The only reminder of last night is from those nasty burps, a mixture of dill, worm, Jack and pure dread.

I haven't talked to Shorty this morning, so I don't know if he's making any headway contacting the other guys. It's probably too early for that. Will he tell the honest truth this time? Cutting the city square, I headed for my usual parking place in a narrow ally way behind the Wednesday Weekly. I have many a fond memory of cutting this square, a tradition back in the day. It is still practiced by the local teenagers today. I'm glad they still do it.

The town square's driving surface had been laid in brick in 1940 and is still preserved in this manner. I still don't know why they decided to use bricks, any more than it has made any sense to keep it this way. Nostalgia is preserved in all shapes and sizes, reasons I should stop questioning, I suppose.

Speaking of nostalgia, *do you want to cut the square* rolled off our lips as naturally as ordering a hamburger and Coke from Cream Land or roast pork from the Kum-back, other local hangouts? Our typical driving route consisted of circling the square a couple of times, then down to the Kum-back, before heading down South Main street to West Highway 72, where we would make a pass through the Bantam Chef, and then head further along 72 to Cream Land. There we would make our turn through Cream Land and back to the square again. Occasionally we parked for a while at any of the three various locations. Actually I'm not sure all existed at the same time. I just remember all three, so possibly my thoughts are a little scrambled this morning. It's my little fantasy so I'll go with it.

Staying straight on South Main and crossing 72 would take us to Cedar Springs, a typical summer time route, because Parson's Mountain Lake, our main swimming hole, was located along the way. We called it Little Mountain because a small elevated mountain rested above the lake, up an ever winding dirt and gravel road. A turnoff near the top would take us up to the lookout fire tower, and passed hidden lake, a lover's lane parking venue.

I no longer ventured to any of these favorite spots, because of their proximity to Cedar Springs, just a little further down the road. From what I had heard, the Fraser-Pressely House still remained empty, but it had been declared a historical landmark. It had been very well maintained for a damn old house. It was a far cry from being dilapidated. The house had been fixed up in recent years by the present owners, even though for some reason, they had chosen not to live there. I bet I could guess the reason.

"Good morning Mister Easterly." I greeted the owner and operator, Webb Easterly, of the Wednesday Weekly. "What's on slate today?"

"Morning back at you, Payne, you look terrible. Did you have a rough weekend or something?"

"Actually I helped with the Halloween jamboree Saturday night and stayed home all yesterday. Guess I got too much shut eye over the weekend."

"I believe I would rest less if I were you," he said, winking and having a coy little smile on that wrinkled face of his. "You don't wear it well."

"Don't worry about me too much. It will probably be my last Sunday just hanging out at home. Do you have any hot assignments for me?"

"Someone broke in and vandalized the high school library over the weekend. The librarian discovered it this morning. Take a few photos and interview her, if you don't mind. It's about time I test the water with your journalistic skills, don't you think?"

"I've been waiting for this moment sir." I am multitalented, and he knew I could write, so why was he claiming a revelation now?

"How about taking a few photos around town too? And please

ask the local merchants how they are preparing for Halloween on the Square Friday."

"You are cutting me loose, aren't you?" I asked in astonishment. It was about damn time. Maybe he was loosening his reins a little. Possibly there was hope for him and me.

"Have fun with it and do me proud."

He smiled as only he could smile, a confident, distinguished looking, southern charmer. He could win you over and make you feel comfortable in just a short couple of minutes. He could be a brother, an uncle, a dad and a friend, all rolled up into one.

That library had been broken into more times than I could count over the years. Vandalism, something my little merry band of criminals seldom did during our marauding excursions. Sure, we trespassed. We did a little discreet breaking and entering and possibly petty larceny, but we never intentionally destroyed property. We had our scruples and morals and a code of ethics... not!

"All right sir, I'll have the photos back to you this afternoon, along with my articles."

"I saw Stan over at the Rough House this morning," said Mister Easterly, in a genuine concerned tone.

"And I bet he was already plastered, wasn't he?"

"No, that's why I took notice. He was quite sober, standing outside and looking in the window. It was almost as if he was saying goodbye to the place. Has he been attending AA?"

I shrugged. "What makes you think he was sober?"

"He was clean shaven. His clothes weren't soiled. I haven't seen him like that in a while. I didn't smell any alcohol on his breath. That was a first too. He smiled and greeted me, and then he said something sort of peculiar."

He had me hooked, line and sinker. All he had to do now was reel me in, so I made it easy and asked, "What did he say, sir?"

He said, "All the little chickens were going home to roost."

"That's it?"

"No," he answered, rubbing his slick bald head. "He said eleven is a lonely number. I thought that song went one is a lonely number?"

"Oh man, there were eleven of us that night," I blurted out, without thinking of the ramifications of my blunder.

"Payne, surely you're not drudging up that incident," warned Mister Easterly, in a rather stern voice. "No good can come out of that abomination. It was the town's darkest hour. We've worked hard to leave the past where it belongs, son."

"Sir, I have respected you all these years, because I thought you were different from the rest of this unforgiving town, but you're no different than them, are you?" I stood astonished by what he had just said. "Support historical Abbeville, and so long as it brings in the tourist, you're happy as pigs in the mud, aren't you? Just keep those bus loads coming, and suck them in with that confederate bull."

"Payne, publicizing that event would have done none of us any good," he attempted to justify his actions. "We had just reopened the Opera House. We were well on the way of establishing Abbeville as a quaint little belle of the south. We couldn't tarnish what so many had worked so hard to build, just for a bunch of hysterical, drunken kids and their wild tales. Sorry to be so frank, son, but correct me if you think otherwise."

"But how else can you explain what happened that night?" I had now raised my voice, and had clenched my fists.

"You all smelled like a brewery that night. We found that marijuana you boys had been smoking." He no longer resembled that kindly southern gent, the man I had respected all my life. I saw him for who he really was, a hypocrite.

"And what about Donnie," I asked. "You think he deserved this too?"

"I have never forgotten about Donald, our star quarterback. He had such a promising football season, until he began hanging out with your corrupted bunch of derelicts." It was his turn to blurt out what he probably wished he hadn't. "He was such a fine boy. He had a head on those broad shoulders. The future belonged to him. His potential was endless. He could have even taken us to the state championship if..."

"If not for us," I finished. "You sick bastard, even you blamed us, so tell me why you hired me in the first place."

"Wasn't it obvious?" You were their leader. I had to keep you close, to ensure you kept the past in the past. The rest would follow by example. It worked flawlessly."

"Until now, and Leroy, you knew about him, didn't you?

You made sure I never knew anything about his accident. You encouraged me to take that vacation."

He said nothing, just stared at the pavement.

"And Lester, the same thing," I shook my head in disbelief. "Shorty, Brody, all of them, I bet you had a hand in making sure they received psychiatric help, didn't you?"

"We never meant to harm any of you kids," he said in that sincere voice of his. "We protected you. We protected the town. I preserved Donald's integrity. How can you be angry about that?"

"You just baited me with this journalism opportunity today, didn't you?"

"Old wounds were surfacing, so I had to do something to distract you, Payne. I knew this was your passion. Mrs. Hill said you had confided in her."

"Mrs. Hill?" The name didn't ring a bell at first. "Sonofabitch, Francis Hill, the vice principal, Madam Chairman herself, what a little snitch."

"She said you were a troubled lad. She feared you were heading down a reckless path. For the record, she was quite taken by you. You shouldn't have taken advantage of a lonely married woman, Payne," winked Westerly. "For the record, she doesn't want you harmed or caught up in this mess a second time. We all feel the same way."

"So she shares her sexual encounters with you, unbelievable. You've probably had her too, I bet. Consider this my notice and resignation, all wrapped into one." I turned and walked away.

"Don't do anything foolish, Payne," he said in that fatherly voice, but it sounded like a warning to me. "It doesn't have to be this way. End your foolishness and all can be forgotten."

"Kiss my ass," I yelled, and then gave him the finger.

This felt worse than the bombs Shorty had dropped on me. Oh crap, I hope he's not in on this too. I couldn't bear knowing that. I've got to make some phone calls.

9

Arriving at my house, I grabbed the phone immediately. "Get your butt over to the house right now. Bring Peter with you. No, I'm not friggin wonderful. I haven't been worth a crap for too many damn years. That's about to change." Then I hung up the phone.

Talking out loud, "Lies, my whole life have been nothing but lies. Mine, theirs, Shorty, who can I trust any more? I need a drink, but I don't have any dill pickle juice."

"Me, you can trust me," mumbled Stan, sitting on the sofa, and shocking me back to reality. I had picked him up on the way, seeing him still sitting outside the Rough House

The phone rang, almost making me jump out of my skin. "That better not be that damn Shorty making up some excuses," I said to Stan. He just sat there with his hands resting on his knees and smiling.

"Okay, your ass better be leaving and getting over here right now, I need you," I shouted in the phone, with authority.

"I miss you too, but I thought we were on for Saturday," answered Cassandra Blake, in a puzzled voice. "I can be there in thirty minutes, if you insist."

"Sure, why not," I said, without thinking. "I could use a friendly shoulder about now."

"Don't do anything foolish, Payne. I'm on my way," she said, hanging up the phone.

What had I just done? Did I really regret inviting her? I

don't think so. She did care about me. She worried about the ramifications of me going back in that house, setting foot on that property again, and what evil might result.

"Eleven," I babbled. "Eleven...that number is a key in this whole mess. Why did you say what you said?" I now diverted my attention to Stan, still just sitting there, hands still folded in his lap, smiling, like he didn't have a care in the world.

"Say what?" he asked me.

"What you told Mister Easterly when you were standing in front of the Rough House...why did you make that statement?"

"I don't remember talking to him. I don't even remember how I got here at your house, Payne. Was I eating a hotdog?"

Had Easterly just set this up, I wondered, just to see how I would react. This is just getting way too weird, way too fast.

The Rough House, an old bar with three pool tables, established in 1932, has been a mainstay on the town square. It is world famous for its hotdogs and still sells those small, glass bottle Cokes. Abbeville even had its own Coco Cola bottling company once upon a time. You can't visit historical Abbeville without including a trip to the Rough House.

Mister Easterly and his cronies had preserved the Rough House's reputation. They had flaunted its notoriety to their advantage, but our little episode didn't even rate a blip on the radar screen. That was about to change. It was time to rattle this town's little perfect Mayberry reputation, and shake its foundation. We needed to let them know we were important too. Our lives did count.

"Stan, when did you give up the booze? How long have you been sober?"

With an almost elfin expression, he squinted, rubbed the side of his face. His cheeks almost appeared inflamed they were so flushed. He perched on the edge of the couch and said, "Last night...I stopped drinking last night. I had this weird impulse to visit your old church off South Main, that Pentecostal Holiness one. They don't really do any snake handling like some folks say they do. They are nice people down there. They welcomed me with open arms."

"You didn't talk in tongue did you?"

He ignored my smart ass question and replied, "We must go

back to the house. It paves our road to salvation, Payne. It will not end until we do."

"You did have quite the religious experience last night, didn't you, even without snakes. Speaking of snakes, look who just pulled into the drive. Woody the Pecker is in the building, or soon will be."

Where had Stan's reliable contagious laughter gone? He sat there solemn as a river stone, blank faced and lost in his own personal la-la land. I feared Bull Street screamed his name too. I sadly missed the tipsy Stan version.

I opened the door and greeted Shorty and Peter, before they had reached the first step of the porch. "Peter is that a snake in your britches, or might you just be glad to see me." The expression on his face told me that he had found no humor in my witty remark, nor did Shorty, standing behind him, giving me the look from hell.

"Payne, you look like dog crap," Peter finally replied. "And that's an improvement from the last time I remember seeing you." He then gave me a big old bear hug.

"Stan is here too." I pointed to the gnome camped out on the couch. Stan managed a friendly wave.

After we completed the meet and greet portion of our agenda, I opened up the floor for discussion. I caught them up to speed on my revelations with my former employer. I wasn't surprised when Shorty told us he had suspected the same thing. Man, it was so comforting to confirm Shorty had not been part of the conspiracy.

"So, did you have any luck contacting the other guys?"

"Stephen will be joining us this afternoon. I have located Larry. His sister, reluctant at first, finally disclosed his where abouts."

"So where is he, and is he coming?"

"He lives at Myrtle Beach."

"Don't tell me he's in one of those all male revues, a pole dancer by night, I couldn't stand that. He doesn't have the equipment for that like old loggerhead over there does," I said nodding, towards Peter.

"Hold onto your socks, dude, because this one is going to shake, rattle and roll you. He's an ordained minister."

"Give me a break. Who in their right mind would certify him to preach?"

"The Catholic church," replied Shorty, waiting for my reaction."It was that damn house that done this to him," I remarked. "But I reckon he's better off going down that path, then where he had probably been heading. Hell, we all should have become preachers or monks or something, after what we experienced that night. Did you talk to him? Will he be joining us?"

"I did. He's on his way from the beach as we speak. He told me he had been waiting all his life for just this moment."

"So, I guess that's it." I had to run the numbers in my head to make sense of them. "Leroy is dead so he definitely will not be joining our little reunion. We don't know if Lester or Charley are dead or alive. Donnie..."

"Brody will be coming with us," Shorty interrupted me. "I'm picking him up in the morning."

"I thought he was in..." but Shorty stopped me short.

"Payne, he needs to be part of this too," explained Shorty. "It could be his only chance at life just like we hope for the rest of us."

Life like we hope to find, that didn't seem like such a bonus. "Well, that makes six of us."

"Seven," said Cassandra, standing in the open doorway.

Seven...my gut told me we needed eleven, but I didn't share these suspicions just yet. It's time to start piecing this ugly jigsaw puzzle together. We needed to jog our memory banks to determine what each of us saw or thought we saw Halloween night 1968.

"Cassandra, I'm glad you're here, but I'm reluctant to drag you along with us into that house. Must I remind you? You were the very one who told me to stay away from it."

"Well, it is obvious you are not going to heed my warnings. You are damn determined to return, so I suppose I can't allow you to do it without me. I might be able to help. I do have insight into these types of matters, even though I don't agree with your decision to go back. I do fear for all of us, if we do this."

"I appreciate your honesty and bravery, but you better hear us out before you decide. Please listen and assert your opinions and beliefs, after we recap that night. You'll be a valuable asset to us by just being an unbiased listener. You can help us decide if we're insane or not."

"I already know all of you are perfectly sane," she smiled, melting me like wax on a candle. "The real insanity lurks in Cedar Springs. I think that is why that house has remained unoccupied all these years."

"You got that straight," added Shorty.

"All right, let's begin," I told the motley crew. "I'll start first."

"You don't want to wait until the others get here," said Peter.

"We'll fill in the gaps for them, when they tell their sides." I insisted on us getting the ball rolling.

"I'm hungry," complained Stan. "Why don't we order hotdogs?"

"Tell you what," our new female member jumped in. "You fellers get started. I'll fix lunch."

"You better order hotdogs instead," I advised. "The cupboard is bare."

"And fries," said Stan. "I love their fries."

"And plenty of dill pickles," I cracked, but only Shorty got that one.

10

I kicked off the stroll down memory lane. I remember how excited I had been about it being Halloween, my most favorite holiday, or at least it used to be. 1968, our junior year, we had not a care in the world. I watched the seconds tick off that huge wall clock in Miss Marshall's Trig class, my final class of the day. I so hated trig. The bell finally rung, signaling my escape. I rushed down the hallway. I dropped my books off in my locker, and then headed to my VW chariot. I was so ready to leave AHS in my dust.

Shorty, you and Brody were already standing by my bug. Brody had a Winston hanging from the corner of his mouth. You had your cheek stuffed with Redman. I'm glad I never took up either one of those disgusting habits but it wasn't from lack of trying.

You gave me a chew of Redman, behind your Dad's shop, just before we were supposed to go bowling in Anderson. Big mistake, I swallowed more juice than I spat, and then puked my guts out. I never took you up on that offer again.

Mama ruined it for me on smoking. She told me when I was just thirteen that if I was going to smoke, not to hide it from her and daddy, just smoke in front of them. If I couldn't sneak around, what was the point? Just as well I suppose, with all my allergies. She never said anything about drinking in front of them.

I recall we drove to my house first. We set the stage for the little white lie. You asked mama could I spend the night with you and Brody. She believed everything that came out of your mouth, rest her soul. She said yes of course. We were all set. I had already asked your folks permission for you to sleep over at my house. We then headed for Five Points to pick up a couple of six packs of that new malt liquor, Hoppin Gators.

Luckily for me, I mowed those five yards for pocket money, and you worked at Busby and Cox's grocery three afternoons a week to support our habit. Weekly allowances didn't hurt either. Yep, we had it made.

"I've got that ratty Styrofoam cooler we used when we go fishing. It's in the back floorboard," I told Shorty. "Pass the cans to Brody. He can put them on ice."

"Man this thing stinks just like fish innards," commented Brody. "Don't you ever hose it out?"

"Just hold your breath until you get it loaded and then close the lid," laughed Shorty. "You're such a whinny little dickhead. I don't even know why we let you tag along."

"Because it cost you too much to keep me from snitching, that's why," boasted Brody, holding his nose with his left hand, loading with his right.

"If you ever even think about spilling your guts, we'll cut your nuts off and feed them to the fish,' warned Shorty.

In the rear view mirror, I caught Brody shaking up a couple of beers, and strategically placing them in the cooler to set us up. Keeping that little secret, I would make sure he got one of them, when the time came.

"It's too early to head to the Bantam Chef and hook up with the rest of the guys. What you say we go to Cream Land for a chocolate shake, and then we can cut the square. We can see what's going on," I said.

"Sounds like a plan, Dude" replied Shorty.

I remember we did our thing until about 5:30, when it finally started getting dark enough for the Trick or Treaters to emerge. I so envied those children still in costume, knocking on door after door. We, on the other hand, had to invent our own form of entertainment, egg tossing being one of them.

Eventually, we were first on the scene in our usual spot, near the fence, the one displaying the menu, located behind the

Bantam Chef. We poured our brew in paper cups to maintain our covert status. A few car loads of girls had already started making their rounds. We acted totally stupid with our antics. I now wonder how we ever got a descent date.

"We didn't get many," chimed in Shorty. "Not with Peter around."

The rest of the guys filed in over the next hour, until the eleven of us were assembled and raising our usual hell, typically reserved for Friday and Saturday. *I still kept the eleven number hush-hush for now.*

"Wasn't that the night Larry got his pecker caught in that wine bottle?" asked Peter.

"No, I think that was another night. Remember it was a Coke bottle," I spoke up. "He was such a stupid prick."

"I recall you could do some damn stupid crap too. I remember you going out with that Murphy gal and shooting off all over her dress and hands, when she tried to help you slip on your condom."

"That wasn't as bad as you at the Auto Drive-in with Marylyn," Shorty quickly responded, knowing all my dirt. "That guy tapped on the driver's window and asked you to remove your foot from the brake, so he and his family could see the movie."

"I don't remember that one," stated Peter.

"Marylyn was giving Payne a full fledged knob job. He was so into it that his right leg was stretched out, pressing the brake to the floor board," explained my best friend, enjoying spilling the beans on me. "The family parked directly behind him couldn't see the movie, because of the brake lights blinking on and off. So Dad walks up and taps on the window. The fogged up windows kept the dad from seeing what was happening."

"I'm sorry. It was a bad movie."

Cassandra walked in, returning from the Rough House with our hotdogs. That put an end to our man talk. We paused to gulp down our meal. That bastard Shorty had removed one of those red wieners and began imitating the drive-in scene. I couldn't say a word, less I draw attention to him, and open up the floor to her questioning.

"Whose idea was it to go to the Rock House?" asked Peter.

"That would have been my bright idea," said a familiar voice from behind us.

"Remind me to lock the doors next time," I said, noticing the gaunt, stick like figure, silhouetting the doorway "Stephen..."

"In the flesh," he replied, stepping into the room, revealing his skeletal physic.

It saddened me to see him like this, but I masked my horror, attempting to remember how he used to look. "Clean shaven makes you look thinner, Wolf Man."

Breaking into a pearly white grin, he walked over and embraced me. I felt I would crush him in my arms. His boney frame was so fragile; I couldn't imagine him lasting another month. I must confess, I did have a fleeting moment of his gayness flashing before me, but our friendship quickly snuffed out those thoughts.

"You look like shit," he told me.

"Every one keeps saying I have that special quality. It's a three step program I'm on."

"Same old Payne," he remarked. "And what do we have here? If it isn't our resident stallion, Peter. You have faired much better than Payne. I was always envious of your gift. We should have all been so blessed."

"If I recall," answered Peter. "You assholes told all of the girls mine was normal sized, just like yours."

"It worked wonderfully until we dropped our drawers, or should I say, until the rest of the boys did," He corrected himself. "I was just a clever little closet pansy back then."

"You pulled it off flawlessly," chimed in Shorty. "We never suspected a thing."

"My dear Wayne Shorty Henderson, you were the first of our little merry band that I confided in, and I do thank you for still treating me the same way."

"You are Stephen and always will be Stephen," confessed Shorty. "Enough said."

"Stan," he giggled. "How could I ever forget Stan Bronson, our comic relief? Your laughter, while embarrassing most of the time, has instilled us into busting way too many guts. How have you been?"

"I'm actually feeling so much better, being here around all

of you," spoke Stan, in the longest sentence any of us had heard him speak from his position on the couch. "Everything is going to be just fine, once we go back."

"And this is Cassandra Blake. She will be joining us. She brings insight and intuition to our merry little band."

"A friend of Payne's is likewise mine," said Stephen. "I do apologize for the vulgar trash talking."

"Larry should be here in a couple of hours," said Shorty.

"And where's Brody?" asked Stephen.

"He will join us tomorrow," I spoke up, saving Shorty from having to explain his whereabouts. "Have you eaten?"

"Thank you for asking but I'm fine," Stephen answered "So what's the plan?"

11

We spent the next thirty minutes catching Stephen up to speed. We would probably have to do the same when the honorable, Reverend Larry McCurry arrived. I mentally prepared for that blessed event. I still couldn't picture Larry with a white collar. I wondered if he would be arriving from Myrtle Beach on that sewing machine scooter.

My wait would be short lived. Larry pulled down the driveway, sporting a brand new Red Mustang convertible, top down, with a straw Panama Jack Hat serving as his wind shear. Stepping from the auto, I didn't see the collar I had expected. Instead, he wore a funky multicolored flowery Hawaiian shirt, pleated and perfectly creased kaki slacks, open toed sandals and dark sunglasses, very un-priestly, I must admit.

He had to top the scales at nearly three hundred pounds. The Larry I remembered had been at least a hundred eighty pounds lighter. A bushy dark mustache occupied his upper lip. He more resembled a pineapple plantation owner than a priest. He looked nothing like the vintage 68 Larry. In his left hand he toted a bottle of wine, more resembling the Larry I expected, except the bottle wasn't shaped like Morgan David or Boone's Farm.

I watched him waddling like a duck, approaching my side door. I cringed, when I envisioned the new Larry running naked through my neighborhood. I sure hoped he kept his pecker out of that bottle of wine. I met him at the door, and when he smiled, I saw the old Larry. Hugging him, I could not stretch my arms around his girth. What a contrast from my previous encounter with Stephen. Larry and Stephen could have passed for the perfect Laurel and Hardy.

"I know what you are asking yourself," Larry nipped it in the bud. "Could this be the result of years of having the late night munchies?"

I laughed, but had thought that very thought.

"I'm afraid not. I'm just big boned. As you remember, my father couldn't take the ridicule inflicted on me, after that night. He moved us out of Abbeville. Eating disorder consumed my every waking moment. Since my parents enrolled me in a Catholic school for my senior year, I just fell into this as a natural escape from that night."

"Should we call you Rev, your holiness, preacher, the next great white Pope, or what?" I asked in my smartass way.

"Larry will do just fine. I'm so glad Shorty called me. I've been thinking about our old crowd for weeks. My nights have been a bit restless. We're going back aren't we?"

I breathed deeply and nodded to confirm his suspicions. I introduced him to Cassandra, and then we visited and reminisced for a while, before we caught him up to speed. We then resumed, comparing notes of October 31st 1968. Shorty began this time, recanting our wild ride to Greenwood to the Rock House.

"As I recall, we decided to follow Stephen home first and ditch his folk's Caddy. It was about eight o'clock by then. Most of us were in some state of drunkenness, some more shit faced than others," he said eyeing Larry and Stan.

"As you guys know, we ended up piling in Lester's Charger and Peter's 61 Impala convertible, six in the Charger and five in the Chevy."

"We were all suckers for exploring those old alleged haunted houses. The Rock House in Greenwood was an easily assessable one. We had visited it numerous times, but we had never had one of those paranormal experiences there. What was the tale about that place?"

I jumped in. "Well, I think this Tolbert guy built it sometime around 1920 or so. He constructed it with stone after he lost his wife and children to a fire in his previous home. He swore he would never let that happen again, as the tale goes."

"I had forgotten about that," said Larry.

"Anyway," I continued. "He moved in his rock solid house, and started being haunted by his deceased family, who apparently moved back in with him. He got the hell out of Dodge. He never returned. I remember one of the reasons we went there was to see the ghosts. The story goes that none of the other owners were able to live there because the same thing happened to them or worse. I never did read anything about what worse meant."

"So, you think it's still empty?" asked Stephen.

"Last I heard it was. Somebody cut down that tree so the second floor so it can't be reached now without a ladder. The stairs inside were already rotted out back in 68. We always had to climb that spindly tree to reach the second floor. As I recall there were just those four big empty rooms on the bottom and the same upstairs."

"Let's hear it for mister historian," mocked Shorty, and then he recanted our 1968 October experience. "Everybody was pretty damned wasted, except for Leroy and Charley, so they climbed the tree first. They gave the rest of us crap after they easily made it to the second floor. The PJ juice was kicking Donnie's ass. Stephen, you weren't too far behind him on the wasted meter."

"Well I had help from a few little magical pills that you fellows didn't know about. I was always messed up on something, but you guys never picked up on my little secret."

"Well, you were ripped and unable to negotiate that tree for sure. You just fell back on your ass, giggling like a little school girl," described Shorty. "That's all it took for Stan to chime in with his wild laughing."

"Giggling like a school girl and queer as a two dollar bill, and you assholes didn't suspect that either" added Stephen. "Damn I was good at that closet thing."

"I knew," spoke up Stan. "I always knew you liked boys, but I didn't tell."

"How could you have possibly known, Stan," asked Steven.

"You copped a feel once during a sleep over when you thought I was asleep."

"I did not. I never did that to any of you, I promise."

"I think you did."

"And I say I didn't. You just dreamed it. I'm not attracted to any of you. You're my friends."

"Okay, I'm sorry for saying it."

I hated all this talk in front of Cassandra, but I must admit it was good to hear Stan open up, more like his old self. Being sober did him good.

"Enough guys," spoke up Peter. "You're going to make the rest of us puke."

"I could certainly do without your male bonding stories too," commented Cassandra, now three shades of red, and eyeing me as if to ask, had I been a willing participant to these perverted acts.

I quickly shook my head back and forth to reassure her I was straight as an arrow and preferred women. I didn't tell her about the vice principle from last night. That could have confirmed my masculinity, but would have gained me no bonus points. Secrets, too many secrets among this wild bunch of ours...I just kept my mouth shut.

"The rest of us eventually made it to the second floor; all except for you two plastered fools. I guess after roaming around in those empty rooms for about thirty uneventful minutes, boredom set in. I think we probably scared the crap out of the ghosts. I believe it was Lester who suggested we ride to the fire tower at Little Mountain," continued Shorty, noticing the puzzled expression on our female newcomer's face. "Parsons Mountain, we all knew it as Little Mountain."

"I remember, we pulled several two car Chinese fire drills along the way," added Larry. "Lester made sure he ended back up under the wheel of his Charger, but unfortunately Stan ended up under the wheel of the Chevy. I still can't believe we allowed him to drive in that condition."

"Most of us were all messed up, with the exception of Leroy, Lester and Charlie. The rules are when we exit and run around the cars, who ever ends up where in a drill, takes that spot. I don't think the designated driver had been invented in 68," I added.

"I'm a damn good driver," Stan whined.

"You've gotten caught DUI how many times now?" asked Shorty. "And your license has been suspended how many times? I've posted your bail at least four times over the past fifteen years. You don't even own a car now, thank God."

"I was talking about back then," clarified Stan.

"We were still quite stupid to let you behind the wheel," reinforced Larry. "You could have killed me, Donnie, Leroy and Payne, who ended up in the car with you."

"He almost did," said Shorty. "He ran that stop sign and did one of those *Dukes of Hazard* maneuvers, jumping that ditch and running through a barbed wire fence, ending up in a corn field. Payne did take over the wheel after that stunt."

"I had to," I added. "Stan had passed out at the wheel."

"It's a wonder any of you survived those years," scoffed Cassandra. "So whose idea was it to go to THAT house, THAT night?"

"Mine," I confessed. "After all, I was the spook house entrepreneur. I thrived on that stuff."

"What was the name of that big three story house with the cellar slave quarters we visited over in Calhoun Falls, the one on the old back road?" asked Larry.

"I can't remember. It was damned spooky as hell," answered Stephen. "Especially those alleged underground slave quarters. Donnie almost caused me to crap my britches, when he flicked on that flash light underneath his chin in that blind alcove."

"You should have seen your face," laughed Stan.

"It burned to the ground not long after we graduated," I added. "Arson was suspected. Vandals, not to unlike us, got a little carried away and torched the place. The name is on the tip of my tongue too, but I guess it doesn't really matter. We visited so many supposedly haunted houses and cemeteries; I can't keep up with them."

"Did any of you ever visit the Ebenezer cemetery on the old Abbeville-Anderson highway?" asked Cassandra, trying to join in.

"Yep, done that," said Shorty. "We bailed out before midnight though. We never confirmed if that devil's head appeared on the evil woman's tomb stone."

"I wouldn't have stayed either," she added.

I can't believe it. We haven't partaken of an adult beverage yet. We haven't even popped the cork on Larry's vintage wine, and he says he has three more bottles in his Mustang. Stan's record for sobriety continues. We have definitely lost our edge.

I was really hoping that our stroll down memory lane would trigger something profound or forgotten about that night, but so far, it, as most of us remembered, just consisted of a bunch of young, reckless, drunken fools looking for the next cheap thrill. I think we could have all gone without Stan's revelation about Stephen molesting him in his sleep. I'll have new nightmares now.

Hopefully our combined recollections of the time spent inside and on the grounds of the Frazier-Pressley House will trigger some long forgotten, deeply buried clues to what actually happened that night. It better, because we're going to need all the help we can muster, before we return.

"Guys, what you say we call it a night, and go for some dinner? I'm famished after the four hour drive and as you can see; my body requires an abundance of nourishment to assert the attention needed to support these events. Fat boy is hungry."

"Well, it is after eight," I said. "What sounds good?"

"Anywhere but the Bantam Chef," laughed Stephen.

"It's Lee's Fried Chicken now. They've torn down the fence, our old hang out spot," spoke up Stan.

"What about Yoder's?" asked Larry.

"It's very popular, but I can't handle that sweet Mennonite Dutch style food." I voted no.

"Then how about the Belmont?" asked Larry. "That's where I'm staying. They have a buffet, or you can order from the menu."

"The Belmont Inn, I've lived here all my life and have never stayed there or had a meal there," remarked Shorty. "It just opened back up a couple years ago."

"Then, the Belmont it is," I replied.

The Belmont Inn, originally the Eureka, right next to the Abbeville Opera House, with its Victorian design, had been the brain child of a Mister P. Rosenburg in the early 1900's. It had its grand opening in 1903. It became the center piece for many vaudevillian troupes and railroad travelers. The inn boasted elegance and fine dinning, with all the best modern conveniences.

By the early fifties the new had apparently worn off, and business declined. Its name eventually changed to the Belmont

Hotel, until it finally closed in 1972. It remained closed until its restoration in 1983 as the now Belmont Inn. Another historical moment presented by the former news hound of the Wednesday Weekly.

Management was probably in for a rude awakening. The boys were back in town and possibly ready to rumble. It was hard to tell with this crowd which way the wind would blow, refined or raunchy. Hedging my bet, I figured we would be etching our mark at the inn tonight, unless Cassandra Blake managed to keep us in check. She certainly had her work cut out for her.

I couldn't help but think how sad it would be without Donnie, Leroy, Charlie and Lester. Assuredly, many a grand toast would be made to our fallen and missing comrades in crime. Less than 100 hours remained before judgment day, four short days to muster up the guts for the return. The number eleven still swirled in the back of my mind.

Tomorrow morning I planned to visit the public library, down South Main, one block from the square, and research Orson Squire Fowler and the Octagon House. That house and its design, the eleven rooms, and possibly the man himself, held the key to unlocking the door to our troubled and tormented souls. We couldn't bring back the dead, but we could certainly do everything within our power to prevent more loses, or could we?

12

The Belmont was still a fine old southern belle. That just sounded like the perfect something that I ought to say, but I kept that thought to myself. I just couldn't form my lips around it, not out loud. Historical garble left such a bad taste in my mouth, since this morning's little discussion with my ex-employer, Mister Easterly; owner, editor, publisher and now full time photographer for the Wednesday Weekly. Did I leave out selfish and lying old fart and sneaky bastard? Now I feel better. I would have felt perfectly comfortable shouting that at the top of my lungs, even inside the bar of the grand old southern belle.

The question loomed precariously in my little pea brain. Would I remain here in my birthplace now? I had always lived here. Abbeville County bordered Georgia. The town was located between the state capitol of Columbia and the city of Greenville. I could be in Atlanta in 2 1/2 hours, the Tennessee Mountains or Myrtle Beach in 4 1/2, or Charlotte, N.C. in a couple of hours. It was the perfect central location. I had never previously thought about leaving, but all that had changed this morning.

I suppose first things first. Wait and see what hand would be dealt Friday. I was never very good at poker. Something told me the house held the winning hand.

"Penny for your thoughts," said a calming voice. "Why don't you allow me to buy you a drink?"

"Sorry Cassandra...bad thoughts creep into the old head from time to time."

"You have my shoulders to lean on, remember."

"And I may take you up on that if you don't watch out."

"The offer is there when you want to cash in on it," she said, waving over the bartender, a rather busty and bouncy blonde with long shapely legs.

"Eyes on me, if I'm buying you a drink," she corralled me in, by placing her hand on my chin and refocusing me on her killer seductive eyes.

"Man thing," I attempted to defend my straying eyes. "We can't help it. We have this magnetic attraction for breasts. It is in our genes."

"Well in case you haven't noticed, I am a woman too."

And what did I do? I took a quick peek, before thinking. Yep, she had two breasts, all right. Returning my focus to her face, she said, "Did you confirm what I told you?"

Math wasn't my best course in school, but I had managed to get by in the real world. I nodded then blabbered "Two nice'uns and they match...your personality, you should be proud of them. They really compliment your eyes and you have two of them too."

"You have such a unique way with words, unlike anyone else for sure. And I'm glad you noticed I have a pair of matching ones, eyes I mean."

I took a deep breath, which was difficult with two feet in my mouth, then said, in my most meaningful, honest and sincere voice, "Maybe when this thing is over, I can pull an entire inventory, with your permission of course." Almost immediately regretting what I had just spilled from my lips, I braced my jaw muscles for the forthcoming facial slap when she replied,

"Possibly, you could work me into your busy schedule tonight, mister auditor, sir. I can't imagine you sending me back up that long lonely road to Due West by my lonesome. Remember there are deer out there."

Before I could respond, "Hey guys, mind if I join you?" asked Shorty, already perching his little fat ass on the bar stool directly behind her. "Larry is making some phone calls from his room. Peter and Stephen are out on the veranda. I haven't seen Stan since we arrived."

"He hasn't been in the bar, if that's what you're worried about," I told him, trying to signal him to leave. He didn't get it.

"Well, he's been off the booze for less than a day, so I would like to keep him sober," explained Shorty. "I'm afraid that one little social drink would do him in, in his fragile state."

"Why don't you take a look in the dining room?"

"Checked there before coming in here," answered Shorty.

"Hi guys," said Larry, still dressed like a normal person, or as normal as a blimp could dress, no priest collar in sight.

I couldn't help but ask, "How come you don't dress like a clergyman? I haven's seen you with one of those collars on yet?"

"I'm on vacation...time off with 'God' behavior. I can still do his bidding in the blink of an eye, if I need too, even out of uniform. Let's eat."

"Peter and Stephen are on the veranda," said Shorty, again. "I'll go round them up. Have you seen Stan?"

"Not since we left Payne's house and arrived here," replied Larry. "You don't think he's fell off the wagon already, do you?"

"That's what I'm thinking," answered Shorty. "Maybe we should fan out, and do a search before we eat?"

Larry sighed, obviously disappointed that we weren't already at the table. I ceased the moment. "Cassandra and I will check the parking lot."

"I'll ask Peter to cut the square with me," said Shorty. "Larry you hang out inside, and I'll have Stephen do the same outside. Let's meet back here in ten minutes."

Ten minutes I thought. That wasn't enough time. Well, actually it was more than enough time, if I only spent five on foreplay. I wanted more than my normal allotted time with Cassandra, so I decided, against my better judgment, that I wouldn't rush things with her. I hoped she didn't push the issue. What I am I thinking?

"Walking around this square sort of brings it all back, doesn't it?" commented Peter.

"It's just the square," replied Shorty. "We parked here, shot moons, tossed cherry bombs, and lusted over all the car loads of girls, not necessarily in that order. Don't go all mushy, nostalgic on me. Surely you haven't lived in Georgia that long?"

"Sorry, I guess I think about stuff more than I used too," he said, almost tearing up.

"I'm sorry, dude," replied Shorty, seeing the pain in his eyes. "I forgot about what you've been through, with that little girl and everything."

"It's not just that. I feel like my life has been one long screw up. Sure we were wild and crazy in high school, maybe a little wilder and crazier than most, but I think it really came unglued after we entered that house. Everything changed and nothing for the good."

"I'm with you, dude. I've had my share of ups and downs."

"A part of me says going back is the right thing, possibly the only thing that might make our lives right, but then another part of me tells me that we could be about to shit and fall back into it big time."

"I know Peter, I've thought the same thing but if we stick together, I believe it will turn out okay."

"Sticking together got us nowhere before..."

"I wish we had the answers, but it's for damned sure we can't go on like this. I refuse to do it. I think we're all tired of it."

"Poor Stephen, even this won't help him, will it," said Peter.

"If it restores his dignity and his sanity, then it will be worth it for him, I'm sure."

"You know, I've been thinking about Donnie a lot, not that I don't always, but this time it has been different. I've been having these weird dreams, too damn real for my comfort."

"Dude, Payne and I have been having strange dreams too. When did yours start?"

Thinking for a second, Peter finally said. "A little over three weeks ago, I reckon."

"First of October," gulped Shorty, swallowing deeply. "Damn, that's when ours started. Larry mentioned something to that effect too."

"And what about Stan...?"

"Not sure, but something caused him to stop drinking like a fish. I have a bad feeling about it."

"Me too," added Peter. "You head down Trinity Street. I'll check out the Rough House."

Standing in the parking lot behind the Belmont, with the street lights reflecting off the hood of the 85 Monte Carlo, I stared into that pair of dreamy eyes. Cassandra Blake had never looked lovelier. There was something about those glowing fluorescent lights that just framed and accented her beautiful features. Why had I not dated her while we were in school? Why, the damn house is why. It ruined everything.

I'm such a pushover for Monte Carlos. My father had bought the very first one in town back in 1970 from Reid's Motor Company. The new generation Chevy looked nothing like a Chevrolet. Shorty, Larry and I can testify to that fact. While driving to Greenwood at speeds exceeding seventy miles an hour, I was nailed by a state trooper. He had met us, and then turned around, and pulled me over at the county line. He wouldn't believe me when I told him the make was a Chevy. 'This ain't no Chev-er-lay, boy.' He finally conceded after walking around it three tines. He only gave me a warning, thank goodness.

Cassandra reminded me of that first Monte Carlo, sleek, new, exciting, with perky head lights. I had less than ten minutes to convey my feelings to her, but for once in my life my tongue felt swollen, way to large for my mouth, preventing me from articulating my thoughts. Like a deer in the headlights, I could not leap out of the way of the rushing vehicle. Yes, I was smitten by her.

She broke the silence, "I don't see Stan anywhere, do you?"

"Stan," still looking like the surprised deer, I finally muttered, "Right...Stan."

"I wonder if the others are having any luck. He's in such a fragile state right now. Anything could push him over the edge and back in the bottle." She continued to have a one way conversation for the most part. "What did he experience at that house to impact him like this?"

"I don't know. He would never talk about it to any of us." I glanced at my watch, time to rendezvous with the others. My window of opportunity had clearly slammed shut.

Inside we approached Larry, standing by a table of free finger foods. He had a hot wing in one hand and a little star shaped half sandwich in the other. A herd of Stan's could have stampeded past him, and I doubt if he would have taken notice. I spotted Stephen, peeping in a veranda window, and I motioned him inside. Shorty and Peter arrived just minutes later. No one had found hide or hair of Stan. He had vanished into thin air.

"Where do you think he went?" asked Stephen.

"He's been so unpredictable, especially with those wild

drinking binges," said Shorty. "I've retrieved him off the street countless times. I have taken him home, drunk out of his gourd. He'll eventually turn up. He always does."

"Let's do dinner and relax," I suggested. "We have an interesting day ahead tomorrow."

"I agree," said Peter. "We can discuss our game plan while we eat."

"Let's do it then," said Stephen, his voice sounding much weaker.

13

"We're supposed to go back. I can feel it. I want to, but I can't," mumbled Stan, huddled behind the trash bin, near the backdoor of the Rough House. "We'll die if we go back there. We'll all die for sure, but what sort of life do we have, if we don't. I can't stand this. The chickens have come back to roost, all eleven of them."

Still sober, he fretted with vengeance over the possibility of them returning, even though he had told the others he wanted to go back. His heart raced wildly. His blood pressure reached dangerous levels. Stan no longer took his one pill a day to keep it in check. He couldn't afford them. His face felt blazing fire hot. His breathing became labored, difficult.

Daylight had dwindled and darkness now surrounded him. His right hand still clutched the pencil in a death grip. He dropped the leather bound journal he had held in his left hand. He had mercifully finished his scribbling; his last testimonial of what had happened to him October 31st, 1968. Stan slummed against the wall and closed his eyes to rest. It seemed it had been forever since he had actually given in to a good night's sleep. The relentless nightmares would give him no peace, no matter how much he drank.

A tear ran down his cheek. He quickly wiped it with the back of his hand, and then his nose dripped a flood of runny snot. He swiped at it with his sleeve. He shook his head back and forth, trying to dismiss thoughts of his pathetic wasted life. He had never married or had experienced a meaningful relationship, all because of that damn old house. He blamed it for all his misfortunes.

The back door of the Rough House opened. Sheldon, the owner, walked over and tossed a couple of trash bags inside the big green bin. Stan melted into the shadows and remained undetected. The door closed, and with it darkness returned to his little hiding place.

He heard a rustling of leaves to his right, but realized no wind stirred. Hearing what sounded like shuffling foot steps coming in his direction, elevated his heart rate even more. The thunderous beating almost drowned out the sound of the foot falls. Sweat poured over his brow and stung his eyes. He blinked uncontrollably to clear his vision, straining to see who approached in the nearly pitch blackness.

He could almost make out movement, but chuckled, remembering how shadows always crept around in his childhood bedroom. He would just pull the covers over his head, and remain like that until the morning daylight chased away the monsters. He had no covers in the ally, so he placed his hands over his eyes, and then he just died. No warning, no pain, he just stopped breathing and faded away peacefully.

The old wino stood over him, kicked him in the foot a couple of times, leaned down and shook him. Satisfied that there would be no resistance, he stripped Stan down to his underwear and claimed everything as his own, including the journal and pencil. He covered Stan's lifeless body with empty cardboard liquor boxes. The wino then scurried off with his treasures, leaving Stan to his cardboard unmarked grave.

Sitting on the grass, trying on Stan's shoes, the old wino heard a noise behind him, heavily breathing and distorted. He turned to see the most hideous monstrosity towering over him, but before he could scream, the thing from a wino's worse nightmare was on him.

14

"Damn good meal," said Shorty. "Sorry Father, I didn't mean to curse."

"Bite me, son," snickered Larry. "Cut the crap, it's just us here, and I know what type of language you fellers are capable of spouting. I used to speak it fluently."

"So you and Cassandra are going to pull some research at the library tomorrow," repeated Peter.

"Yep, I want to follow a hunch about the house's architecture, the man who designed it, Orson Squire Fowler."

"Stephen and I will see if we can dig up any dirt on the Pressely or Frazier families," confirmed Larry.

"Good luck. Folks around here don't take kindly to questions about that place," I warned him.

"I've got to drive to Columbia and pick up Brody. We'll meet you tomorrow afternoon at Payne's," said Shorty.

"Guys, I have a doctor's appointment in Greenville," said Peter. "I'm not sure how long it will take, but I'll call the Belmont and leave a message at the desk before I head back. Larry, check the desk periodically, please."

"Are you still going through with that surgery?" asked Shorty.

Peter just shrugged. He did feel better here among friends, but he would not have them as a safety net forever. "If you don't mind putting me up Shorty..."

"I would have it no other way."

"Stephen is bunking with me," added Larry. "I have two

queens in my suite."

"One queen, unless you're coming out of the closet too," laughed Stephen.

"Uh, I have an extra bedroom at my place if you really would rather not drive back to Due West tonight, Cassandra." I actually said something worth while for a change, and kept to the script previewed in the parking lot.

"That sounds wonderful, but you'll have to let me borrow a tee-shirt or something. I left in such a rush I didn't pack a single thing, not that I had planned to stay."

"Tee-shirt, tooth brush, whatever you need," I smiled.

"Perfect host aren't you?"

"Perfect indeed...Guys, call me if any of you see Stan, and I'll do the same. Something stinks about him just vanishing."

The others confided they felt the same way.

"What you say we plan to meet at my house around two tomorrow afternoon," I suggested.

"Two PM it is," confirmed Larry.

We arrived at my place. I was quite nervous about this. I was questioning my intentions, and almost regretting I had invited her to stay, almost. I stood in the kitchen staring into space like a moron.

"I took liberty to take a shower," shouted Cassandra from the hallway.

She walked to the door. "How do I look in your Atlanta Braves jersey?"

I chanted like an Indian, and completed a series of tomahawk chops to show my approval, noticing her breasts, then her eyes, unfortunately in that order. She noticed the sequence too.

"So, are you still seeing twos?"

"Lot of good things tends to come in pairs. Did you find the tooth brush I left you?"

"Kissable clean...head to my toes."

Having a surge of boldness, I grabbed her by the hand and pulled her against me. Her breasts were as full and soft as they looked. Clutching her firm butt with both hands, I felt no panties. I immediately became aroused and she noticed the transformation.

"I don't think we'll be messing up those bed covers in the

spare bedroom tonight," I advised her. "That is unless you prefer to sleep alone."

She smiled. No words sometimes speak volumes. Caressing led to a deep passionate kiss. Suddenly I became clumsy, unsure if I should really be doing this. I had developed a conscious. She sensed my hesitation. She was cautious too. After all, we had waited a lifetime for this moment. It should be special.

Before I realized it, I was assisting her in slipping the shirt over her head and easing her butt up on the bathroom vanity. Standing flat footed was a new position for me. I guess this would be special, but not as I had envisioned. We awkwardly proceeded like two inexperienced eleventh graders.

Just like that, it was over. I stood there red faced and embarrassed. She just smiled and kissed me deeply, no apologizes required. I'm a one shot wonder, so what can I say. I had royally messed this up for her, possibly not for me, but definitely for her. Since when did I care if a woman got theirs before me, never; but this time felt different. It seemed I had somehow cheated her. Boy I was treading in new waters and I liked how it felt.

There was nothing to do now, but head to bed. We snuggled under the covers, and I began apologizing again. She smiled and kissed me deeply. Then just like that, with a Midas touch, she soon remedied the problem. After the marathon, we both lay spent. For the first time in a very long time I had forgotten about the house on the Cedar Springs Road.

A ray of light from a gap in the bedroom curtains, zeroed in on my eyes, blinding me like one of those laser trackers from a sniper's scope. I rubbed the crud from my eyes. Blinking, I stared at the digital clock on the night stand until it came into focus. 9:11 AM, I had not slept this long without the assistance of alcohol in forever. I ironically felt rested and rejuvenated.

Yawning and then taking a deep morning breath, the bed sheets smelled of sweat and raunchy sex. This had been missing from my bed for way too long. I felt wonderfully cheap and dirty. I had my back to my new bed buddy. She was glued to it like my shadow, one arm draped around my chest, one leg curled between my legs. Her tits pressed against my back, felt like the nipples of two pacifiers.

She emitted a comforting sound, a cross between a little

puttering 2 cycle engine and kitten's purr, her version of a snore, blowing against the back of my neck. Her breathing was sensual and deep, if breathing can be described as sensual. It comforted me and just felt so perfect.

Trying not to disturb her, I carefully raised her arm, eased my legs from her one planted between them, and rolled out of bed, landing clumsily on all fours. I turned expecting her to be awake and smiling, but instead she had instinctively turned to her other side, and had pulled the covers up to her nose. She looked like an angel; best I could tell, only seeing the back of her head under the covers. I have a vivid imagination.

I had this incredible urge to cook breakfast and serve her in bed. She had already served me there quite well. I opted for a quick shower first to wash off the residue of the night's escapades. It clung to my lower extremities like sticky molasses. I smiled when I realized my face felt the same way.

After a lengthily soapy shower, I glanced in the bedroom to see her still buried under the sheets. It must have been as good for her too or she was just very tired. I opted for the first version.

I scurried down the hallway to the kitchen, pitter pattering barefoot and shirtless, wearing only a pair of silky Mister Peanut underwear. I was ready to prepare a breakfast worthy of a queen. What I found in the refrigerator was a carton of two eggs, a half chunk of molted extra sharp cheese and one shriveled bell pepper. In the freezer compartment I discovered a chicken pot pie, three banana popsicles and a frozen bottle of Miller Lite. I had forgotten putting it there.

Panicking, I began flinging open the kitchen cabinet doors. There, on the second shelf, I spied a can of Spam. Perfect, I had my breakfast menu. I heard the shower running, so breakfast in bed would no longer be an option. I stifled the urge to join her; figuring desert might be served afterwards, banana split ala Payne style.

Basking in a sudden flash of afterglow, I had no inkling of the perils facing my fellow investigators in town. Life can be so unfair. We were the poster boys to prove it.

15

"Are you okay in there?" asked Larry, rapping on the bathroom door, hearing Stephen searching desperately for a Buick.

After about a minute of non stop regurgitating, Stephen finally mustered up a weak response, "Just part of my morning ritual, my version of purging my system to maintain my boyish figure. Don't try this at home."

"I should go on your program to shed some of this blubber," consoled Larry, through the still closed door.

"Trust me. My version is the kiss of death, literally."

Pastor Larry whispered a little prayer, wishing he could do more for his friend. Aids was not an uncommon sight to him. He had witnessed far too many other hapless souls wasting away to nothing, falling victim to this cruel disease.

He feared he would soon be forced to read Stephen his last rites, and bless his soul for the next journey. He certainly didn't cherish doing this for his dear friend, but he had accepted that responsibility long ago. After all, it was his chosen profession. He wasn't sure if Stephen was Catholic, but doubted it really mattered.

Stephen emerged from the bathroom, looking much worse than Larry remembered from just a few hours ago. His eyes were sunken dark and deep, cheek bones almost protruding. He had the look of a dead man walking. Remarkably, he remained upbeat.

"Well, are you up for a quick nine at High Meadows this morning, before we start our research?" He mustered a wink and a smile.

"I haven't thought about that nine hole course in years," exclaimed Larry, "Probably, because I suck at golf. I gave it up the year after we graduated."

"So I guess that would be a no..."

"That would be a hell no."

"Watch you mouth Reverend."

"I'm just keeping it real. God knows my limitations and my handicap. Are you hungry? Never mind. That look tells me I asked a stupid question."

"Larry, I just hope I make it long enough to see this through," he sighed, pulling out an already pre-rolled joint from a case on the nightstand. "Don't worry, it's legal. I have a prescription for my condition...sort of. I wrote it. Can I offer you a toke?"

"Nah, fire it up and enjoy. It should help the nausea and relieve some of the pain."

"And hopefully give me a case of the munchies," Stephen mustered up a chuckle.

"I don't need a joint to motivate me for that," laughed Larry, rubbing his prominent belly. "I'm going to miss you Stephen."

"Same here," replied a tearful Stephen. "I have no one to blame but myself. Life's choices can be cruel sometimes, but I have no regrets, except for going in that damned house."

"Hey, we had done it countless times, and had never encountered evil spirits before. I don't know why that particular time was a game changer."

"So you believe in evil spirits. Do you really think the house is haunted?"

"There are forces at work out there much greater than us. I'm a man of the cloth now, but I can't deny or dismiss what I witnessed that night. Can you?"

"I've thought about it a lot. I'm sure all of the guys have, and I still don't know if I believe what happened. I mean it happened. I know it did but I'm just not sure it happened like I remember it did. I was so wasted."

"I'm not sure I totally follow you Stephen."

"Okay, tell me your version then I'll tell you mine and let's see if they match."

"Fare enough, here goes but I'm a little fuzzy on the details too, compliments of one bottle too many of Boone's Farm Apple wine."

"You don't have to explain that to me," grinned Stephen, buzzing from the reefer. "Like I said, I was probably more wasted than any of you that night."

Larry started with his version of the episode. Well I do remember we parked at the foot of the fire tower road at Little Mountain. The two car loads emerged, everyone whooping and hollering like a bunch of wild men, our trait. I think Leroy, Charley and Lester were the only sober ones, but then again they always were. Personally, I couldn't have been around us sober.

I'm not sure who was more stumble down drunk, me or Stan. I'll give that honor to Stan, only because I remember being there and I'm sure he probably didn't.

Donnie was doing his usual, trying to pick a fight with all of us. That PJ always brought the worst out of him, such a violent inner soul. No one had seen this side of him but us. To everyone else he played the role of the personable and cordial All American Quarterback. He had such a promising college and professional career ahead. I suspect that's why the town took it so hard and blamed us, the band of drunken misfits.

I think Payne suggested us forgoing climbing the tower road and then the tower. He suggested us checking out the creepy unoccupied house instead. Halloween, it sounded like the perfect way to end our night before heading to the river to camp out. I remember hoping Stan had another 8-track besides *Neil Diamond* belting out *Crackling Rosy*. He wore that one out the last time we crashed at the river. We all loved exploring those old houses. The Rock House apparently had not satisfied our appetites that particular night.

I don't really recall which car I ended up in, and don't remember much about the drive there. Next thing I do remember is that we were stumbling down the drive. At least I was stumbling. We had maybe three working flash lights between us, but the full moon helped guide the way. I'm sure glad you didn't transform into a werewolf.

We unintentionally began spurring off into three or so groups, huddling with the ones that possessed the flash lights. I ended up with Payne, a flash light owner, and Shorty. I'm not sure how the other groups panned out; who was with whom. Payne decided to explore the log cabin first, that one adjacent to the main house. We followed like two little trailing sheep. Payne loved exploring haunted places. He's always been fanatical about horror and science fiction crap, more so than the rest of us combined.

Shorty stopped to take another piss. It seemed like he pissed about every fifteen minutes when drinking. I think he's cursed with a small bladder and active kidneys. Payne checked the cabin door, locked. He walked, and I stumbled clumsily, around the side, checking the windows. Ironically, all the panes were in place, none broken. Finally he found one unlocked in the back and eased it up. It made a spine tingling creaking sound, perfect for a haunting.

He clambered in, and I followed. I'm not sure what happened to Shorty because he wasn't behind me. The window slammed shut after I cleared it. I dropped onto the filthy floor, landing belly down. It scared the crap out of both of us. Payne dropped his flash light. Man it was suddenly darker than my worse nightmare. We laughed it off. He banged the flashlight with his hand until it finally flickered back to life.

What little furniture occupied the one room cabin looked incredibly old and thickly layered with a ton of dust. I felt like we had just walked out of the *Time Tunnel*, one of my favorite television shows by the way. It wouldn't take us long to explore the one room.

Old glasses and dishes occupied a cupboard, most were cracked or broken. An assortment of tarnished silverware laid claim to a drawer. The beam caught sight of a crudely constructed bookshelf, only one book rested on the top shelf, almost out of reach. Standing on my tip toes, I managed to retrieve it. It was an old bible with a tattered binder, dog eared with the outer layer of pages yellow and brown colored. After flipping through a few pages, I placed it down on the bottom shelf. Having not found my religious calling yet, it really didn't hold my interest.

A peculiar smell burned my nostrils. It smelled of hard earned sweat, not sickening like someone well past due for a shower. I had smelled that same type of odor somewhere before, but couldn't place where at the time. I remember where and who now though, Mattie, my black nanny. She always had this odd body odor, not offensive, but it caused me to associate it with black people for some reason, a young's boy's perception.

That very same scent hung in the air of that cabin. It hadn't been there when we entered. I should have asked Payne if he smelled it, but I didn't think it was that important. I was too drunk, I reckon. We stayed in the cabin less than five minutes. We exited through the front door, unlocking it from the inside. There was still no sign of Shorty.

We could see lights and shadows coming from a couple of windows of the huge three story house, a result of flashlight toting buddies already scouting out the premises. Payne hated it when someone else entered one of these old houses before him, but he had chosen to look in the cabin first. Snooze, you loose.

We made our way across the overgrown lawn, almost thigh high in places. The tall massive oaks with thick long branches spread like open arms. I don't know why, but the sight of them sent a shiver down my back. They appeared poised to snatch us up before we reached the porch, which spanned the full width of the house. The trees allowed us to pass in peace. I feared that they would grab us on the return trip.

We could hear hoots and laughter from inside. I recognized Donnie's voice, and then Stan's. Payne nudged me, saying to watch this. He snuck onto the porch and located a window. He highlighted his face with the flashlight then banged on the window, screaming a customized Payne style scream. It worked flawlessly. It startled the hell out of them, not that they would ever admit it.

I peered in a second window. I saw Lester, Donnie, Leroy and Charley disappearing up a narrow stairway. Stan sat in a corner, chin resting on his chest, on the verge of passing out. He still clutched an Orange Tommy bottle. I figured you must be with Stan, Peter and Brody in the adjoining room. I still didn't know where Shorty was, but he was there without a flash light, because we only had three.

Payne and I entered through an open doorway. I sat down beside Stan. I tried to revive him, but he just spewed incoherent gibberish, before bursting into his patented contagious laughter.

It worked, because I laughed too, at what, I had no idea.

Payne disappeared, exploring the bottom floor, leaving Stan and me in the dark, all except for the moon beams. I could hear the footsteps on the second floor above us. I'm not sure if Stan heard anything, but he continued to burst into bouts of laughter, never opening his eyes. I didn't know what he had found so funny.

I suddenly heard a yell like a banshee from outside. It didn't sound put on. I crawled over to a window, leaned with my back against the wall just adjacent to it. I was leery of peeping out, fearful that something would be looking at me from the other side. Hearing a second scream and recognizing Shorty's voice, I mustered up the courage to take a quick peek.

What I am about to tell you, I have not shared with anyone, except the good Lord above. I'm not sure if even He believed me. Shorty ran across the front lawn, flailing his hands like he was swatting at a swarm of mad hornets. In the moonlight I could detect no swarm, but I did see an odd smoky apparition, some twenty feet behind him, drifting effortlessly in his direction and keeping pace.

It took shape off and on as it moved, almost had human features. I do believe it sensed me at the window, because it stopped abruptly, just hung their slightly above the ground. I saw a face looking directly at me. Let me tell you, it wasn't a happy face either. I dropped from the window and crawled at hyper speed back toward Stan, but Stan was gone. I was alone, in the dark and no longer feeling the affects of Boone Farm Apple wine.

Now that I think about it, that face looked ancient, almost primitive and it was feminine, in a scary sort of way. It was definitely not a modern day apparition, if indeed that's what it was. I could hear the thundering footsteps, sounding like they had reached the third floor.

What I did next was strictly impulsive and cowardly. I bolted out the door, with reckless abandon. I didn't look back or stop running until I was safely in the back floor of Lester's Charger. I had my head buried under the floor mat. I remained there until I heard the door open, and Lester asking me what the hell I was doing. I almost pissed in my pants when he opened that door.

He asked me what was wrong. I sat on the edge of the seat, and just told him we needed to leave. He told me to stay put. He would go round up the others. I kept a watchful eye on the lawn and house, could see the light from one flashlight on the third floor. I wondered where the other two flash lights were.

I heard more screams. These sent chill bumps down my arms. They didn't sound playful either. These sounded genuine and in trouble. I slunk back down like the coward I was, to my floor mat safe haven, where I remained until some of you returned.

16

"I must say Payne, I never knew Spam could be a culinary experience," remarked my house guest.

"It's a gift;" I replied, "All of us great chefs can take a few simple items and create a work of art for the palette."

"Well I must commend you then. You're the gift that keeps on giving, old great one."

"You wore me out too."

"I'm sorry you're tired," she moaned, in a mockingly disappointed way.

"I think we missed doing it on the kitchen table last night so we didn't complete the world tour of every room."

There she went again, with that smile, the one that dares me to do stupid stuff. I flung the paper plates and cups from the table, not breaking a single one. We completed the tour, and then took another shower together, finding a new way to scrub-a-dub-dub. Drying off with a towel, she finally reminded me, "This has been wonderful, but shouldn't we be heading to the library? It's almost noon."

"Like this," I replied. "We should put on some clothes first."

"I can slip back on what I wore yesterday. I'll pick up a few things this afternoon, if you wish me to stay?"

"What you're wearing is fine," I replied, tugging at her towel. "And you have an open invitation."

"Perfect..."

Within twenty minutes, we were at the library and inquiring

about any information Miss Riley Wilson may have on Orson Squire Fowler or his writings. She was most helpful, recognizing his name and his link to the house's design. Luckily she was new in town, and didn't know me or my interest in the subject. I suppose a little paranoia had set in for me, thinking a conspiracy was out to shut us down. No horde of vigilantes stormed the library.

We discovered that Fowler had been born in 1809. He had been laid to rest in 1887, and to my surprise, had been quite a character. His first publication, *Perfection of Character*, supported various forms of self culture. He was a proponent of phrenology. Neither Cassandra nor I knew what the hell that meant, so we paused to research the definition. We discovered it was the science of studying bumps and fissures on the skull to determine personality traits. He would have had his hands full with this bunch of knot heads.

Reading on, it mentioned him being the creator of the octagon house design. We knew that already. He authored several sex manuals. We didn't know that. Now we were talking, a man after my own hard. Fowler was a regular one stop shop with his belief in women's rights, when it wasn't cool back in those Victorian times. He stood up for kid's rights and was against child labor. He could have run one of those dating services back then, dabbling into marriage counseling, sex education and finding the ideal mate.

He proposed ideas about hydropathy, another term that baffled us. It had something to do with curing diseases with water. The old boy didn't like tobacco use or women wearing tight corsets, but yet he wrote sex manuals. Apparently he had an opinion on just about everything. He was way ahead of his time.

"He was really into that phrenology crap," I remarked, growing tired of reading about it. He and his cronies practiced what they preached.

"Even Mark Twain got into it, and took a few humorous shots at Fowler," added Cassandra. "It really took off and many believed in it."

"Here we go." I said, "Now were getting to the ties with the octagon design."

The article stated that *his phrenological studies had*

persuaded him that the field of architecture would be his next forte. As he explained, every man could be his own architect. No apprenticeship was necessary if one were endowed with strong phrenological organs of INHABITIVENESS (Love of Home), and CONSTRUCTIVENESS (the ability to build). Architecture was then but child's play.

"Well doesn't that just say it all," I said, scratching my head, wondering what the hell we had just read.

"Look here," she pointed to a sentence mentioning his publication of The Octagon House, *A Home for All*. "He wanted all houses to be built in the octagon shape. He even designed schools and churches with the same thing in mind."

"It says here that the octagon architecture had been around even before Fowler tried to claim credit for it," I added. "There are all sorts of buildings mentioned as early as the 1600's. I can't tell a lie. George Washington even had an octagon shaped barn and garden house in Mount Vernon. Not to be outdone, Thomas Jefferson built an octagon shaped house in Virginia. There was an endless list of octagon homes, their owners and locations.

Fowler was obsessed with the design. He professed that the design could be adapted for any sized home. He even came up with inexpensive materials like gravel, lime and sand, his version of concrete. He proclaimed his design was healthier, cheaper to heat, and a centrally located spiral stair case would provide better air circulation, and the windows, plenty of light.

He even built a humongous version in New York with sixty main rooms and forty other rooms and closets. His staircase was seventy feet high and enclosed in glass. On the main floor he could transform four octagonal rooms into one large one with a series of folding partitions.

The man was amazing for sure. This monster house had central heat, hot and cold running water, indoor flushing toilets, a rain water collection system, lighting from natural gas, both a water filtration and gravity-fed water system. He even had an early version of an intercom system, using speaking tubes as he called them. Dumbwaiters kept the food moving throughout the various floors.

Something else caught my eye in the article. It was exactly what I had hoped to find. I read it out loud to Cassandra. "Listen to this," I prepared her.

One such unit is at the Genesee Country Village Museum just southwest of Rochester, New York, built in 1870 by Erastus Hyde and his wife Julia in Friendship, New York. He was a homeopathic physician and herbalist, while she was a Methodist minister. They had become involved in the then popular Spiritualist Movement which began not too far from Rochester. Their wooden, octagonal house, by virtue of its plan, was perfect for spiritualist séances, since it had no deep corners which could harbor evil spirits during their séances with the spirits of the dead. Naturally, in time the house came to be considered haunted. The building was dismantled into 6,000 numbered pieces in order to move it to the Genesee Country Village Museum where it has been carefully restored and furnished in the proper Victorian fashion of its day. Legend claims that the workmen involved in the restoration of the building were bothered by the fact that their tools moved of their own accord into different places from which they had been left, and the Museum Director's dog always refused to go into the building when its master entered it. Nonetheless, it is a most popular building in the Museum Village today, despite the overtones of its haunted nature.

"Pay dirt, now we're on to something," I announced. "I just knew that peculiar design had a connection to all of this."

"So you believe it is the design instead of circumstances shrouding the house."

"It could be both. The house design might just provide the perfect door, a portal for restless spirits like that house in New York. Seems like that physician and his wife thought so."

"Odd don't you think, that a Methodist or any minister would be involved in spiritual séances."

"Brain storm," I shouted almost too loudly in the confines of the library. I caught a few stares. "We have the best of both worlds."

She looked puzzled. "I know I'm going to regret this, but what are you talking about?"

"You...you're our medium, gypsy woman. And we have Larry, our own Catholic Priest. This plan is falling into place wonderfully."

"I'm not so sure the Catholic Church would buy into to this,

Payne."

"Hey, they perform exorcisms, don't they?"

"I think a Priest has to ask permission and lay out his case first. We don't have that sort of time, not if you're determined to do this Friday. It's Tuesday if you haven't forgotten."

"Believe me, Mondays and Tuesdays will forever be etched in my memory; thanks to you for making those memories so vivid and wonderful."

She smiled. "We still have five days to go.

"I know. We haven't desecrated my carport and utility room yet."

"Washer or dryer," she replied, then rolled her eyes.

"I'm certainly having a positive influence on you. Your sarcastic wit has really improved in just two short days. I've brought you down to my level."

"I learn quickly, but seriously, I'm not sure about bringing in the church without permission. We don't want to get Larry defrocked."

"You let me worry about Larry. He was one of us before he ever became one of them. He can cut a few corners for the cause. He's got as much at stake as we do. I've got to find the John. What about you?"

"I'm fine."

I got in one last one. "Doing it in the library opens up more possibilities, but we better wrap this thing up so we'll be at the house before the others arrive. I promise. I will make it up to you."

"You're unbelievable. I'll read on, and see if I can uncover anything else while you're gone," she said, patting me on my ass.

17

"Well, that about does it for me," said Larry. "What do you remember about that night, Stephen?"

"Well contrary to what you thought, I wasn't with the others as you suspected. With my addiction, as you all know about now, I slipped off behind one of those enormous oaks to burn one. No one really noticed. I popped some magic pills too."

"Well, most of us were too trashed to care. You concealed it well though."

I had several rolled joints in my boot and fired one up. I watched the flash lights beaming wildly across the yard. My buddies were whooping and hollering like a thousand maniacs rushing toward that house. It reminded me of an attack of marauding Yankees on the unsuspecting southern rebels, residing safely inside. I expected to see the plantation set afire, the women raped, the slaves set free but only after the place had been properly pillaged.

I had quite a buzz going on when I caught sight of another flashing beam, heading in the opposite direction. Curious and totally wasted, I followed to find out who had branched off away from the old mansion. At the time, I had no idea it was you and Payne, until I closed the distance. I never saw Shorty either.

You had already entered the cabin by the time I caught up. I fired up a second joint. I watched you guys from a side window. I had planned to scare the crap out of you. The surprise was on me. I felt someone touch me on the shoulder from behind, rather firmly I must say. I whirled around to see which one of you were messing with me. Nobody was there. Now that was just too damn creepy. I shrugged it off, thinking I had really lucked up on some good shit with that last dime bag I had purchased. I would have to remember where I bought it.

You two didn't stay in there very long. After you left, I went inside, figuring no one would be coming back anytime soon. I could do my thing undetected and uninterrupted. That spook house crap didn't really interest me. Getting ripped did.

"Don't take this the wrong way. Larry, but I didn't really enjoy being around straight people like you guys when I really got stoned. I feared I would mess up and reveal my secret. I wasn't ready for that. Staying in my closet was much safer back then. I wasn't sure if you guys would still like me if I confessed I was queer. Have you ever smoked weed?"

"Can't say that I have but I must confess. I took a couple of those diet pills while trying to cram for a test once. Aren't they some sort of speed?"

"I don't think they will require any Hail Mary's."

Attempting to enhance my metaphoric state, I dropped some acid. What happened next, I am not completely sure was real, or induced by the acid trip, or both. Possibly it just opened my mind and channeled the events to me, transforming me into some sort of spiritual magnet. Today, reflecting, I'm still not sure what I experienced.

Enjoying the ambiance of the deserted log cabin and under the influence, in a severely drug enhanced state; I journeyed down a familiar road, questioning my sexuality. The road forked. I stood there juggling my options. Who was I really? For a young adult, this is an extremely difficult question. I should know.

The right path leads me to a safe place, where I would not be ridiculed and tormented for my life style. The left path; however, opens up an ugly can of worms, where I must defend daily who I am. There I would have to hide my sexual preferences from the public eye. It could leave me lynched by my nuts, still alive and screaming, only if I am lucky.

My head told me to take the safe route and avoid conflict, live to love another day. My heart said, screw it and live my life like I saw fit. In 1968, that left fork would be a daily battle, brutal and one that I may not survive, living here in the south. I always picked the right fork then, buried myself deeper in the closet and my drugs. I suffered from depression, but I didn't know it. My addiction didn't help.

"I know I've drifted away from the point of this exercise, to remember what happened that night, but to me that was a very important part of it."

"Stephen," said Larry, in a priestly tone. "It's your turn, your story, you tell it your way. I would not have judged you back then, nor will I judge you now. I love you for being Stephen and my friend. Please continue."

I sat there, backed into a corner, sitting on the floor, a corner that depicted my life perfectly I suppose. I heard noises, far away at first, or maybe it just seemed far away, because I was tripping. I snuffed out the joint and fanned the air furiously, thinking you had returned. It seems silly now. You weren't my parents, so why was I so intent on hiding the truth. I guess I associated my secret drug abuse with my secret life style. Exposing one would expose the other.

I thought I saw movement from the corner of my eye. An abundance of moonlight filtered in the three cabin windows, and because my eyes had adjusted, I could see the single room clearly. Darkness had always been my safe zone. I possess cat eyes to some extent. I stared, trying to figure out what had moved. I detected a sound and movement from the opposite direction. I swirled too late. I saw no one.

I broke into a giggle, one that would even make Stan proud. You know the one. I willed myself to stand. That in itself was a major accomplishment. On wobbly legs, I held onto the wall for support. I inched my way toward the book shelves. The sounds and glimpses of movement intensified, but it didn't deter my quest to reach those book shelves.

Just as my hand made contact with that bottom shelf, some one hurled a plate. It shattered just inches from my hand. In slow motion I fell backwards, losing my balance and crashing to the floor on my ass. Laughing out loud, I eased up on one knee, and held onto the side of the book shelf. I attempted to stand.

A cup, and then a glass crashed just above my head. Shrapnel rained down on me. Suddenly this wasn't so funny. I yelled for you bastards to stop. I turned to face whichever one of you was pulling this crap. The room remained empty. I saw no hiding place for the chunkers. This really freaked me out. Someone was throwing that dinnerware and getting too damn close.

I leaned against the wall. I waited for the next projectile. A couple of minutes must have passed and nothing happened. Satisfied that this phenomena had to be drug induced, I turned to examine the book shelves again, unsure why they so intrigued me. A fork buried into the wood, grazing my left pinky finger. No one could be that accurate with a fork. Besides, forks don't easily stick into wood.

Panic set in. A drug induced trip had gone unpredictably bad. I tried to convince myself that this was impossible. How many countless times had we visited legendary haunted places, and walked away in a drunken stupor, scoffing that nothing really haunted those places. I had never contemplated what we would do if faced with a ghostly encounter. I thought, only Payne could appreciate this moment.

Before I regained any semblance of composure, a spoon whizzed by my right ear, its handle buried an inch deep into the wood. Now that one really got my attention. Spoons are not built for dart throwing. At that moment, I had a somewhat uncontrollable religious experience. I grabbed that bible off the top shelf. I started begging for forgiveness, for being so wasted, and in the wrong damn place.

A vicious cold blast of air slammed me, rocking me backward. The window panes rattled. I heard a door open and slam several times, not unlike how I slammed a door when pissed off at someone. I clutched that bible to my bosom. I thought about clicking my heels together and screaming there's no place like home at the top of my lungs. I would have done it to, if I had thought it would have gotten me the hell out of there, even to Kansas.

I never saw an actual materialized entity, like you said you saw, but I had seen enough to know that it was time for me to make like horse shit and hit the trail. Exit stage right, man, and I hauled ass. At first the door would not open. How could it be jammed? It wasn't jammed when I entered. Fighting with that door knob, like I was fighting for my life, it finally opened.

I hauled ass and leaped into Peter's Chevy, thanking my lucky stars that the top was up. After scanning the darkness for pursuers and satisfied there were none, I fired up my last joint, and I just waited. I had no idea you were hiding in the Charger, or I would have been in that backseat with you.

"So," spoke up Larry. "We had to wait almost twenty years before we shared our experiences from that night."

"Well, I guess all of us shared a few tidbits with one another, but after how the public treated us, especially Payne, we just clamed up to avoid more humiliation. It was the sort of public humiliation I had tried to avoid all my life. Go figure that one, Padre."

"A gay drug addict," whispered Larry. "You wouldn't have stood a chance in hell in this town."

"That's a fact, Jack."

18

"Welcome back and not a minute too soon," said Cassandra. "Read this," she said, pointing to the article.

"We've got to get back to my house, so just give me your version on the way," I said, gathering up the scattered papers and walking toward the exit.

"It seems Mister Fowler was more into sex than we had originally read. Not only did he write books, he conducted lectures on the subject. He believed in radical reforms for marriage, parenting, and he really treaded on thin ice with his spin on changes of sexual attitudes."

"Well like I said earlier, he had an opinion on everything."

"It seems he could pack a house at first with his lectures, whether society believed in his concepts or not. I guess sex is always a drawing card."

"It is for me."

"He finally crossed the line when he wrote a book called *Creative and Sexual Science,* assisting married couples in how to love scientifically. In that book he included stuff like explaining how men and women had the duty to promote sexual vigor, signs of sexual conditions, how young men could increase a woman's love without shocking them and so on."

"It would have been a best seller today."

"There's plenty more about the life and times of Orson Squire Fowler, but I don' think it will help our cause, not anything to do with that old house."

"I trust and value your opinion," I answered, exiting the library.

"Well if it isn't my former, ace photographer," said Mister Easterly, in a not so affectionate tone. "So what brings you to our fine county library? Are you placing an application and starting your new career, Payne?"

"I used to look up to you as a father figure," I told him, looking him square in his beady little eyes. "But that was before I knew what a son of bitch you were. Now excuse us, or should I just say move your ass out of our way."

"Now there's no cause to be crude, Payne. Then again, I suppose you've reunited with your class of high school hooligans. You've obviously digressed, and have reverted to your old ways."

Now I'm not a violent person. Actually I'm a chicken by nature. I avoid confrontations, especially physical ones at all cost, but with a clinched jaw, and an even more clinched right fist, I decked the old bastard on that south main side walk. It hurt my hand like hell, but felt pretty damned rewarding.

"If you stand back up before we get in our car, I'll knock the hell out of you again," I warned him, before opening the door for Cassandra. "And if you're thinking about suing me or pressing charges, just remember, I know where you live, and no restraining order will prevent me from bringing over my gang of hooligans, and beating you within an inch of your life. We have no witnesses that I just threatened you, do we sweetheart?"

"Oh my, look Payne, that sweet looking old man just fell," mocked Cassandra. "Should we call an ambulance or help him stand?"

"Not just yet," I replied. "But you better jot down the number. We could still use it."

I watched in the rearview mirror, while he actually stayed down until we put about a hundred yards between us. I might have won that battle, but I suspected this war had a ways to go yet. My gut told me we were probably outnumbered and outgunned. We had them where we wanted them, I smiled.

When we pulled into my street, I saw Shorty's car already parked in the drive. He and Brody were already inside. Shorty knew where I kept my emergency key.

Entering, I saw Shorty sitting on the den's sofa, sipping on an adult beverage. It was Jack and Coke I suspected. "Where's Brody, in the bathroom?"

"He's not here," answered Shorty, bottoming out his drink. "He refused to come, changed his mind or better put, he plain freaked out, and had to be restrained with a straight jacket, and then medicated."

I felt like a spent condom on a deflating erection, poor Brody. "How are you holding up?"

"Forth drink so far, but check back with me after a couple of more."

"What happened?" asked Cassandra.

"When I arrived, he had his bag packed. He was anxious to leave. Then dumbass-me, I started talking about the house and our plans. He just lost his cookies, and started raving and ranting like a lunatic. He knew we were planning to go back, so I'm not sure what made him snap. I had told him yesterday on the phone, that we were returning. He seemed fine with it; actually excited, I thought."

"Is there anything we can do?"

"Pray he doesn't have to stay there forever, Payne. I need another drink. Can I fix you one?"

"Yeah, I'll have one with you," I told him, not really wanting one, but knowing he didn't need to drink alone.

"Fix me one too," said Cassandra, giving me a little wink. "Make it a light one though." She laid a big old wet one on me after Shorty cut the corner. "We're going to work through this," she assured me.

Shorty returned with a round of drinks. "I really hoped Brody would be able to join us."

"I regret it for him. Do you know what frightened him so?"

"I do. And it wasn't that far off from what terrified the crap out of me that night. I've never shared it with anyone, including Brody."

"Not even Peter," I twisted the dagger just a tad, knowing how Peter confided in Shorty. He was after all, the better listener.

"No one," exclaimed Shorty. "We sort of let you take the fall for all of us. That was so wrong. I'm sorry, Payne."

Stephen and Larry walked into the room, taking us by

surprise.

"Okay boys, what did you learn today?" I asked, trying to change the subject.

"Payne, we let you down I'm afraid," spoke up Larry. "We didn't get around to researching the house, but we compared notes from that night. We should have told what happened back then, but we were spineless little bastards."

"Anything earth shattering?"

"You tell us what you found out," answered Larry. "And what happened to each of you that night, and then we'll recap our tales."

"Fine," I said. "Has anyone seen Peter yet? And what about Stan, has he turned up?"

"No on all accounts," replied Stephen.

We shared what we had uncovered, concerning the house's design and Fowler. Neither seemed surprised or overwhelmed. They didn't ascertain the significance yet.

"Payne, I've told Stephen what I saw that night. He shared what happened to him with me, both inside the log cabin and in the house. Now you guys need to tell us what happened to you that night. Like our encounters, it screwed up your worlds too. Afterwards, we'll pile ours on."

A necessary evil, I knew we had to eventually cross this bridge, and I guess today would be that day. Denial better served my purposes. My purposes were not necessarily on the top of the agenda. We should begin.

"Look," motioned Stephen, pointing to the large picture window.

We saw Peter pull up in front. We decided to delay our discussion until he could be part of it. Putting all of our cards on the table seemed long overdue. We all had sort of remained in denial, too embarrassed to confide in one another. Some best friends we were. Now we had an opportunity to cleanse our tormented souls, unlock the mystery from 1968, and free ourselves from this curse.

"Well?" I asked first.

He shrugged, "I decided not to do it."

"Not to keep your appointment?" I prodded.

"No, I kept my appointment...sort of," Peter explained. "I

decided not to have the reduction surgery."

"Just curious, what changed your mind? Don't get me wrong, I'm glad you did."

"The doctor," he noted, with an accented smile.

"Did he tell you it was too dangerous?" asked Stephen.

"Nope, after one look, she said it was the most incredible creation she had ever seen. She said it would be a crime to destroy the ninth wonder," he gloated. "I may have embellished that last part. She has some ideas about special fittings and restraining rings that should prevent mishaps."

"Sounds like a very special doctor," commented Cassandra. "Too bad she is your doctor, I see a little sparkle in those eyes."

"Yep, it's not ethical to mix it up with a patient," agreed Peter. "She expressed that to me just before she removed herself from my case, and referred me to a colleague. We have a date Saturday night, so let's not screw up Friday."

"You are certainly blessed in more ways that just that one," expressed Larry. "You are surrounded by those who love you."

"I know," answered Peter. "So what did you boys find out?"

"Did you see Stan on your drive through the square," I asked.

"I'm afraid not," answered Peter.

"It's not the first time he has dropped off the face of the earth," spoke up Shorty. "When he gets on one of those drinking binges, he could end up almost anywhere. I suggest we get started. He will eventually show up."

Larry and Stephen decided to give us an abbreviated version of their experiences first. After finishing, Peter's only comment was, "I don't guess you have any PJ?" I seconded the motion.

"You and Donnie were the brewing experts," chuckled Larry. "My motivation came from a wine bottle."

"I sure do miss Donnie," said a solemn faced Peter. "I hope we uncover the answers."

"That's the intent, dude," said a slurred tongued Shorty, already feeling the results from a seventh Jack and Coke.

"I'll start," volunteered Peter. "Might as well just get it out of the way."

Stan was just too ripped to climb the stairs, so Brody set his butt down and told him to stay put. He didn't resist. Hell he couldn't even stand up on his own. He just sat there, mumbling and laughing out loud. We figured he'd be all right until we returned for him.

Lester, Charley, Leroy and Donnie ventured off, exploring the first floor. I could hear them several rooms away. Brody and I cautiously made our way up the stairs. Between the PJ and Hoppin Gators, neither of us was feeling any pain either.

Just as we reached the second floor, I heard Brody gagging behind me. I turned just in time to catch a spew of his puke on my tennis shoes and jean cuffs. The stench overwhelmed me, and I cut loose too. What a pair of spook hunters we made. One tried to out up-chuck the other like we were dueling pukers.

Brody crawled on hands and knees, just inside the first room at the top of the stairs. He waved me to go on. I was spent too. I sat down beside him. After a couple of minutes he toppled over on his side next to one of those huge old luggage trunks. I knew he was done. I told him I'd grab him on the way back down, then started doing the room to room exploration of the second floor. I first deserted Stan, then Brody; what a friend.

I was surprised to see scattered pieces of furniture still occupying the house. I could hear the others on the opposite side of the house, still on the first floor. Donnie's voice blared out louder than the others, but I figured that was the PJ talking. Lester had tried one cup, but those other two boys were tight assed non drinkers.

Suddenly it dawned on me that I was alone in the middle of that house on the second floor. I had a panic attack and twirled around, thinking I heard boards creaking behind me. I had never been alone in one of those spook houses before, and let me tell you, it wasn't a good feeling. There's not a brave bone in my body. I'm not ashamed to admit it.

With the PJ juice raising hell through my blood stream and still feeling puny, I became totally disoriented. I wasn't sure which way to go to return to Brody. That's when I saw lights coming from underneath a door on the opposite side of what looked like some sort of den or sitting room. I didn't hear the normal yelling and laughing. I figured it was some of the guys messing with me, like always. I smelled set-up.

I yelled, telling them to kiss my royal butt. I wasn't scared of their crap. The light grew brighter. It looked too bright to be one of our flashlights. My eyes began running, like I had grit in them. I found it hard to breath. I yelled at them again. The light underneath that door didn't waver or diminish. It sort of pulsated. Flashlights don't pulsate. Drunks don't think clearly, either.

I inched my way closer, shinning my own flash light, scanning the door. I decided it must be a closet. I got to within a couple of feet and my flash light flickered, then went out. Other than the moon rays causing weird shadows, the room went deathly black.

I took two quick steps, grabbed the door knob with my hand for a change, and jerked it open. A light ten times brighter than a strobe blinded me, and then I got slammed by this incredibly powerful whoosh, knocking me backwards, into the air, feet sprawled out in front of me. It felt like a freight train had run over me. When I shook the cobwebs, I was flat on my back, over ten feet from the door.

My skin tingled from head to toe. My teeth ached to the gums. The tips of my fingers felt hot and burned. My ears were ringing, like someone had exploded a cherry bomb just inches away. I had crapped in my pants. The room was black as pitch, and then from the other side of the room, magically, my flash light came back on. I was spellbound.

Embarrassed, I impulsively slipped off my pants, cleaned up with my underwear and hid them in a fireplace. Just as I put back on my shoes, I heard a blood curdling scream. I recognized Brody's voice. I grabbed the flash light and followed the scream, a scream that seemed endless. Just before I arrived, the scream became muffled, and then stopped all together.

I reached the stairway. Brody was not where I had left him beside that trunk. The whole episode, including me cleaning up, had probably lasted less than five minutes; precious minutes too many.

I heard a low whimpering sound, almost like a winding down siren. It emitted from that trunk. I hesitated, and then opened it, remembering what had just happened with that door. Like an approaching ambulance siren, the volume continued to increase at an astounding rate. I mustered up one large spurt of courage, grabbed the leather handle, flipped the metal latch on the lid and jerked it open, flash light aimed like a rifle.

Wide eyed and yelling, like he was being murdered, lay Brody, curled up in an almost impossible human position. I tried to calm him down, but he just continued to emit this ear bursting cry. I covered my ears, shouting for him to stop, but he wouldn't. I then did an unforgivable thing. I slammed the trunk lid back closed, and this time, he hushed up. The deathly quite scared me even more.

I dragged the trunk to the next room with Brody packaged inside. I just sat there on it, as if I was trying to hatch an egg. I don't know to this day why I did that, but I did. That's the last thing I remember until Shorty woke me up.

I can still feel that lick he gave me square on the jaw, after I told him Brody was inside. He almost broke it. I certainly deserved the beating of my life for doing it. It wasn't like me to act like that. The PJ had nothing to do with my reaction. I had lost that buzz after everything started unfolding. Puking helps sober your ass.

Shorty shook his head back and forth, and then bottomed his eighth drink. He should have been in a comatose state. "I still have a hard time with what you did, but I do forgive you, Peter. I know it wasn't you. That house messed with all of us. You didn't put Brody in that trunk."

"I feel directly responsible for Brody being institutionalized," sighed Peter. "I deserted him."

"Peter, like I just said, you didn't put him in that trunk, but I know who did."

"Guys, it's almost 6 PM," advised Cassandra. "I've ordered pizza. Why don't we take a little break?"

"Wise woman," I said, giving her an affectionate hug. We just seemed right for each other. Of course that's my opinion.

19

A rusted and dented 1979 green two door Buick Electra pulled onto the grass, just off the asphalt road. It chugalugged to a stop, black smoke puffed from its exhaust pipe. The occupant glanced at the time, 5:11. It would soon be dark. The autumn days had become shorter. The driver grew nervous and anxious with the setting sun. From this angle, seeing the entire house was nearly impossible and maybe a blessing.

Fingers thumped the steering wheel, playing no particular tune. The house and its surrounding buildings stood in tact, protesting the hand of time. The house was darkened and unoccupied. It had been like this forever. The driver routinely parked in front, searching for answers, but daring not to enter the property.

Staring from window to window, specifically those located on the third floor, the driver took a long pull from the paper bagged pint bottle, Southern Comfort, sweet tasting but affective. Empty beer cans decorated the back seat floor. Empty potato chip bags and hamburger wrappers adorned the front seat and passenger side floorboard.

The driver checked the mirror for any oncoming cars, and noticed blood shot eyes greeted the view. Hands trembling, paper rattling, another long swig of the brown whisky met fevered and cracked lips. Like a sudden electrical shock, a leg cramp struck the driver's calf with such vengeance, the driver yelled out loud.

Stifling the out burst, the driver quickly glanced to the house, as if thinking it would react to the sound. It didn't. Approaching headlights from a curve directly ahead, signaled it time to leave, so the driver took a quick left turn, and was gone by the time the other car passed in front of the old house.

Tears ran down the driver's cheeks, a tightly clenched fist pounded on the dashboard, knowing the past could not be changed or reversed, fearing what might have to be done next to protect the future. Meddlers, all of them, they would have to be stopped before death claimed them all on the Cedar Springs road.

20

"I always had a fondness for cheeseburger pizza," smacked Larry.

"Looks like you've fulfilled your fondness then," snickered Shorty, poking Larry in the belly.

"You had only one piece," remarked Cassandra to Stephen.

"My appetite sort of comes and goes. It's on the go right now."

"Are you in pain?"

"Nothing I can't tolerate, and if it worsens, I have medication and the reefer. Life is good."

"Shorty, are you all right?" I asked him.

"I reckon none of us are really all right, are we, dude?" he answered me, without the previous slur in his speech.

"Are you up to telling us what happened to you?"

"I reckon now is as good a time as any. I owe it to Brody to tell what we know. Let me drain the snake first."

A car slowed out front and stopped. I walked toward the front door to see who it was and it peeled out, racing down the street. I only caught glimpse of one tail light, as it made the turn at the end; the other light was burned out. I figured it was just kids showing off. That's the way we used to behave.

"Quite a group of testimonials," remarked Cassandra, wrapping her hands around my waist from behind.

"I still find it hard to believe we waited this many years before we did this. I'm just as bad as the rest of them to a certain extent."

"We're going to lick it," she said. "And I'm sorry you received the blunt of the town's fury."

"It wasn't planned. It just happened. We were stupid kids."

"All right love birds," snapped Shorty. "Do you want to hear what I've got to say, or just mossy off to bed?"

"You've got the floor," I said, bowing and pointing him to center stage.

"Well you boys have spun quite the yarn about spooks and all the scary crap, but I guess mine is not nearly so spectacular by comparison. Don't get me wrong. It got my attention, making me haul ass across that front yard. I still can't to this day explain what was chasing me. Larry got a better look at it than me, because I was too sacred to look behind me. I reckon what happened to Brody got next to me worse than my own experience, but I'll start with mine first."

Like you fellers have already pointed out, I didn't enter that cabin. I dropped my beer and went back to the car for another one. I thought I saw somebody standing next to Lester's Charger, but when I got there I didn't see anybody. I figured it was one of you messing with me. I called you out.

That was a big mistake, me cussing and throwing rocks in the bushes. One rock bounced off one of those big oaks and it slammed against Lester's front fender. I couldn't see if it made a dent, but I suspected if it had, Lester would surely kick my butt. A second rock hit the side of the car. I had only thrown one.

I figured you boys knew better than to be throwing rocks at that Charger, so it had to be somebody else. I crouched behind an open door and I called them out, cursing them what-fer. I guess I struck a cord with that rock thrower, because the next thing I knew, the car shook back and forth like someone had a shoulder against the opposite side.

I lost my balance and tumbled to the ground. The car continued to rock with vengeance. From my perspective on the ground, I could see underneath to the other side. I didn't see any feet. The perpetrator wasn't standing on the opposite side. Just as quickly as it started, it stopped.

The headlights came on. I peeked inside toward the driver's side. The driver's side door was closed and the window was rolled up. The radio blared on, and the horn began blowing. I had seen and heard enough. I haul assed in no particular direction. The doors slammed and I could feel something breathing down my neck. I heard this damned awful yelling, and realized it was coming from me.

By the time I had stopped running, I was behind the house. I saw flash lights on the second and third floors. I made my way up a back stairway on the far end of the house and up to the second floor. That's where I found Peter sitting on that old trunk.

I heard movement inside. I jerked Peter off of it and peered inside. After seeing Brody there, I reckon I cold cocked Peter pretty hard, and then I got Brody out. With Peter's help, we made it back to the first floor porch. I wasn't ready to return to the cars right yet. I wasn't fully ready to forgive Peter, either. Brody's life has been one screwed up mess since,"

"You said you knew who put him in that trunk," I reminded him.

"Donnie locked him in it. He was in one of his damn combative moods, PJ induced of course."

Brody told me he felt something tugging at him. He woke just as Donnie pushed him backwards into the trunk, calling him puke breath. He struggled to get out of the trunk, with Donnie stomping on his fingers. Brody said he remembers the likes of Leroy, Charley and Lester trying to intervene, but Donnie would have no part of it. He pushed them away, slugging Charlie and Leroy, before Lester just finally stepped back.

"That's not the half of it. What happened to him inside that trunk is what sent him to Bull Street," sniffled Shorty, overcome by his own story.

"Here," I said passing him a straight shot of Jack and a paper towel. He wiped his nose and turned up the bottle.

"Brody said there was something inside that trunk with him. It was biting and pinching and scratching him, breathing a foul smell in his face. I believed what he said."

"We do too," I assured him. "Did you see the bite or scratch marks?"

"Be honest with you, I didn't think to look. Brody said it was a living hell inside there. Ya'll didn't know it, I reckon, but he was highly claustrophobic back then. He's not so bad now, but back then it was really bad."

"Donnie was a piece of work," I said.

"A piece of dog crap when he got ripped," clarified Shorty. "And we always let him get away with it, didn't we. He was mister super jock, the big shit quarterback. Well justice was served, wasn't it?"

"You didn't?"

"Nope, but I might would have, if someone or something hadn't beaten me to it."

"Well Payne, that leaves you," said Peter. "What's your story?"

"It's late," spoke up Cassandra. "Can't this wait until in the morning?"

"Well I reckon we've been waiting almost nineteen years," said Shorty. "Another night won't matter."

"No argument from me," I gladly admitted to them.

"Maybe Stan will show back up tomorrow," said Larry. "Can we have a quick prayer before we part ways, so I can justify this as a business trip?"

Everyone laughed and bowed their heads.

21

The Tuesday morning dawn came earlier than usual, or at least it felt like it to me. Cassandra clung to my back like my shadow again, the arrangement becoming way too comfortable, at least for me. I was tempted to have my way with her again, but I fought off the urges, and slipped from the covers instead.

After a quick shower, I began calling the guys to give them their wake-up calls. The clock said 8:11, and it was time for all sleepy heads to be up and at'um. Some were readier than others. Shorty fell into that other category, ole Jack taking its revenge.

We decided to meet at the Dutch Oven for breakfast, another Mennonite restaurant, just up North Main, a half block from the town square. I liked their food better than Yoder's because it didn't taste sugary. Don't misunderstand me, Yoder's did a booming business, and was a must stop place for tourist buses, but it just wasn't for me.

The Mennonite community had exploded in Abbeville and the surrounding area. With them, they had brought a vast assortment of skills; seasoned carpenters, electricians, builders, welders, fabricators and plumbers, you name it, and they did it. No one worked harder or did a better job. We soon learned to call them first when we had a problem.

Their religion instilled them to build their own churches and schools. At first, our small town wasn't sure they were ready for this invasion of oddly dressed folks, buying up all the country side real-estate, but quickly the locals warmed up to the newcomers, and embraced them with open arms. Soon the Mennonites blended in as if they had always existed here.

Cassandra and I arrived first, securing a table large enough to seat seven, in hopes that Stan would show up. Larry walked up from the Belmont on the opposite end of the square. Soaking wet with perspiration, he smiled, and crashed down in a chair like a felled tree. The chair creaked and moaned, protesting his arrival.

"I don't guess you saw Stan on your jaunt here," I asked.

"I'm afraid not," huffed and puffed a still winded Larry. "Coffee and water with lemon," he said to the waitress.

"And where's Stephen," asked a concerned Cassandra.

"He may join us later," sighed Larry. "He wasn't having a very good morning, I must sadly report. I fear his situation is reaching grave proportions."

"Cruel disease," I commented. "Speaking of cruel, Shorty looks like he's been road hard and put up wet, then run over by a truck." I pointed to him, spotting him feeling his way through the front door like a blind man.

He flagged down every waitress, as he made his way toward our table, "Coffee, I need coffee, black, thick, strong and I need it ASAP."

Shorty flopped down next to Larry, testing the chair's weight capacity by the shear force of his delivery. "Larry, please work a miracle and heal this throbbing head of mine."

"Miracles are reserved for the work of Saints, I'm afraid. I'm not there yet. Have you tried a beer and tomato juice? It always helped me."

"Do they serve them here?" asked Shorty. "If so I'll start with a six pack of beer and a quart of mater juice. My designated driver is parking the car. He should be here in a few minutes."

Peter entered and was quite the contrast from his badly hung over passenger. He whistled a catchy tune, and greeted everyone in an exuberant tone. He did not resemble the remaining cast of 68, still plagued by that night or last night.

"Good morning good people." The joy of being alive bled from every pore. "What is everyone having, because I'm buying?"

"He's been like this all morning," cursed Shorty. "It's damned disgusting and getting very old."

"What puts you into such a wonderful mood?" asked Larry. "You seem so blessed this morning, Peter."

"I just woke up this morning, feeling the burden lifted off me after our series of confessions last night. For once I feel things are going to work out for all of us. Absolutely nothing could dampen my spirits."

Eavesdropping had not been intentional, but we couldn't help overhearing the conversation from a nearby table, three gentlemen I didn't recognize. "Yep, I heard he was just in his underwear, buried under a bunch of boxes, just outside the back door of the Rough House," said old man Barnes.

"And I heard he was the resident town drunk, sort of like Otis on the Andy Griffin show," added Vic Hall. "Someone said he drank like a he thought there would be no tomorrow."

"Do they expect fowl play," asked Gregg Wilson.

"I haven't heard anyone say yet?" answered Vic. "Who would have wanted to kill a poor guy like that? Some say he didn't have anything of value."

"Excuse me," I apologized. "I couldn't help but overhear. What happened? Who's dead?"

"Some local guy is what we heard," answered Gregg. "We're staying at the bed and breakfast, further up North Main. I'm sorry I don't remember the poor fellow's name."

"They found him dead behind that Rough House bar, near the trash bin out back," added Vic. "They think he had been there all night."

"Thank you and I'm sorry I disrupted your meal."

I looked at the others. I could tell they were thinking the same thing. This wasn't good.

Shorty finally broke the silence. "You reckon it could have been Stan?"

I shrugged. "There's only one way to find out. You boys and girl sit tight while I go to the sheriff's office and do a little snooping."

"But you're not with the newspaper now," advised Cassandra.

"They might not know it yet."

"I wouldn't bet the bank on it," added Peter. "Remember, you're in Abbeville, and you quitting the paper would have been big news, not to mention you decking the owner and operator of the newspaper."

"So, then I'll call in a few favors. Trust me, I will get an answer."

"I think I'll grab breakfast to go and check on Stephen," Larry informed us.

"I'll just stay here with Peter and Cassandra," said Shorty. "Do you have any mystical healing powers that could stop this pounding headache, Cassandra?"

"Try decapitation," chimed in Peter. "It would get rid of the ugly too."

"Bite me," snapped Shorty. "Damn I hope it wasn't Stan they found."

22

"Good morning Officer Price." I sucked up and greeted the officer with the utmost respect. "I heard you found a body behind the Rough House."

"And I heard that you quit the Wednesday Weekly," he fired back.

"Career improvement on my part," I replied. "Anyone I know?"

"You know I'm not supposed to divulge that information until we've contacted the next of kin."

"You owe me Jimbo. I got those Turkey Federation tickets for you, remember."

"You don't let anything slide do you, Payne. Keep this under wraps or the Sheriff will have my balls. We found one of your old classmates, Stan Bronson. We figure he had been dead for quite some time. Someone had stripped the body down to his underwear."

"Was he murdered?"

"You don't give up do you?"

"I have two Ducks Unlimited tickets," I baited him. "They could be yours with the right answers."

"You're an asshole."

"An asshole with tickets," I rebutted.

"Damn it, Payne! I don't think the officer on the scene detected any obvious wounds," answered my frustrated stoolie. "But he was buried under a bunch of cardboard boxes like someone tried to conceal the body, and his clothes haven't been found. There is something fishy for sure. The autopsy should tell us more."

"Thanks Jimbo," I said shaking his hand. "I'll drop off the tickets at your house."

"Keep your nose clean and out of this you hear, Payne. I would hate to see you get caught up in another mess."

"What can I say. I'm a mess magnet," I answered, my heart pounding in my chest, still trying to digest the horrific news about Stan. "I don't work for the paper anymore, so you won't see it in print."

I exited the back door of the courthouse, where the sheriff's office was located. I took the back alley walk on my return trip to the Dutch Oven. There it was; yellow crime scene tape, less than a block from the sheriff's department. Stan had died beside that big green dumpster.

I paused and squatted down, gagged and almost became sick to my stomach, visualizing him buried under those boxes. I tried to think. Both of Stan's parents were deceased, but he still had one brother. I seem to recall he had moved to Texas. Stan had taken his secret about that night to the grave. His torment had ended. Ours hadn't.

I couldn't help but question, could the house have reached out to him here? If it had, none of us could be safe. I thought about Leroy, Charlie and Lester, one dead, two missing. Had the house gotten them as well? And Stephen, a walking dead man; was his affliction the result of a curse or just unprotected sex. There was Brody. Without a miracle breakthrough, he could be locked away in an institute for the insane for the remainder of his life.

What about the rest of us? A bright yellow stretch of tape could as easily be in our future too. Boy, we sure squandered our golden years. Even stupider, we were determined to dig it back up at all costs. What were we thinking? We weren't.

The creaking backdoor of the Rough House opened, causing me to fall backward off balance and onto my ass. "I figured I would find you here," said Cassandra, arms crossed and rolling her eyes.

"How did you know it was Stan?"

"Premonition," she replied. "I wish I could explain or control it. It just comes in waves when I least expect it."

"Did you actually visualize Stan here at the crime scene?"

"I know where you're going with this," she said, lending me her hand and pulling me to my feet. "I don't see actual visions, or dead people, or anything like that. It's more like a feeling that just comes over me. I know when something has happened or the potential is there for something to occur, if left unchecked."

"So what do you feel for us?"

"It doesn't work like that, sweetie. It's not like one of those Eight Balls that you shake up and ask it a question, and then like magic, an answer materializes. I have no control over it, but personally, I see a long and loving future for us. I guess I always have."

"You're not admitting you've had a crush on me, are you?" I asked, not believing my ears.

"I guess you could call it that, but you got caught up in that night and we just sort of went our separate ways."

"Your premonitions suck then, because I liked you back then too and you're right, that house messed it up for both of us."

"Well just maybe that evil house of yours has some redeeming qualities, if it is responsible for bringing us together after all these years."

"I wouldn't give that house that sort of credit just yet. I think it has something else in store for us. I call it my premonition, and now you're a part of it, against my better judgment."

"Come on. The others are still waiting for us at the Dutch Oven. Larry returned with Stephen in tow."

"How is he?"

"He's a gamer, but I fear not for much longer," she said, looping her arm under mine and leading the way.

"I wish we could reverse his curse."

"While Aids is certainly a curse to those inflicted, I don't think there's a cure or a secret potion that will prevent the inevitable. I hate it too. I haven't known him long, but I like Stephen."

"You'd love him more as the wolf man," I grinned. "Remind me to show you *The Night of the Monsters* when this is over."

"Was he in the movies?"

"Yep, he was a star in a classic," I boasted proudly.

A star indeed thought the watcher, having overheard the conversation. Queer through and through, you mess with fire, you get burned. All of you are messing with a blaze that will descend on you like a fire storm. This truth will not set you free. Death waits for you, if you dare return. It knows your names.

For another fallen, I bid you farewell. I hope you wore clean underwear, for that's all you had. Death is a chameleon, a shape shifter, a repo-man, the tax collector, and it takes what is rightfully his.

Nineteen years is an eternity without answers. Answers can deliver death. Life or death, choices or not, see you on the other side. In a puff of black smoke and grinding gears the Buick sputtered away.

We returned to our table. Cassandra and Larry had been right. Stephen did look like warmed over death.

"Have you eaten anything?" I asked him.

"Just grits, the southern breakfast of champions, but it at least stays down, especially if I top it with Texas Pete."

"What about you, shit for brains?" I asked Shorty.

"Feeling just fine," he boasted. "I took Larry's advice and I downed me a mater-juice and Miller Lite. The second one was a charm."

"One is usually sufficient," added Larry.

"What did you find out?" asked Peter.

"I believe the look on your face tells us what we didn't want to hear," said Stephen. "It was Stan, wasn't it?"

I nodded and dropped my head, choked back the tears, and said, "Someone stripped off his clothes, and then concealed him under empty liquor boxes behind the trash bin."

"A proper burial," said Shorty. "Stan would have liked it, being that close to the Rough House."

"Any suspects?" asked Peter.

"Nope...they haven't called it a murder yet."

"So what next?" asked Larry.

"They've got to contact his next of kin."

"Simple enough, Dude," responded Shorty. "He just has that one bother, Mitchell. I believe he's in Oklahoma."

"I thought he was in Texas."

"Texas, Okalahoma, Arizona, its somewhere westward, same difference," shrugged Shorty. "Five bucks says he doesn't come back for the funeral."

"But Stan was his brother," protested Cassandra.

"Mitchell pretty much disowned him after Stan turned into a drunk," explained Shorty. "I think he really cut him loose after that Halloween night. We weren't very popular in town, that's for sure."

"And that damn Charley just made it worse with his stretched truths and blame," added Peter. "He was always a big pussy. Oops, sorry Cassandra, I forget you're part of the gang now."

"I think I'm getting use to the colorful language."

"He was always a liar," agreed Shorty. "Whatever one of us did, he usually claimed it had really happened to him."

"Except that night," said Stephen. "He threw all of us under the bus, especially Payne. He claimed no responsibility for what had happened."

"I still don't figure him the type to join the military," added Larry. "And then Nam claimed another victim, the fate of so many in that dreaded war."

"MIA," I spoke the words. "Like Lester, he fought a different war. Lester's war was between him and his wife. I still wonder what happened to him."

"Is this diversionary tactics, Payne? You still haven't told us what happened to you that night," Stephen reminded me and the others.

"Not here," I replied. "Let's go somewhere private. We still need to mourn Stan first."

"What about the Lake Secession spillway," asked Shorty. "That was always one of our favorite spots? Stan loved it there."

"Donnie's girl friend always wrote all of our excuses when we laid out of school," chuckled Peter.

"Candy Kane," we sounded like a chorus speaking her name.

"I think I've heard enough," said Cassandra. "Spare me any sexual conquests."

"What about Little Mountain, instead?" asked Shorty. "Stan loved it there too."

"Isn't that a tad too close to Cedar Springs?" asked Larry.

"No guts, no glory," smiled Shorty.

"No brains, no gains," I added in my two cents.

"Look," explained Shorty. "We don't even have to go down the Cedar Springs Road. We can come in from the other entrance, McCormick Highway."

"I reckon it is as good time as any for us to test the water, and make sure we really want to do this," added Stephen.

"You guys are just plain crazy," exclaimed Cassandra,

"All our lives," agreed Larry. "I'm in, Lord help us."

"Are you having a premonition?" I asked her.

"How do you guys say it? It's just has a gut feel to it."

"We can pile in my Town Car," advised Peter.

"Bogey at three o'clock" announced Shorty, pointing toward the restaurant's front door.

"Mister Easterly," I sighed. "Just what we don't need..."

"And he's heading this way," added Cassandra.

"And he has a damn sour looking scowl on his face," remarked Stephen.

"Good news," mentioned Larry. "There are no law enforcement officers with him."

"Or lawyers," chimed in Peter.

"I think we can take him," said Shorty, flexing his muscles.

"Well Payne, I see you've assembled most of the likely suspects," said Mister Easterly, bending over with both hands resting on the table's edge. "I suppose you've heard about the unfortunate departure of one of the town's most distinguishing figures."

I started to stand, but Cassandra placed her hand on my knee assertively to persuade me otherwise. I unclenched my right fist and flexed my fingers impatiently, waiting for him to piss me off with his next statement. I had trusted and worked for this man my entire working career. Sadly, I had never been a good judge of character. This certainly added an exclamation point to my handicap.

"Stan Bronson, your cohort in crime," continued the Wednesday Weekly owner, "Most likely our finest citizen died from acute toxic alcohol poisoning, a sad ending to a most outstanding and astonishing life."

I caught movement out of the corner of my eye and realized Shorty had stood to his feet. Cassandra tightened her grip on my knee. It wasn't an affectionate clutch.

"Don't worry, Payne," advised Easterly, smiling and keeping his voice low, so that just our table heard him. "His death will not make the front page. It will be a mere footnote in the obituary. He embarrassed himself and this town with his pathetic displays of public drunkenness."

Peter had now joined Shorty, arms crossed and clinching his jaw. Cassandra's death grip caused me to flinch, and give her a firm look.

"Dead in his skid marked underwear," head shaking, Easterly pushed his luck and the buttons of Stan's friends. "It should have been him back in 68, not Donald. Stan Bronson is a nobody now, just like he was a nobody then."

Larry and Stephen stood in tandem. It almost appeared choreographed. Easterly paid neither of them any attention, keeping his eyes locked on mine. He hardly blinked, nor did I.

"Just plain simple white trash," he continued. "Not worthy of our landfill..."

Cassandra sprung to her feet, like a Jack in the Box. She caught me by surprise. I followed. We stood six strong, still silent. The other patrons had taken notice of our theatrics.

"Please, act like the vandalistic, ruffian scoundrels you are," encouraged Easterly. "I have plenty of witnesses this time."

I can't put into words the rage that burned inside me. I'm sure the others were just as insulted and pissed. One drop of Easterly's spilled blood would put us into a shark feeding frenzy.

I brushed past his shoulder, heading to the exit. One by one, my five cohorts in crime followed, each making sure they brushed or bumped him as they passed. The Dutch Oven grew silent as a church when the preacher says 'let us pray'.

Easterly stood there, facing our empty table. He never turned to watch us file onto the sidewalk and toward the square. No one spoke. We walked in double file until we reached the towering granite confederate monument in the center of the square.

"He's got to pay for that," spoke up Shorty.

"And he will in due time," I assured all of them.

"He was just baiting all of you," said Cassandra, "But I'm in if you want to kick his butt."

"I have the bruises to show for your restraints," I said, rubbing my right leg and knee.

"Let's load up and cut the square, then head for Little Mountain," said Peter. "And we do it in style, down the Cedar Springs Road!"

"Amen," added Larry.

"I wish we had a cherry bomb," remarked Stephen, sending us all into an outburst of laughter. Only Stan's contagious laugh was missing.

Easterly walked from the restaurant to the stares of the remaining customers, still deathly silent and aware something of significance had just occurred. He paused on the sidewalk to straighten his tie and tug on his belt. He then turned and walked briskly toward the square, making a hard left at the corner.

His destination was the sheriff's office, where he would enquire if any further information had surfaced about Stan Bronson's death. Natural causes, he needed to hear natural causes and not extenuating circumstances or possibly murder. It would be tough to keep it from the headlines if his death was flagged as suspicious."

He couldn't count on the sheriff to keep it under wraps either. He was his own man, operated by the book, and had not been corrupted by that event in 68, like so many others. He greeted a couple of deputies then enquired about the sheriff. The Sheriff was home nursing a bad back.

Less than five minutes later, he departed, distraught at the news, suspicious circumstances. Thankfully no one had spoken foul play or possible murder, leaving him a glimmer of hope. Then again, maybe he needed a distraction. He would think on his options.

Easterly walked into the Wednesday Weekly office and sat at his desk. Flipping through the phone directory, he swiftly made half dozen calls, keeping his dialogue short and to the point. Hanging up, he eased open a file cabinet drawer, and he retrieved the bottle of Johnny Walker Red. He placed it on his desk. He rotated it, reading the label while eyeing the liquid sloshing around inside.

He glanced at the wall clock. He watched the minute hand click to eleven past ten. He unscrewed the top and poured a double shot in the Abbeville Opera House logo coffee cup. Holding it with both hands, he just sat there for almost a full minute. He held up the cup and completed a silent toast to Donald Ray Clark. He gulped its contents in one long swallow. He repeated this ritual until the fifth showed half empty.

The phone rang. He answered it. It was the call he had been waiting for. He told the caller, "Do it."

23

Little Mountain had been our childhood swimming hole. Called Parson's Mountain Park, it later became one of our favorite late night party and drinking spots. It had not changed a whole lot. The 28 acre manmade lake looked so small now, but had once been enormous in our youthful eyes.

To us, it had been grander than the Smokey Mountains, but actually the single mountain only topped out at eight hundred feet. Size doesn't always matter. It was our mountain. Geologists called our mountain a monadnock, their technical term for a mound of hard rock left when all the surrounding land erodes away. Somehow that just doesn't roll off your tongue. Do you want to go to the monadnock tonight? That wouldn't get my juices flowing.

It was a rite of passage to hike or drive the winding dirt and gravel road to the turn off at the tower road. The spur took you to the fire tower that overlooked the surrounding country side. Although the ranger station located at the top of the tower wasn't assessable, we still climbed the steps to one platform shy of the top. There we admired the fantastic view whether in broad daylight or intoxicated, concealed by the cloak of darkness. Often, an endless sky of stars filled the night. Most sensible folks climbed it to breathe in the fall colors. We did it on drunken dares.

Other Little Mountain points of interest, the four civil war-era gold mines, were fenced in to protect and preserve them, and keep vandals out. While we didn't vandalize the mines, we did climb over the fences and toss out various dares, but never actually attempted to enter the caved in tunnels. We were often drunk out of our gourds, but not necessarily that stupid, on most occasions anyway.

A more popular and beneficial spot had to be Lost Lake. The dirt road wasn't easy to find. There were no markers pointing the way, thus spurred the lost lake legend. Little Mountain's version of lover's lane, secluded, on a red clay packed road, was nothing picturesque. If optimized to your advantage you could reap plentiful rewards. The lake, a cattail filled hole of dirty water, could work its magic, only if the two participants were there for the same reason. Getting lucky really meant getting lucky.

A stones throw, the way the crows flies, lurked the Frazier-Pressley House, waiting our return. We tempted fate by just being this close, but fear eluded us. Stan's death and Westerly's defiant attitude had instilled a sense of purpose, of determination and possibly a splash of bravery. Six sad souls had previously been unsure and unwilling to whole heartily accept destiny. Now we seemed surer of what we had to do. It was one of those 'damn the torpedoes' moments, whatever the hell that means to a gang of misfits.

Standing six strong, five short of our original number, much preparation and detective work lay ahead before Friday's visit. We had less than four days remaining until our personal reckoning day. I sensed a battle loomed ahead. This time we would win the war hopefully. We had to or else.

We sat at one of several wooden picnic tables located near the water's edge. All but Cassandra had been here before, so the significance of the lake really didn't register with her. Again, it seemed so tiny, now inserting new meaning to *Little Mountain Lake*.

"All right dude, you've tip toed around this long enough. We've given you way too much leeway," advised Shorty. "Spill it. What really happened to you that night? No holding back, tell the truth and nothing but the truth, so help you Stan."

I took a deep breath, and then let it out, a long and winded sigh. This didn't come easily for me, but I knew it was my turn to talk. Cassandra placed her hand in mine. It felt much better than that previous hand to my knee and leg. From her I gained the strength to speak.

I didn't experience what Larry said he had experienced in the cabin. He was right. You all know it. I always like to be the first one in one of those old secluded houses. I should have gone to the house before going to that log cabin. I regret that decision. I might have prevented some of what had happened, if I had.

"I shouldn't have left you there, Larry, with Stan and no flash light. That was so stupid and thoughtless on my part. Stupid, stupid, stupid..."

"Don't sweat it. We had never been spooked in an old house before, unless we instigated it," chuckled Larry, his belly shaking like Jell-O.

I ventured off to explore the first floor, more intrigued than ever by the house, supposedly because it was still partially furnished and in stellar shape. It reeled me in as effectively as a Venus Fly Trap lures its unsuspecting prey. I heard the others on the second floor. I should have gone up, but I'm way too meticulous. I have to take it one floor at time. It's my own personal rule, just like not crossing in the mall from one side to the other. I have to visit all the stores on one side before covering those on the opposite. It's some sort compulsive disorder, I suppose.

While I found each room fascinating, I detected nothing of value or interest. I sensed no ghosts or goblins. I'm not sure how much time expired by the time I returned to the foot of the stairs. Neither you nor Stan was where I had left you. I had heard the wild screams earlier on the second floor. They had been muffled from my end of the house.

As I ascended the stairs I heard the other crowd already on the third floor. I could barely make out Donnie's voice, cursing and trying to instigate a fight with someone. I never understood why he always picked fights with us when he got wasted. We were his friends. It didn't make sense. Everyone chalked it up to the PJ. I think these tendencies had deeper, darker origins.

When I reached the steps, those leading to the second floor, I could hear that Donnie had really lost it this time. He was going at it full throttle with somebody. I heard a loud thump, like the deadweight of a body crashing to the floor, somewhere above me. More yells erupted. I couldn't make out what the voices were saying. That's when I heard glass breaking.

The glass breaking really pissed me off. We were never malicious in our little trespassing ventures. We sort of had an unwritten code of ethics, not to trash the places we explored. I didn't appreciate one of us intentionally vandalizing the house. Old houses were sort of sacred to me.

I did something I absolutely never do. I skipped the second floor, and then made my way to the third. Do you realize how difficult that is for me to do? I never saw Peter, Shorty or Brody or that trunk. I'm speculating that Shorty hadn't got there yet. Peter was probability already in his stupor, and Brody in that trunk.

Before I reached the top floor, all yelling and scuffling had ceased. Matter of a fact, I heard no voices at all. I paused half way up the stairs, chilled to the bone, and suddenly overcome with fear. Something else I never do, I never get scared in an old house or cemetery. I smelled a strange almost burned odor, but not really burnt. My flashlight flickered out. Someone brushed by me, ascending the steps.

I tapped the flash light. It came back on. The beam captured a bloody faced Stan on the top step, almost causing me to tumble backwards. I grabbed the rail just in time. When I redirected the light, Stan was gone. The malt liquor from those Hoppin Gators was making me woozy. Its funny, it only took less than four cans to do that to me back then. Four of anything now doesn't even wet by whistle.

I regained my composure, and stabilized my shaky legs, and then I completed by climb. Scanning the room with the flashlight, I could not find Stan. He was injured. I had to locate him. The room contained an assortment of hard cane backed chairs, a couple of small end tables, but not much more. It reminded me of a doctor's waiting room. Maybe I thought that because Stan was hurt.

All remained deathly quite. I no longer heard the guys muffled arguing. It was creepy. I normally like creepy, but this wasn't normal creepiness. The room smelled musky and dusty, undisturbed and preserved, and just a tad eerie, what I'd expect of a spook house.

The floor creaked as I made my way into the next room. Pushing the door open ever so slightly, I still expected one of you dips to pounce out in front of me. No pouncing occurred. For the first time, I noted no dusty footprints on the hardwood floor but my own. I quickly determined the guys had gone in the opposite direction.

A creature of habit, I continued my journey in the direction I had selected, figuring I could catch up with the others soon enough. I stressed over not touring the second floor first, but vowed I would do so on my return trip.

Each room contained an assortment of old rickety furniture, until I entered the last one. It contained a massive wooden, oddly crafted desk. I couldn't believe no one had pillaged it, but figured moving it down the three flights of stairs would be no easy task for a thief. Bookshelves from floor to ceiling adorned two walls, bookless of course. Other than a couple of destroyed chairs, the room was empty. Boy, so easily I had forgotten about Stan, enthralled by the house. It had me mesmerized.

I didn't know it then, but after yesterday's research, I assume this was possibly the good doctor's office. The most recent owners had maintained it as such. Odd, I thought I smelled tobacco smoke, but none of us smoked cigars or a pipe. It was a pleasant smell, almost soothing. My eyes became suddenly heavy. I chalked it up to the booze. I tried to shake it off.

Wooziness persisted, but I wasn't going to let it get the best of me. I walked over to the desk, and began opening the drawers. I didn't really expect to find anything. It was just an impulsive action, my need to know if anything interesting might just be inside. Other than a couple of lead pencils and crumpled note paper, the drawers were empty.

I retrieved the pieces of paper. They crumbled in my hands, returning to a chalky, dusty substance. I don't know why, but I ran my hand underneath the center drawer. I felt something attached there. I removed the drawer, flipped it over and sure enough, tacked to the bottom was a yellow, dingy envelope, still sealed with some sort of wax crest. I couldn't make out the writing on the outside. The ink had long ago faded.

I heard another commotion from one of the floors below, and

I stuffed the envelope inside my shirt for safe keeping. I retraced my steps to the stairs. There, I saw a slew of foot prints headed in the opposite direction. Leroy, Lester, Donnie and Charley were certainly quiet as mice. I suspected an ambush somewhere ahead.

Planning to counter their attack, I clicked off my flashlight, and I relied on the moon beans offering enough filtered light. I was also quite proficient at hide and scare. Inching along the wall and purposely staying out of view, I peeped through the first door. I no longer smelled tobacco, but I did smell a woman's perfume instead. My senses were being bombarded by so many curious odors.

For sure, none of us wore perfume. Only Leroy and Charley even shaved. I wasn't sure if either of them used after shave cologne. I certainly don't remember ever smelling any on them. The dizziness returned. I became light headed, overwhelmed by the overpowering sweet fragrance. I grabbed the door facing to maintain my balance.

My stomach felt like a dozen butterflies had just emerged from their cocoons and were testing their wings inside my belly. My vision became blurred. My ears ached as if they were being invaded by a million singing Cicadas, their seven year return confirmed.

That's the last thing I remember, until I was being shaken violently, an invitation to return among the living. I heard voices, loud, distant and shouting voices.

"What have you done, Payne?"

"Snap out of it," yelled another.

"Come on man, wake up," shouted a third.

Blinking quickly and almost robotically at first, everything gradually focused in. Standing over me, I recognized Charley first. Lester, and then Leroy looking like two bookends, was standing beside him. My back was against a wall. I was sitting, legs spread eagled.

I started to rub my face. I sensed something sticky and wet on the fingers of my right hand. I held up all five fingers inches away from my face. Someone aimed a flashlight at me. I saw what looked like blood dripping from my finger tips. A gash ran through the center of my palm. I felt no searing pain from the fresh wound.

I asked them, "What happened?"

Charley replied, "You tell us."

I shook my head, "I don't know. Where am I?"

"What do you mean where are you?" asked Charley.

"You're still in the house," confirmed Lester. "You're on the third floor."

"Yeah," I answered "This is the last place I remember being. How did I cut my hand?"

"It looks like you did it on that long sliver of glass," said Charlie, pointing to a bloody dagger shaped piece of glass, lying by my side.

"Where did that come from?" I asked, still having no recollection of the accident.

"From that broken window," replied Lester, directing me to the window with a nod. The window was just above my right shoulder.

I tried to stand, but I sat right back down with a crash. "Is anyone else hurt?" I asked, still unsure why I asked that question.

Leroy dropped his head, but remained speechless. Lester rubbed both hands through his greasy hair. He shook his head wildly in disbelief. Charley finally answered my question. "We think Donnie is dead." He eyed the window, then me.

I turned and propped up on one knee, holding onto to the windowsill. I peered through an opening where glass had once been. I could make out a figure on a jutted out section of roof two floors down. I looked at the guys, and then returned my stare to the sprawled figure on that rooftop. I realized it was Donnie's lifeless body, arms and legs contorted in the wrong direction.

"That's it. I don't remember another thing about what had happened. I still regret I'm the one who wanted to explore that house. Donnie was dead, I was cut and I couldn't remember a damn thing, reasonable doubt in any court of law."

24

The Buick Electra, hidden down a secluded fire lane, its driver with high powered binoculars, watched the six perched atop and around the lake shore picnic table. The driver varied the field of view from one troubled face to the next, pausing on the female, still not recognizing her or understanding her connection with the group.

Without warning, the woman shifted and looked directly into the lenses, her eyes penetrating; unlocking the secrets of the driver's tormented soul. Eyes squinting, she seemed to focus on the watcher's camouflaged hiding place. Her full lips moved, mouthing something while she held her gaze. Her lips formed the words, *someone is watching us*. The binoculars fell, hanging by a strap around the watcher's neck, shaken by the uncanny perception of this female.

Another vehicle pulled into a parking place, the opposite end from where the Town Car had been parked. A van with dark tinted glass concealed the occupants from view. The watcher eased further back into the tree line and brush to maintain an anonymous status, still shaken by the female's premonition.

"I tell you, I have this feeling we're being watched," she repeated a second time, still looking toward the elevated parking area.

I held my hand above my eyes to block out the sun. I strained to detect movement, but saw nothing. "Are you sure?"

"Oh I'm sure. I can't control these feelings, but I'm rarely ever wrong."

"I need to relieve myself," said Larry. "I'll retrieve that chilled wine from the cooler. After all, it is officially afternoon now, half passed twelve. I'll take a look around just in case."

"I'll go with you," remarked Stephen. "My bladder aches for relief too."

"Hurry back girls," grinned Shorty.

"So you really don't remember what happened," stated Cassandra.

"Nothing about hurting myself or Donnie falling out that window..."

"It got real ugly too," added Peter. "The town blamed all of us for Donnie Ray Clark's death, especially Payne."

"I think being a juvenile is the only thing that kept them from trying to build a case against me for possible involuntary homicide."

"That damn Charley didn't help our cause, telling everyone about how they had found you bleeding and next to that window," cursed Peter. "Abbeville's star quarterback was dead as a door nail and under suspicious circumstances."

"Everyone still thinks I killed him. Who's to say I didn't. I sure don't remember, and the circumstantial evidence was there."

"Why would you have possibly killed him?" asked Cassandra.

"Don't know," I shrugged.

"And none of you admitted what you had experienced at that house, until now."

"Well, we hinted at it during the initial questioning phase, but frankly, we were catching so much grief about Donnie's death, one by one we clammed up. Our parents and lawyers recommended it was not in our best interest to babble our crazy talk. It would just make things worse for us, further tarnishing our credibility."

"I still can't believe you didn't share these details with one another until now," said Cassandra, shaking her head, bewildered. "You were friends for goodness sake!"

"We were still kids, badly confused kids, taking poor advice, and trying to move on with our lives," I answered.

"What was in that envelope?" she asked.

"What envelope?"

"The one that you said you found in that desk."

"I never opened it."

"Where is it now?"

"I'm not sure. So much was going on back then, the envelope didn't seem that important."

"I sense it could provide a piece of the missing jigsaw puzzle. You should try to find it."

"Another premonition..."

"Just gut this time," she smiled.

Larry and Stephen relieved themselves at the park's facilities. Now chatting up a storm, and making their way toward the parking lot, they passed between the two changing buildings, men and women's. Two black hooded figures stepped from behind one of the buildings, blocking their path. Fearing the worse, they turned to exit the other way, finding two more hooded figures, these carrying sharp serrated hunting knifes, preventing their hasty retreat.

"Well," spoke up Stephen. "It's a little early for Halloween, but nice costumes just the same. Those multipurpose hoods make the perfect candy collectors, if you plug up those eye holes. Where did you purchase them, Klans are US, one size fits all? Haven't you heard boys, the KKK so isn't in this year, and they're supposed to be white, not black."

The four menacing hooded nightmares closed ranks, now standing within a couple of feet, exposing the pure hatred in their eyes. The largest of the four, well over six feet tall, big boned, solid as rock, spoke first, "Well what do we have here, the fag queen and her fat ass queer steer? You girls been in that John playing pitch and catch?"

"Please stand clear," demanded Larry. "I'm a priest. You wouldn't wish to harm the clergy, I'm sure."

"And what's he," asked a second hooded, "an alter boy?" He then delivered a knee buckling fist to Larry's kidney, sending him tumbling into the arms of a third hooded demon.

Supporting Larry by the chin, the brut delivered a round house left to his right cheek, putting him out and down for the count. Countless kicks to his lifeless body prompted no response. The forth had pinned Stephen's arms behind him.

"Let's just see what makes this little feller so special," said the monster sized leader. "Let's give him a proper southern welcome. Klan, I assure you, we're worse than any KKK."

"Guys, I must warn you. You really need to just back off. You're playing with fire." Lights out, Stephen was clubbed from behind.

25

"I think they really let me off to minimize any bad publicity and potential media circus. For the record, Donnie's death was listed accidental. While it was still in the news for a few days, local star athletic and all, it soon fizzled out, just like the town's leadership had hoped. Thinking back now, Easterly probably defused it."

"It didn't change how the community hated us," added Shorty. "Especially, you, Payne."

"Yeah, in most people's minds I was still a murderer of sorts. Some still give me wide berth."

"Why did you stay in a place where the people hated you so?" asked Cassandra.

"I was just a kid, and pig headed, I suppose. This was my home. They weren't going to drive me away. Plus, I didn't have the answers for what happened that night. If I left here, I would never know. I don't know what gave me the idea that the answer would miraculously just drop out of the sky, and all would be behind me. Eventually most forgot. Easterly eventually offered me the job at the paper. I just tried to move on."

"Didn't work so damn good did it," said Peter. "I know. I tried too."

"Leaving the state didn't help you. And look at the others, whether they stayed or left, their lives remained a mess. Oddly, we're the lucky ones."

As if on queue, we looked up, and saw Larry stumbling in

our direction, holding a naked and lifeless Stephen in his arms. We rushed to meet him, Shorty taking Stephen from his arms just before Larry collapsed to the hard red clay ground.

"Is he dead?" asked Cassandra.

"No, he's still breathing," I said, unable to ignore the precarious bruising and bleeding.

Cassandra retrieved some water from the fountain, and dabbed Larry's face until finally he came around.

"What the hell happened?" asked Shorty.

"We were attacked, four of them, up by the changing rooms," coughed Larry.

"Who did this?" asked Peter.

"I don't know, they were hooded," cried Larry. "They attacked us. They dragged us inside the women's changing room."

Each of the large square cinder block buildings had an open walk through entrance, no door and no ceiling, walls about sixteen feet tall. They were used by swimmers to disrobe, change in and out of bathing suits. On many Friday and Saturday nights local teenagers used them as make-out rooms. Discarded condoms routinely littered the cement floor.

"They knocked me unconscious. I woke up on the floor, still clothed," whimpered Larry. "I suppose they didn't really want to desecrate a man of the cloth. I might have a couple of cracked ribs though."

"And what about Stephen?" I asked.

"I don't know. I found him like that, his clothes shredded to bits and him unconscious also."

"It's obvious what that did to him," whispered Peter.

"I'll kill the son of bitches that did this," shouted Shorty, running toward the scene of the crime.

There was no stopping the mighty little bulldozer, so Peter just followed him instead, as back-up, just in case they located the perpetrators. I covered Stephen with my jacket, not knowing what else to do. Cassandra ripped a second piece of cloth from her blouse, dampened it, and then washed his bloodied face.

Stephen's eyes flickered, and he opened them, started flailing wildly with his hands. Realizing it was us; he relaxed, and spoke in an extremely weak voice. "I got them where I want them;" he smiled "None of them used protection. They're the ones that have been royally screwed. Never do this to a man with Aids. I tried to warn them. Dumbasses, they wouldn't listen."

"You do have an interesting defense system," I told him, clutching his shoulder.

"And they will too one day, hopefully," his voice becoming weaker. "Payne, the bible..."

"Bible," I shrugged.

"The Bible from the log cabin," he whispered, blood now trickling from the corner of his mouth. "I took it that night ... still have it...might come in handy...my place in Spartanburg, under the mattress...read...hand written inscriptions...1868...I think the house wants it back...she wants it returned."

He breathed in deeply, chest heaving against my arms. I was holding him in my lap. His eyes suddenly stared blankly skyward. He jerked, puppet like, then his suffering ended. Stephen was dead. My friend was dead. No silver bullet killed the wolf man. I couldn't help thinking that five of us remained to finish what we had started. We owed it to Stephen. We owed to all of them. Friday seemed so far away. Maybe we shouldn't wait until Halloween night, I thought.

"We couldn't find anybody," said Shorty.

"They're gone and Stephen's clothes are trashed," added Peter, clutching them in his hands.

"He won't be needing them," I answered. "Stephen's dead."

"Damn it," snapped Shorty. "What do we do now?"

I just shook my head, not knowing how to answer his question. My thoughts drifted back to that night. The four of us had rushed down those stairs to check on Donnie's condition. We found Larry, Brody and Shorty on the second floor. Something was going on, but we didn't take time to ask them. We just passed them by.

When we reached the outside, we saw Stan standing over Donnie's body. Stan's face looked fine. It wasn't beaten or bloodied like I had remembered seeing him on that third floor. Other than him appearing dazed and wild eyed, he looked like Stan.

I kneeled down and checked Donnie's pulse. He didn't have one. Dead, the two story fall from that window, and the superstar was history. What were we supposed to do now?

"Dude, what are we supposed to do now?" asked Shorty again. "Earth to the mother ship, do you hear me, Payne?"

"We take him to town. We tell the Sheriff what happened," I answered.

"You know they're not going to believe us, just like last time," warned Peter. "They'll think we killed another one of our friends."

"You know he's right," nodded Shorty.

"Guys, there's something you need to hear," spoke up Larry, tears rolling down his rounded cheeks. "Those hooded creeps told us to get the hell out of town or else, just before they kicked our asses. One specifically said for us to stay away from that house. I vaguely remember that just as I was coming to. They meant it."

"Maybe we should put Stephen on ice until we finish this," suggested Shorty. "I'm not going to allow them to bully us. This isn't high school."

"Obviously not, these maniacs mean business," said Larry.

"Tell you what," I replied. "Let's take Stephen to his house. He told me to retrieve something from there. When this is over we'll make things right for him. Keeping it under wraps might be our only chance, as bad as I hate to agree with Shorty."

"You're all talking crazy. You mustn't do this," advised Cassandra. "It's wrong. It's so wrong. There's been a murder here."

I touched my hand against her cheek and told her, "Everything about this, so ain't right. You can bow out of this if you'd like to Cassandra. It might be best if you did, but we've got to take this to the end. We don't have a choice. Exposing this stops us dead in our tracks. The wolf man would have wanted us to finish this."

"But the way things are going, none of you will live to see the finish line," she began to cry. "I don't want to lose you, Payne, not after just finding you. Totally against my better judgment, I'm in, and I will go along with whatever you decide. I may not like it, but I'll see it through, for Steven, and God help us all."

"You're stealing my line now," spoke up Larry.

She tried to muster up a smile. "Do you think Stan's and Stephen's deaths are connected?"

"Sure seems too coincidental, doesn't it," said Peter.

"I don't know what to believe any more," I answered. "But we better stay on top of our game, or we might just end up like them."

"Let's go if we're going to Spartanburg, dudes. I'd like to be back in Abbeville before dark," said Shorty.

"What's the matter Shorty? Are you afraid of the dark?" asked Peter.

"No, I just like to see what's sneaking up on me," he answered. "Night wasn't Stan's friend, remember."

"Before we go, will you join me in a prayer," asked Larry.

We bowed our heads while Larry delivered one that brought the house down. I didn't talk in tongue like my grandmother, but I think I came close. I knew at that moment, I was a changed man; to be determined if that will pan out for the good or not.

We loaded Stephen in the trunk of the Town car. We didn't like doing it, but we all agreed our options were limited. We stopped briefly at the Belmont to allow Larry to clean up and change clothes, and to retrieve Stephen's keys. His wallet from his tattered pants provided us with his address. The ride there and back would take almost four hours. It would be dark thirty before we got back to my house.

A deputy sheriff's cruiser was parked out front when we arrived back at my house. I was glad we no longer had Stephen's corpse in the trunk.

"This can't be good," whispered Cassandra.

"It's all right. It's Jimbo Price, nothing to worry about."

The lanky deputy stepped from the shadows of my carport, and ambled in our direction, pausing only to spit a mouthful of tobacco. Jimbo eyed us suspiciously. Maybe I was just paranoid.

"Autopsy is in. Stan Bronson died of natural causes, a heart attack. He was supposed to be on blood pressure medicine, but apparently he hadn't taken his pills in a long time. None was detected in his system. Payne...his heart just stopped...end of story. I snuck a peak at the autopsy report. "

"Then what happened to his clothes?" asked Peter.

"We don't know. Somebody must have stripped him down after he died, but there was no foul play involved, best we can tell. His blood alcohol level was zero. I just thought you might want to know that too."

"He died clean and sober," smiled Cassandra. "Thank you Lord."

"I'll let you know if anything else turns up. I'm sorry about this. I know you were friends."

"Jimbo," I addressed him with the utmost curiosity and concern. "An autopsy in less than twelve hours, that doesn't happen in Abbeville. Most take days, some weeks. How was this one completed so quickly? Something smells fishy."

"You're right, Payne," he answered, scratching his ear, and spitting more nasty juice. "I thought it was damn peculiar too, but somebody wanted this done real bad and real quick, and it got done. Coroner must have been itching for something to do, I reckon or..."

"Somebody wanted to hang this thing on us," spoke up Shorty. "That's why they wanted to know."

"Or they just wanted to quickly brush it aside," I commented. "Sweep it under the rug like they've done before. We can't have any bad PR for the quaint little historical town, now can we? What would that do for tourism? Slam, bam, thank you ma'am, Stan is just a bug on the windshield!"

"You fellers don't know how much trouble I'd be in for just telling you this. Sheriff would have my nuts, roasted and served on a silver platter. Payne, like I told you before, try to keep your nose clean and out of this. That's all I've got to say. It's done, closed and leave it at that. For the record, I liked old Stan, but hated seeing him throwing his life away like he was doing. Keep the report under your hats, please."

"Thanks Jimbo, you take care," I replied, almost tempted to tell him about Stephen, and what had happened at Little Mountain Lake. I figured the timing was wrong for now, even though I knew I could probably trust him. I'd tell him when this was over.

Good news, his death and Stephen's were not connected. At least we have no serial killer or curse stalking us. Stan's death had been of natural causes, and Stephen's had been a brutal attack at the hands of four black hooded, bigoted vigilantes. It suddenly hit me. They were both actually dead, and in less than twenty four hours, just gone. Maybe that house didn't want us to return after all. A curse has a way of working out things.

I tried to brush it off. We're expected to do this when people throw their lives away or suffer from terminal illnesses. I caught myself thinking they're better off. Dead is not better off, no matter what the reason. Sure, Stan was a pathetic drunk, but he had possibly turned the corner, and was ready to defeat his addiction.

Stephen, his days numbered, ravished by an unforgiving sickness, but he was still full of life, and determined to see us solve this mystery. He could have gone to the grave knowing the answers, the truth about that night, but had instead, had his life snuffed out by those worthless bastards. I agreed whole heartily with Shorty. Someone or something would pay for this.

Everyone bunked at my house for the night, agreeing there might be safety in numbers. The number eleven hadn't worked so well, I reminded myself, with six dead or missing, one loony tunes and now the surviving four possibly one step away from either outcome. My one regret was pulling Cassandra Blake into this. She could be in grave danger now too.

I had two extra bedrooms and a couch that converted into a queen sized sleeper. Cassandra bunked with me of course. The others had their own beds. Exhausted, we decided to give our mission a well deserved break. We'd pick up where we left off Wednesday morning. One by one, sometime after midnight, we filed like zombies into the kitchen.

Yes, adult beverages were on demand to chase away the night's goblins of insomnia. This would be both a short and long night. We were battle worn soldiers, and our forces were dwindling.

"We're one hell of a rag tag bunch of sorry looking asses," Shorty put it so eloquently. "How are you feeling big boy?"

"Sore and hurting physically, but more suffering from a heavy heart," replied a somber Larry. "I should have been able to do more. I let Stephen down. I'm such a pussy, no offense meant Cassandra."

"None taken," she said. "I'm pretty much a pussy when it comes to that sort of thing too." She smiled and gave Larry a hug. "You did all you could do for goodness sake. There were four of them and they had knives. They targeted Stephen because of his life style preferences. You're not to blame."

"They targeted him because they didn't know about me," explained Larry. "I'm a man of God now, but before, I found myself attracted to males, always had. I just never experimented with it. I have never had a male on male encounter. I fought the urge, the relentless desire, tooth and nail, trying to convince myself I wasn't like that. Finally I faced the truth, I was a homosexual. My faith has been strong; however, and I practice celibacy. Satan still tugs and pushes from time to time, but I can honestly say I have never crossed that bridge. I don't shun homosexuality, never have, and never will. I have just chosen not to follow that path. My work is my salvation."

"I always thought you were queer," spoke up Shorty. "In a good sort of way," he added, walking over and giving Larry a big old bear hug too.

"I'm a thirty five year old virgin," he laughed. "Neither man or woman have tasted the fruit of my loins. They don't know what they have been missing."

"I applaud you," congratulated a tearful Peter, clapping his hands, and giving Larry a standing ovation. "If I would have had your strength and determination and faith, an eleven year old girl would still be alive."

Eleven, that number triggered my thought pattern. I grabbed my notepad, and began reviewing my chicken scratch again, jotting down other entries. After about ten minutes, I gave it up, my exhausted brain unable to devote the attention and reasoning to complete a fair assessment. We jabbered and talked old times. Larry called it fellowship.

The stove's clock warned me it was almost 4 AM, and if I hoped to get any sleep, I should act on that now. Cassandra had bailed out on us two hours ago. I'm not convinced she was actually sleepy. I think she just thought it best to give us some male bonding time, sensing we needed it. When I eventually joined her, I crashed like a falling tree. She snuggled up to my back. It just felt right, like it had always been.

Unable to nod off, I switched on the radio, catching the tail end of Night Train and DABO-DOO's show. I hadn't thanked them for picking up that casket from the jamboree. I listened now while they talked their foolishness. Those boys could adlib with the best of them. They had the perfect radio voices, very theatrical at times. Night Train always said he had a face tailored for radio. Soon, I was out like a light, no reflection on them, just tired as hell.

26

"Good morning you two," smiled Shorty. "Bet you could use some coffee and a shower."

I gave Shorty the finger. "Black and keep it coming. Where are the others?"

"Larry said he just needed some air and time to meditate. He took his fat ass for a walk, go figure. Peter is gone to pick up a copy of today's paper to see if Stan made our prestigious weekly news."

"I think I will go take that shower," remarked Cassandra, winking at Shorty. It was good to pull the wool over his eyes.

"Need any help?" I asked, sowing the untrue seed.

"Thanks tiger, but I intend to depart this shower cleaner than I entered," she replied, giving me a swift pat on my butt, as she passed. We had pulled off our scam flawlessly.

"Love, ain't it just grand?" chuckled Shorty, which resulted in my second finger of the morning, left handed this time.

"This is such a cluster isn't it, Shorty?"

"That's putting it lightly," he answered, handing me a mug of brew. "Two dead qualifies it for something worse. Do you think we're doing the right thing? I mean, going back to that house after all these years."

"Sounds like you're having second thoughts," I commented, taking my first sip.

"Second, third and forth...I don't know what we should be doing. For nineteen years this has eaten away at me like a cancer, but I guess it beats the alternative, being dead. We're above dirt. I don't do dead so damn good."

"Yeah, somebody doesn't want us to go back for sure. We know Easterly is certainly one of them. I just find it hard to swallow that he could be behind or even involved in that attack yesterday. We're talking murder here. This is serious shit."

"Yep, that's the way I would categorize murder, Dude," he grinned, and held up his coffee mug, toasting my revelation. "Are you thinking conspiracy?"

"I don't know. I just don't see this town being that vengeful over something that happened almost twenty years ago. What is there to gain from it?"

"Tourism is a major money maker here now, whether we buy into it or not. Abbeville oozes history. Easterly told you he would not tolerate any bad publicity."

"Today bad news sells better than good news unfortunately," I explained. "Ironically this town would probably be overrun with reporters and curiosity seekers, if it turned out to be the site of a famous serial killer or even a legendary haunted house. Look what happened with the Amityville Horror; books, movies, and everyone flocking in to see it first hand."

"We could be movie stars or famous authors, or just plain dead and part of the story," scoffed Shorty. "I don't know Payne. Something tells me the worst is yet to come. Call it my own little Cassandra style premonition."

"Are you stealing my thunder in here?" she asked, standing there toweling off her hair, wearing nothing but one of my Hard Rock tee-shirts, that barely reached below her you know what. "Don't worry boys. I won't be parading around like this all day, only until I dry my hair. You can tuck your tongues back in your mouths and wipe the drool from your chins. No wonder we're the dominating species. All of you are so predictable and so easily manipulated."

Before we could validate her assessment of the male race, Peter came barging in the back door like a fire breathing dragon. He slammed the newspaper on the table, and then threw up his arms in disgust. "There's no mention of Stan anywhere, not even in the obituary. He deserves better than this, damn it."

"Cover up," chimed in Shorty. "Deaths are always a big deal

in that paper. Everyone pages to the obituary to see if their name appears in the print. You don't think the town is not going to notice this too."

"I concede. Easterly intentionally excluded it, but that might be okay. I agree Stan deserved better, but it diverts any unwanted attention away from us. He's played right into our hands, if you really think about it."

"I might agree with you except for what happened yesterday," theorized Peter. "By not being in the lime light, we're just making it easy for more attacks, aren't we?"

"Good point," I said. "But the kind that attacked Larry and Stephen wouldn't be deterred one way or the other. Let's face it. We're it, unless we decide to go public. Right now that would be incriminating. We've moved a dead body from the scene of the crime and to another county. We've hampered a potential police investigation, regardless to our motive."

"Shouldn't Larry be back by now?" asked Cassandra.

I panicked when I heard those words. I could see the same fear on the other's faces.

27

Larry had set out walking in no particular direction. He wasn't a distance walker and not much on exercise period, but he had covered almost a mile. He was still putting distance between him and Payne's house. He had a lot on his mind, especially after the death of Stephen. Contrary to his revelations and confessions of last night, he now again questioned his faith and sexuality. Apparently being influenced by a tugging Satan, whispering contradictions in his ears, he tried to clear his head.

He whispered numerous prayers as he walked, for Stephen, for Stan, for the others and mostly for himself. He pondered had he really been true to himself, not giving his homosexuality an opportunity to develop.

He had experimented with straight sex in high school, but had never actually had intercourse with a female. Sure, he had received that one hand job from Patty Carver at band camp, but he could have just as easily received one of those from a gay guy. Patty did have a thick mustache, come to think of it, he remembered. Connie Burton had even shown him her vagina, but the lighting wasn't that good under the bleachers to see much more than just her thick, black, bushy pubic hair. He had at least seen one.

Rachel Woodward had let him feel her tits once. She had melons as big as his head, but then everything about her was huge. He still couldn't remember ever getting that thrilled by any of this contact with females. He was hopelessly gay.

His greatest joy by far had been during those alcohol induced wild nights with the guys, when he would strip and streak through the parking lots or other venues. He had felt so liberated and free, streaking. He was an exhibitionist, but only when intoxicated. Those were the good old days, when everybody was still alive.

He figured he had probably pulled plenty of embarrassing stunts while under the influence of Boone's Farm or Mad Dog 20-20. The guys had told him about many of those embarrassing moments. All in all, his youth had not been as troubled as Stephen's probably had. He hadn't struggled that much with his uncertainty about his sexual preferences until after high school.

Larry remained so deeply in thought that he never sensed he was being followed. The green Buick Electra trailed him, almost a hundred yards away, inching along, keeping pace and its distance. He had reached a stretch of no houses, a spot where the side walk ended. He now walked on the asphalt, still doing battle with Satan and his emotions. He wasn't sure who was winning.

He also failed to see the truck parked in the edge of the woods, where two of the black hooded figures waited for him to reach their location. Head down, arms swinging by his sides, he watched the terrain directly below his round belly. He was fearful he may step on a piece of gravel or loose asphalt that might send him tumbling face first. He could almost imagine grinding his knees and elbows into the rough surface. He was neither a seasoned walker or sure footed enough to be doing this, but he pressed onward. It wasn't streaking but he made the best of it, fully clothed.

At least he walked in the lane toward the traffic like one was supposed to do. The ambushers lay waiting on the opposite side of the two lane road. He didn't know that, and if he had, for all practical purposes, it would have gained him no real advantage. Truth be known, he couldn't outrun a tortoise, even for a short sprint, especially after having already walked this distance.

Their quarry, the portly priest, had reached the mark. Baseball bats in hand, the two thugs sprinted toward the road where Larry only focused on the black asphalt beneath his feet. It was almost a blessing he hadn't seen what was coming.

The car horn blared from behind, causing Larry to almost

stumble and fall. Slowing and regaining his balance, he turned to look for the source of the honking horn. Instead he spotted his would be attackers. They were less than thirty yards away, and sliding to an abrupt stop at the sound and sight of the approaching Buick Electra. They did an about face, and ran like frightened squirrels, trying to avoid an automobile's tires. The hooded feigns quickly disappeared in the thick brush.

The green blur roared past Larry, not enabling him to see the driver through the darkly tinted glass. He did throw up a waving hand to thank who ever steered the smoking behemoth, for possibly saving his life. He then quickly reversed his course. He maintained a steady retreating pace that even surprised him.

No one followed. The potential ambush had been thwarted this time. Glancing back, he saw the Buick had turned around and pulled to a stop, monitoring his progress and ensuring the attackers stayed at bay. He mumbled a little prayer for the mystery driver, legs cramping and lungs burning, hurried as best he could back toward Payne's house.

Cassandra first recognized Larry marching in our direction, nudged me, and pointed. I pressed the accelerator and sped to close the distance. He looked almost dead on his feet, wringing wet from head to toe, face as red as a matador's cape.

Veering from left to right, it appeared he would fall any second, and fall he did. He crashed onto the grassy shoulder, next to the road, as if he had just been shot. He rolled over on his back, resembling a beached whale. I slammed on the brakes adjacent to him. He was laboring to breathe. Shorty and Peter leaped from the back before the car came to a complete stop.

"Are you okay, Dude?"

Larry sort of nodded to confirm he was all right. His color, white as chalk, lips purple, and skin almost sticky-clammy. He could have been pegged for the lead zombie in Night of the Living Dead. His chest heaved, the big man sucking in air like a vacuum cleaner, then exhaling like a leaf blower.

"What are you doing, practicing for the Boston Marathon?" asked Peter.

Cassandra and I arrived just in time to hear him say, "God just encouraged me to tell Satan to go back to hell. I belong to the Lord and will forever do his bidding, end of story."

We looked at one another, rolling our eyes and shrugging, clueless to his rants. The big man had apparently completed a profound religious experience. I was just glad he wasn't speaking in tongue. We eventually got him to his feet and into the car.

He recapped his experience with the two hooded men, and what he thought was a 1979 green Buick Electra, referring to the mystery driver as his personal avenging angel. Against my better judgment, I had decided to pay Mr. Easterly a little visit, but the others had talked me out of it. They said I shouldn't with Stephen lying dead in his condo. It was a convincing argument, I had to admit.

We decided that none of us would go anywhere alone until this was over. I didn't buy into the Klan being responsible. The black hoods dispelled that possibility. A person or persons simply didn't want us digging up old bones. I just wasn't sure how deeply the conspiracy might go, or if indeed a conspiracy actually existed. The fact that two of my dear friends were dead as a result troubled my miserable soul.

We sat around my den, no one saying much of anything. We looked like a bunch of whipped little puppies. I certainly had no answers, which rated me as a very ineffective leader. I don't remember being nominated. I must have volunteered. I glanced at my watch. Noon approached, two and a half days remained, if indeed we planned to do this Halloween night. I still believed we had to wait until Friday. I just wasn't sure what specifically compelled me to stick to this plan.

I fingered my notepad, resting on the loveseat beside me. Cassandra sat on the other side of me, but I wasn't fingering her. Sex had dropped off the radar screen. My mind couldn't wrap around sexual gratification right now. Besides, I do believe I love this woman sitting next to me. But right now I envisioned being back at that house, replaying what I remembered, attempting to trigger anything that I had forgotten.

I glanced around the room, attempting to read the thoughts of those staring off into space. We resembled carcasses. All we were missing were flies and circling turkey buzzards and the depiction would be perfect. Gloom and doom, we had them both corralled.

Cassandra finally broke the silence, "Where's that old bible we retrieved from Stephen's condo?"

"Still in the trunk of the Town Car," replied Peter. "I'll go get it."

"Let me," spoke up Larry, holding out his hand for the keys. "It requires the scrutiny of an expert. I'm sorry guys, but you don't qualify."

"Have at it, Pope Laurence McCurry," smarted off Shorty.

"Payne, what about that letter you found?" asked Cassandra, "Do you still not remember what happened to it?"

"Not right off...let me go mining later in those boxes in the closet. I can't imagine I would have trashed it, but then again, it has been over nineteen years."

"Hey Dude, what have you been writing in that notepad over there," asked Shorty, pointing to the loveseat.

"I suppose it's my think pad. I've just been trying to make the pieces of the puzzle fit."

"And have you had any luck?" asked Peter.

"Just theory right now..."

"Why don't you share what you've got so far?" pressed Cassandra. "Maybe we can help."

"I don't know. I'm reaching. It might not make any sense."

"We're all reaching, Dude, in case you haven't noticed."

Larry returned with the tattered bible, already thumbing through it and muttering to himself. He flopped down in a recliner, clicked on the lamp resting on the side table. His mouth twitched and eye brows fluttered as if he suffered from some form of epileptic seizure.

"All right, here goes" I said, retrieving my scribbling. "But try not to laugh."

"Look Dude. This is so way beyond anything funny. In case you haven't noticed, we're fighting for our sorry lives, and we're not exactly winning. Just read it."

28
THE ELEVENS

"Please try to exercise open minds. That shouldn't be too difficult for most of you. Cassandra you are exempted."

Larry folded the bible across his Humpty-Dumpty belly. He gave me his undivided attention. Shorty cracked a cold one. The foam flowed from the long neck opening. Shorty sucked on the bottle like a leach after blood. No beer droplets escaped.

Peter yawned, dark circles under his eyes, signaling the ordeal was getting the best of him. Cassandra snuggled next to me and rubbed the back of my neck. It reminded me I hadn't taken her up on that massage yet, but she had compensated me handsomely, so who's complaining.

I had not shaven in the last couple of days, but with a beard there wasn't much to shave. I had avoided looking in any mirrors, almost vampire like behavior. I feared what this ordeal may have done to me also. I felt like I had aged twenty years, something neither Stan nor Stephen would be able to experience.

I opened my notepad and stared at my entries. With just over two days remaining, could my scribbling amount to a hill of beans? I would let the others be the judge. "Okay, it sort of started clicking with me after we dug into the history and architecture of the house. We were young and stupid back in 68. None of us really noticed just how unique that house design really was."

"Tough to see unique under the cloak of darkness with only flashlights," interrupted Shorty.

"Not to mention most of us weren't feeling any pain," reminded Larry. "Boone's Farm, PJ, Hoppin Gators and Orange Tommy's tend to cloud one's eyes for details."

"The house is made up of three octagon designs and eleven rooms," I began in as much detail as I could remember. I explained the house layout and the uniqueness of its unique design. I included briefly the history of the designer, Orson Squire Fowler and his beliefs. I recapped the Pressely and Fraser connection. That alone didn't spur any great revues. Only Cassandra understood the significance.

"Keep in mind that eleven room design," I prompted them as I continued. "Historical Abbeville was instrumental in the south succeeding from the United States, eleven southern slave states to be exact."

"So we have eleven rooms and eleven states," recapped Shorty. "So what?"

"1968, eleven juniors, that would be eleven, eleventh graders in a town where eleven states split from the homeland, ventured into the house of eleven rooms. Are you seeing an interesting pattern now?"

"That's a lot of elevens so far," remarked Larry.

"I haven't even gotten started yet."

"I'm on the edge of my seat," added Larry.

"Leroy died eleven years ago in 1975. Charlie went MIA in Nam with ten other men, eleven counting him. Lester disappeared in 1979, eleven years after we visited the house in 1968." I paused to watch for their reactions. I had hooked them; well, almost everyone.

"You're into this eleven thing aren't you?" remarked a skeptical Shorty. "I'll check back with you once I've tossed back my eleventh cold one."

"Some of what I am about to cover may be a little sensitive but it should help me make my case."

"Do it," encouraged Larry.

"Peter, you started your landscape business in 1975, right?"

"Yep," he hesitated then said, "eleven years ago. Damn..."

"Three years later in 1979 and eleven years from 1968, the tragedy happens, taking the life of the eleven year old girl. I'm sorry Peter, I know this it not something you wanted me to bring up."

"It's all right. It happened. There's no hiding it or denying it. I could be in jail now but they wouldn't involve the police, for good reasons."

"The father of the girl was trying to ensure his family had jobs." I could see this one wasn't making sense, until I did the math for them. "He and ten others, not counting the dead girl, equal eleven."

I could feel Cassandra trembling next to me. She was getting it. Now I had to convince Shorty. "Shorty, remember some of our discussions about us living eleven miles apart."

He half ass nodded, and took a swallow of beer.

"You told me that Stephen called you late, at 11:30 to confess he had Aids. Then when you and I discussed the house here that first night, I glanced at the time and it was 6:11 PM. You've also been seeing that shrink for eleven years now."

"So I guess you're going to tell me next we have eleven planets or stars all lined up," he scoffed, but I could read him like a book. I had him too.

"What he's saying is for whatever the reason, you eleven juniors were somehow the key that opened a door, the trigger for what happened in 1968," spoke up Cassandra. "And the elevens have continued to impact your lives."

"So what exactly does that mean?" asked Shorty, trying not to buy into it. He wasn't fooling me.

"I don't know that yet, but I have one more thing to add. Larry said that the Buick he encountered..."

Larry finished my sentence. "It was a 1979 Electra, I'm positive."

"Subtract 1968 from 1979 and we have 11," chimed in Peter.

"This is a beginning," added Cassandra. "I feel it as strongly as I have ever experienced anything before."

"Then you're going to do back flips when I read this to you," smiled Larry, opening up the bible and thumbing to an earmarked page.

29

The 79 Buick with its engine switched off, parked in the edge of the pines. The driver watched the pick-up pull from its hiding place. Two previously hooded men pulled into the highway and drove away. They were confident that no one had seen them trying to have batting practice with the chubby priest. The Buick followed. The driver recognized the passenger of the pickup, but not the driver.

Following for eleven miles, finally the pickup pulled up a long winding and secluded drive. The Buick's driver parked and followed on foot, undetected, sticking close to a hedgerow covered by kudzu. The two were joined by a second pair, one a huge mountain of a man. These were the four from the lake attack; how convenient thought the Buick's driver.

The big one seemed irritated that the other two had failed in their mission. He walked inside, and from a window could be seen making a phone call. By his reaction, the news he had just delivered wasn't taken well either. He hung up the phone, throwing up his hands, and storming around the room highly pissed. He continued his ranting at the others.

The Buick's driver took advantage of the situation, stormed into the house, catching the four totally by surprise. Uniquely masked and waving the razor sharp machete, he yelled, "This is for Stephen Pool and Larry McCurry, you sick bastards!"

30

"I have found several hand written entries strategically hidden within the pages of the bible," started Larry. "The first entry was made in 1863, two years into the Civil War. Guess what, that makes it eleven years after the original construction of the Frazier-Pressely House in 1852. By the miss-spellings and almost broken language, I would suspect this had been written by a possible Haitian slave, female it appears."

"What was her name?" asked Cassandra.

"Her signature is tough to read, but I think it is something like Claudette L'ouverture. My guess, she worked on the plantation in some high ranking position, from the best I can tell from some of her scribbling I've been able to decipher. Her writings indicated she was a troubled soul. I fear she was in some sort of perilous danger. I am paraphrasing what I have read of course, because it would loose something in translation if I read it out loud as scribbled."

"I can feel her pain too," confirmed Cassandra, chill bumps rippling down her arms.

"There's mention several times of Vaudou. I think she means voodoo."

"You mean we're talking zombies and sticking pins in dolls," blurted out Shorty.

"Over exaggerated in their culture by the horror movies, I assure you. Voodoo was simply a religion. Satan and creating zombies was not the premise of voodoo."

"What makes you such a damn expert on this bull shit?" asked Shorty.

"You're talking to a priest, Shorty," Cassandra reminded him. "Watch your mouth."

"I'm talking to Larry, the same Larry that we hauled home countless times because he had passed out from his wine, the same guy who got his little pecker stuck in that coke bottle, mister take his clothes off and run naked through parking lots," answered Shorty rolling his eyes. "He's no preacher to me."

"Point taken, but to answer your question, dickhead, I studied many religions, and the Haitian culture was one of them."

"Let him get on with it, Shorty," spoke up Peter.

"Voodoo had many gods. Ghede Ghede is the god of the dead in the voodoo culture. He's wise and is supposed to have all of the knowledge of the dead. He's the undertaker, always dressed in black and wearing dark glasses. There are others of his retinue, Baron la Croix and Baron Cemetière. Mama Bridgette is the goddess who protects the graves. There are many more, good ones and evil ones."

"I agree with Shorty," I interrupted. "what does this have to do with what's in that bible?"

"Two symbols appear numerous times. The moon for one, and the skull and crossbones."

"So are we talking pirates or zombies?" asked Shorty.

"The moon is the symbol for a not so nice spirit, Kalfu, the spirit of the night and the source for darkness. From what I remember, he's a sonofabitch, very dangerous."

"Must I remind you too, that you are a man of the cloth," chastised Cassandra.

"Sorry my dear, I'm guilty by association. They bring it out of me."

"Okay, so we have the moon man," said Peter. "Who does the skull and crossbones belong to?"

"Bacalou, and he's an extremely evil spirit."

"What do these evil spirits have to do with the woman and us, and what is written in the old bible," I asked.

"Well, I can't say for sure, but here's what I do know. This woman was convinced these two spirits were wrecking havoc on her life. She mentions a bokor, which is a sorcerer, and a Lutin, which is an anabaptized child. She refers to this child as her eleventh, a boy."

"Eleventh, now we're getting somewhere," I said, grinning proudly.

"Can you fit the pieces of the puzzles together to make sense to us slow witted southern boys?" snapped Shorty.

"These evil spirits were apparently trying to possess her eleventh child. She sought help from a bocor, who lived either on the plantation or near by."

"She was trying to protect her child," nodded Cassandra, visualizing understanding the situation.

"She was trying to save her child's soul," explained Larry. "I fear he might have already been dead."

"A protective mother," said Cassandra. "I like her already."

"That smell," recalled Larry, not much louder than a whisper. "In the cabin, I smelled her. She was there when Payne and I entered the cabin. I knew the scent smelled familiar. It oozed that of a hard working Negro, and again, not offensive to me. The scent was almost soothing from my childhood memories. A black woman took care of me while my folks worked. She had that odor."

"One or both of the spirits must have attacked Stephen in that cabin," added Cassandra. "He's the one who stole her bible. They were trying to protect it, because she wrote of them in it."

"Or maybe she didn't want Stephen to take it," added Peter.

Out of no where, Shorty blurted, "Eleven times."

"Yeah, where have you been?" asked Peter. "We've been talking eleven for a while now."

"Brody," he sighed. "No one mentioned Brody's connection and I knew if I did, I would have to take this crap seriously."

"So what are you trying to say?" I asked my best pal.

"He's in that hospital again, because he tried to take his life. It was his eleventh attempt in the past nineteen years. I had never told anyone this before. Those damn spirits attacked him in that trunk and left him like this."

"Let's take a break," I advised, but the boys were into it now.

"Any idea what this eleven stuff really means?" asked Peter.

"Eleven is a powerful number," answered Larry. "I don't even know where to begin. It is significant in almost every culture.

It's predominant in the bible."

"So much for a break," I muttered. "One thing is for certain. It's significant to that night and us. I have a hunch where it originated. Fowler and the house's design play into it big time. We just have to figure out why and how. Hold your thoughts, and we'll get to it in a while, Larry."

"I'm going to read on and see what else I can determine. She hid these entries in this bible for a reason, and it wasn't from the spirits. She was afraid of someone human too."

I glanced over at our newest member, and saw she had this most peculiar look on her face, almost as if possessed. Before I could ask her what was wrong, she blinked several times, and then looked at me and smiled. I didn't press the issue, but I should have.

31

Easterly dialed the number for the eleventh time but still received no answer. He tossed back another shot of straight scotch, extremely troubled by this predicament. He could not just drive over there because he must remain anonymous in the matter to them and to the community.

This was not going as he had planned. Easterly sorely regretted having had the previous confrontation with Payne. Too much was now out in the open. This posed more serious consequences. He had to somehow determine how bad the situation had gotten, without incriminating himself.

He had just wanted them to deliver a warning, not inflict any injuries. What they had actually done could jeopardize everything. He kicked himself. He had crossed a line he had never considered crossing before. He found himself on the wrong side of justice. He contemplated how to move forward without digging the hole deeper.

Easterly picked up the phone, deciding to cash in on another favor. This would be his final lifeline. He had no other options at his disposal. There would be no turning back now, even if he had to dirty his own hands, something he had never done before, either.

He threw the shot glass across the room. It slammed into the wall, accidentally shattering the picture frame displaying the photograph of the 1968 Upstate Conference Winning football team. That year the team was just one game shy of winning the state title.

His son, Donald, held the trophy high and proud. His bastard son never knew he was his real father. No one knew, except his biological mother, who died giving him life due to complications in the delivery room. A stranger, a good man, had raised him as his own, while he could only watch from the shadows of obscurity.

That ruthless band of rebels had been the cause of his son's untimely death. He never understood why Donald had taken such a fondness to their outlaw shenanigans. He could do nothing to prevent it without confessing his own sins. Easterly had used the tourism angle as an excuse to justify his actions pertaining to the ten remaining little shits, which had taken his only son away from him.

Now that his wife was deceased, his two daughters grown and living out of state, and Donald's surrogate Dad in a nursing home with some terminal illness, all bets were off. It was time to even the score. He couldn't believe he was thinking like this, but lines had already been crossed. There could be no turning back. He had waited much too long for revenge.

32

The 79 Buick Electra, driver sweating profusely, had been previously invigorated by his encounter with the four hooded men. Rectifying the situation had been so gloriously satisfying. He now returned his attention to the band of investigators. Revisiting that house on the Cedar Springs Road would only deliver more evil and possible death to those who dared venture inside.

While no one had been harmed there since that Halloween Night, those who attempted to live there had soon found it not worth the trials and tribulations offered. The existing owners had made several attempts to sell it at below market value, but had been unable to unload it. The house's well earned and deserved haunted reputation had nixed all opportunities. Most realtors simply refused to list it, many having experienced strange occurrences when they had tried to show the house to a prospective buyer.

In the past year the owners had even tried to donate it as a historical site to the county, but they had been turned down on their offer. It was on the national register, but the county cited that renovation would be too costly, and maintenance, taxes and so forth beyond budget. The owners knew the real reason for their reluctance, finally throwing up their hands, and paying the taxes, and allowing the wrath of nature to eventually reclaim it as its own. Oddly, the house seemed to thwart nature's attempts as if immune to decay and time, forever preserved for eternity. Evil refused to die.

33

I tried to rummage through scores of unmarked boxes in the closet, searching for that envelope. So far I had come up empty. I could not remember what I had done with it. Possibly my brain had blocked it out. The logical place would have been in that shoe box, but it wasn't there. Drawing blanks, I gave up.

I watched Larry flip through the bible's pages, frequently stopping and jotting down notes as he did. My emotions covered the spectrum anticipating the outcome of opening Pandora's Box.

I am convinced that the eleven roomed house had somehow opened a portal to the Haitian evil spirits. I thought about the octagonal house and the mention of it by virtue of its plan, to be perfect for spiritualist séances. I wondered if I had just stumbled onto the key. I decided to consult my roomy, our resident medium and spiritualist.

"Miss Blake, have you ever conducted a real séance?"

"Just for the fun of it with some girl friends..."

"I was just thinking..."

"You want to have one at that house, don't you?"

"Well...octagonal houses were thought to be spiritual conduits, from what we've read. I just thought by having one, we might just be able to contact that Haitian woman, and get to the bottom of this."

"You're really serious, aren't you?"

"Only if you're willing to give it a shot. I don't think the reverend Larry would make our best medium, do you?"

"What if we conjure up one of those evil spirits?"

"I thought séances were for the dearly departed, the human kind, and not gods or spiritual entities."

"A spirit is a spirit. I don't think it's like calling a direct line to the person you wish to speak to."

"Well, that's the way it works in the movies. You summon Uncle Bob, you get Uncle Bob. The table lifts up, the curtains blow around, lights flicker, and then the spirit talks through the medium."

"Payne, we're not playing look into the crystal ball with voices from beyond, and pretending make belief spirits are answering us. This could be potentially dangerous, if we don't know what we're doing. Those on the other side do."

"So you really believe this stuff can work?"

"I deal in premonitions, not spiritual dial up. I believe that house has a mind of its own, or at least has spiritual minds that own it. I don't think we can control or manipulate this to serve our needs."

"But all we want to do is ask it or her a few questions," I turned on the sad puppy dog look.

"And if we somehow get a wrong number..."

"We hang up the phone."

"We better discuss this seriously as a group, because we can't have a séance with just the two of us"

"Don't worry. I'm sure the boys will be all over this."

We retuned to the den. Shorty and Peter huddled on the couch in deep discussion, both sipping an adult beverage. Larry still had his nose buried in the slave's bible. The clock glared 7 PM, not 11. Where had another day gone? Time no longer on our side, only two days remained. We needed to shit or get off the pot, so to speak.

The phone rang and disrupted my plan. It was Jimbo Price, my deputy stoolie. They had found Stan's wallet and clothes in the possession of a local vagrant. He had confessed to taking them off a corpse. Stan was already dead when he had found him.

Jimbo said the poor wino had been delirious when he wondered into the station. He had demanded that the officers put him behind bars to protect him. He feared a giant one eyed, devil monster roaming the night. He smelled of something rot gut. He had been feeling no pain when he entered the station. The Stan Bronson mystery had now been solved, case closed.

I filled in the others, what Jimbo had just disclosed to me. We made one final toast to Stan, and moved on to the next thing on the agenda, the significance of the elevens. Larry had the floor once again.

"All right, so tell us oh great one, why elevens?" asked Shorty.

"I'm not sure why, but I can tell you what I remember about the number eleven. Hold onto to your butts. Here we go."

"Can the theatrics, Fryer," snapped an impatient Shorty. "Just get on with it."

"Eleven is a Master Number in Numerology and Astrology. Unfortunately, it can mean sin or peril. People with this number can be lured toward the unknown. It can bring with it the gift of spiritual inheritance."

"How do you retain information like this?" asked Cassandra.

"I've always sort of had a photographic memory."

"Is that why you double exposed yourself," chuckled Shorty.

"Lay off him," I warned Shorty. "This is no kidding matter."

"No kidding, you've seen him naked too," laughed Shorty. "And I can only cringe to think what he would do to the streaking world now."

Larry ignored Shorty. "Think how eleven has influenced every day living. Many sports are played with eleven players; our football, Soccer, Cricket and even Field Hockey. A Rugby ball is eleven inches long."

"Like you know something about sports," lashed out Shorty, finding it impossible to just shut the hell up.

"Cut him some slack," warned Peter, punching Shorty in the shoulder.

"Mash, one of my favorite shows ever, was based on a 1968 Novel. The television show ran for eleven seasons and had eleven main characters. And speaking of wars, World War I ended on the 11th hour of the 11th day of the 11th month." He smiled, proud of how he rattled this off effortlessly.

"Apollo 11 was the first space ship of ours to land on the moon. A rocket must travel at over 11km per second to escape our gravitational pull. The average weight of a heart in a grown man is about eleven pounds."

"Enough," screamed Shorty. "I'm having an eleven overdose. We get it. You know this eleven shit. Tell us something about eleven that could have affected what has happened to us."

"Let's take a little breather," I told Larry. "This is fascinating, but you're about to OD me too."

"Sorry, I get into this stuff, as you can tell."

"Ignore them," smiled our only female. "I'm impressed."

I knew the number eleven was important, but I needed fresh air, overwhelmed by this sudden wealth of knowledge. I stepped into the backyard and breathed in October's chilly night. She joined me, snuggled up to my back, and placed her arms around me. I wished it could remain like this. Friday loomed. I feared the worst, fresh out of optimism.

An unmarked cruiser slowed as it approached the drive. The off duty highway patrolman inside eyed the house for any signs of the occupants. Blinds were pulled, doors closed, so the house offered no glimpse of his targets. He had a debt to pay, and then he would be free and clear to run his own life, make his own decisions.

With a gloved hand, he reached under the seat. He retrieved two quart sized Ziploc bags. One contained pure cocaine and the other an assortment of previously confiscated illegal capsules and pills. Either one alone would keep these bumbling idiots up to their asses in lawyers and court appearances. To ensure there was no possible plea bargaining, he fondled the third bag resting on the passenger side seat, a bloody knife with Stan Bronson's blood on the blade.

That dufus, Jimbo, had been so easily manipulated with false information, information he had predictably delivered to Payne, stating the coroner had found nothing suspicious about his friend's death. Knife wounds would support the crime. His brother-in-law, the coroner, would back up the story, because he owed the officer.

The wino presently in custody would be the witness to the attack. Winos could be bought so easily. The Sheriff, still down in his back and laid up at home, would never know any better. That job would soon be his anyway, with the delivery of the next blackmail scheme. Like a well oiled machine, there would be no screw ups this time.

When he finished planting the evidence, he would drive up and check on those four assholes that messed up the lake threat. He had warrants for their arrests, legit drug related and robbery charges. Loose ends would be tidied up.

Parking the cruiser behind a shed at an unoccupied house two doors down, he made his way back to the outside utility room, where he would conceal the evidence. He would tip off other officers, anonymously of course; allow them to make the bust. This was almost too easy he thought, checking for any sign of life, before he slipped into the single automobile carport.

Reaching for the utility room door, he felt a tap on his shoulder. He turned and stared hell right in the eye. The blow delivered swiftly, crumpled him into the waiting arms of his assailant. Placed into the back of his cruiser, knife confiscated, drugs stuffed inside his shirt, he was driven eleven miles away, setting a scene worthy of playing out on the Opera House stage.

The trip back would not take long, not at the speed he traveled. The redeemer would stop only long enough to make an anonymous phone call to the police department. Diversionary tactics, not what the mastermind had envisioned. Smiling, the driver of the Buick drew satisfaction, knowing again the puppet master had been outwitted. Insomnia inspired innovation. Sleep was for the weak.

34

"Guys I promise to keep this quick," advised Larry. "I'll cover a few biblical elevens, if you will bear with me."

"Eleven us to death, Dude," spouted Shorty. "But I don't see where it's getting us?"

This stuff really scared the crap out of Shorty, but he was too stubborn to admit it. The rest of us weren't so proud.

"Let's just get through this," remarked Peter.

"Larry, I'm with you on this," reassured Cassandra. "Please continue."

I had nothing to say. I was already convinced eleven had something to do with our dilemma. Nothing Larry could divulge could possibly impact what my gut already told me. The eleven, I suspected, had nothing to do with the bible or any friendly spirits. It had our number, no pun intended.

"Elevens can be good omens. Jesus appeared eleven times after his death, the ultimate in ancient Spiritualism. Joseph had eleven brothers. David had eleven mighty men. Jesus told eleven parables on his way to his death."

Larry rattled off scripture after scripture, containing the number eleven, for at least another ten minutes. My eyes became heavy, and I'm still amazed I didn't scream uncle. Cassandra sat on the edge of her seat, hanging on his every word, very supportive. I could see it in their eyes. Peter and Shorty had already bailed, and just let it run its course.

I snapped back to attention, when I heard Larry mutter the

word, Hadees. He said it occurred eleven times in the New Testament. Hadees had been translated as Hell, ten of those eleven times, and as grave one time. He made references to death, destruction, punishment, calamity, and torment, all beyond the grave. He lost me again when he began speaking of Hebrew Sheol, Greek Hadees and Saxon translations. Finally the bleeding stopped. So what did all this mean? Larry's audience had no clue.

"So tell me old great high priest, just what the hell does your babbling amount to, and please speak English," said Shorty.

"I was merely attempting to illustrate to you the significance of the number. Good verses, evil verses, indifferent, it appears all the time."

"I'll stick to my guns here," I stepped up to the plate. "The octagon house's eleven rooms are spiritual connections. There were eleven of us, eleventh graders. The slave woman plagued by those dangerous spirits somehow created some sort of alignment with us that Halloween night. That unleashed hell on earth for us, a curse, an abomination, call it what ever you want. It latched onto our lives. It hasn't let go of us since. Going back is the only chance we have of undoing it for those of us that remain."

Shorty stood, clapped, giving me a one man standing ovation. I bowed, and then gave him two fingers, right and left. He smiled and returned the greeting.

"Do you want to hear what else she wrote in the bible?" asked Larry, dropping the other shoe.

"Not without a drink," responded Shorty.

"Amen," added Peter.

I stepped out onto the carport, just as an odd set of tail lights passed by on the street. I walked to the corner for a better look. I identified the 79 Buick Electra, making a left turn at the intersection, three houses away. Peter's Town Car blocked all others so I yelled, "Peter, road trip, now! It's the Buick!"

The four inside poured out of the doorway like an extremely tiny horde of ants spilling from their hill. Even Larry had pep in his step. In less than a half minute, we were burning rubber in semi-hot pursuit. The tale lights were nowhere to be seen.

We passed one, then a second intersecting street, and Shorty yelled, "Buick at three o'clock! The bastard has his lights off."

Peter slammed on brakes, threw it in reverse, all in one motion. It's wonder he didn't strip the gears or even worse, drop the transmission. The Buick was already on the move, and leaving us in a cloud of spewing black, oily engine dung, reminiscent of *James Bond,* implementing a smoke screen. I figured we should be able to follow the Buick's smoky trail, just like following Hansel and Gretel's bread crumbs.

How did that go you ask? Not so good. Soon we were engulfed in the choking fog, and had lost sight of any tail lights. Eventually we followed the all too visible swirling crumbs but missed the Buick's right turn. By the time we realized our mistake and back tracked, the dissipating cloud of blackness offered no clue of the direction it had taken.

We had been unable to close the gap and make out the license plate, so we remained clueless to the avenging angel's identity and his or her role in our lives. Obviously we were of some significance to the driver. We returned to my house, and decided to take turns on watch for the night, just in case the 79 made another appearance.Peter volunteered to take the first turn. Shortly after everyone had retired to their bedrooms, he became restless and troubled, decided to take a drive. He deserted his post, drawn by forces he could not resist, leaving the house unguarded and us, open game for intruders.

35

A massive crime scene had exploded at the secluded driveway. An assortment of emergency vehicle lights illuminated the darkness. The Sheriff had found it necessary to suck it up and forget about his ailing back, to head up the investigation. Officer Jimbo Price, oozing exuberance, had never been involved in anything of this magnitude, five bodies, one a state highway patrolman.

Mister Easterly glanced at his watch, 11:11 PM. He paced nervously at the base of the drive, lost in an ocean of television crews from the three major venues and news paper reporters from surrounding counties. Our tiny town was about to make the national news, and for all the wrong reasons. Forgetting about the impact on tourism and those responsible for his son's death, he prayed no trails led back to him.

"Jimbo," remarked Sheriff Campbell Burdette, squinting, his back throbbing worse than a thousand tooth aches, "I've never witnessed such a damn ugly mess in all my thirty one years in law enforcement. We have a dead cop here, on my watch. No police officer has ever died on duty under my watch before, except for that sorry ass Bryson Myers back in 67. He got caught with his britches down, had a massive heart attack in the middle of him screwing that white trash whore in the Long Cane Cemetery. We could have covered it up too, if those meddling kids hadn't been hiding and watching his fat ass bob up and down like a cork in the back seat of his police car. Plus the whore got pinned underneath him, and was stuck there until the ambulance arrived."

Jimbo just nodded, too occupied to be very interested in crap that had happened twenty years ago, when he was just a chap in diapers. He tried to stay focused on the coroner and the investigating team's progress, taking notes in his little black book, and mentally storing away what he had seen and heard up until now. The coroner struggled with the task. The fallen officer was his brother-in-law and coconspirator in a plan gone terribly wrong.

The patrolman had a knife buried in his chest, handle deep. His weapon was still holstered. Arrest warrants had been plucked from his shirt pocket. Three of the dead men's names were on those blood stained warrants.

An assortment of drugs were scattered on a coffee table, presumably owned by the four dead men. Jimbo knew all of the departed by first and last names, real bad asses in the community, all with various arrest records, ranging from drug possession, assault, public drunkenness, and disorderly contact to resisting arrests, spousal abuse. You name it, and they had been busted on it, or had skirted the legal system, and had gotten away with some of the alleged crimes. Their crime spree stopped here, thought Jimbo.

A machete, still clutched in the dead patrolman's right hand, had apparently been the weapon used to hack them to pieces. Jimbo jotted in his notebook, *why had he chosen a machete and had not used his revolver?* Something smelled. This scene just didn't quite add up.

Two men had been decapitated, a third's head hung on by a sliver of flesh and bone, and the forth, the largest of the four, had been gutted like a deer. Jimbo Price contemplated the possible scenarios. Had this been an arrest gone bad, or could it have been the result of a corrupt officer, asking for more than the others thought he deserved?

Even a bigger mystery loomed in Jimbo's mind. Who had phoned in the anonymous call? Had a sixth person been present and witnessed the crime, escaped by the skin of his or her teeth?

"Jimbo, sit tight here," ordered the sheriff. "I've got to face the music with that horde of news folks at the end of the drive, and then I've got to do something about this back of mine."

"On top of it chief," saluted Jimbo.

Easterly watched Sheriff Burdette's car approaching the swarming news media, licking at the chops, each ready to scoop the story. He simply blended into the crowd. He would allow the others to ask their questions. He could no longer control the situation.

Ten minutes later the worse possible scenario unfolded. Five were dead, one had been an officer, all five owing him favors, none successfully fulfilling his requests. A plus, this distraction would allow him to handle the other situation with little notice, but he would have to do it alone now. Stan Bronson's untimely death would go unnoticed, with no need now to stage a crime. Too many news personnel in town altered his original game plan.

The million dollar question, who had murdered his five gun slingers? He didn't buy into the machete welding officer story, which the sheriff had confided in him, after addressing the other reporters. Those four good old boys would have eaten the patrolman's lunch, if he had threatened them with just a machete. There's no way possible he would have ever been able to hack up all four. He was supposed to arrest them, not murder them.

Payne and his crew of misfits could not have perpetrated something so horrifically gruesome, or could they? If they hadn't, then who would do something like this? Who had a reason to do it? Could it have been a mere coincidence that they all ended up there at the same time, and had been murdered by an unknown assailant, a real drug deal gone bad? Easterly had too many questions and feared the answers.

It would be a week before he would have to print anything in his newspaper. By then it would be history, instead of news. Right now he had to figure out what those others were up to. He still intended on punishing them for Donald's death, now that he had all of them in one basket. 'Chickens have come home to roost.' Stan Bronson had told him. They were going to venture back into that house, he could just feel it, but why, why would they even want to?

He returned to his automobile and just sat there for a few minutes, head on the steering wheel, attempting to regain his composure. He took a draw of whisky from the flask, then a second and third, until it had bottomed out. It didn't help cure his mood.

The watcher propped against a news van, eying him intensely, mood changing from pity to spite. Like father, like son, hiding behind the booze, and allowing it to dictate his actions. Donnie had known the secret. He had chosen turning to his Purple Jesus beverage instead. He had figured his real father would never tell him the truth, ashamed of the bastard son. His anger, more pronounced under the influence, prompted Donnie to always take it out on the ones that cared about him, all except for his paternal father.

That house had changed everything. Donnie could possibly have still been alive now, if not for that house's interference. His rage had become amplified, by just being there that night. The superstar quarterback had completely lost control, more so than ever, and the ramifications had been deadly.

The media circus continued. Seeing enough, the watcher faded into the background and disappeared. Easterly plotted his next move.

36

Abstinence overturned. After making love to Cassandra, she had been able to find sleep quickly. I wasn't convinced I had contributed to her crashing slumber, as much had the events of the day. It hadn't had the same impact on me. A rare case of insomnia had stricken me. I was too damn sober, and didn't even crave a drink.

The digital radio alarm clock on my night stand glowed almost 2 AM. I decided I might as well relieve Peter, and take my watch earlier than the 3 AM scheduled time. Slipping on my jeans and ratty old Falcons sweatshirt, I tip toed, bare footed, down the hallway toward the den. I didn't spot Peter, so I headed for the kitchen.

Just as I cut the corner, Peter entered the side door from the carport. "See something?" I asked, almost causing him to leap onto the kitchen counter top.

"Watch that crap. I was just getting some fresh air, clearing my head."

"Catch you some Z's. I couldn't sleep. I'll take over."

"Suits me,' he said, grabbing a soda from the frig, and disappearing down the hallway.

I stepped out onto the patio to check things out, the concrete much too cold on my bare feet. Just before stepping back inside, I heard a pinging sound. Cautiously following the pinging and clicking noises, I discovered the sounds emitting from Peter's Town Car. I felt the hood, warm to the touch, the engine in cool down mode. Peter had just returned from somewhere, and he hadn't mentioned it. I shrugged it off, thinking maybe he had just been in the car listening to the radio, but why would he have run the engine? He could have been chilled, fired up the heat. I thought better of my assumptions.

I rummaged through the refrigerator after returning inside, opting for a root beer and chunk of sharp cheese. I settled on the couch in the darkened den, watching the street through the picture window, drapes wide open. All appeared to be quite.

It suddenly dawned on me that I had no job. I pondered my next career move, but had no solutions to improve my unemployment situation. I had maybe eight hundred bucks in my checking and about two grand in a credit union savings account. With both a house and car payment looming, that wouldn't take me very far. I could grovel and ask for my job back, but I've never been good at groveling.

The Wednesday Weekly had been my only real job. I had never given any thought what I would do, if I wasn't working there. I would have to consider that, but not tonight. Procrastination took the reins. My focus returned to the house, and what might be waiting for us there. I had even shut my bed buddy from my thoughts. I tried to remember what I had done with that damn envelop, but still drew blanks.

Headlights approached, so I rushed to the window to identify the vehicle. False alarm, it wasn't the green Buick Electra we had followed earlier. The late model vehicle's style looked vaguely familiar, but I never fancied myself much of a car expert. Cars were cars. Makes and models never drew my interest. It never slowed. Soon it had sped out of sight at the opposite end of the street.

I heard thunderous snoring from down the hall. Shorty could rattle the window panes. He occupied his bedroom alone. Peter and Larry had decided to bunk together in the third bedroom. Peter stretched out on an old cot retrieved from Shorty's place, opting to give the oversized priest the queen sized bed. He had laughed, saying the queen bed best suited Larry's demeanor. I could detect sporadic broken snoring coming from that room. Larry was not in the same league with Shorty. I sadly missed Stan and Stephen.

The commotion from the Buick had disrupted our Bible study. Larry had not finished reviewing and sharing the slave lady's entries. I spotted the bible, open and resting on the end table next to the recliner Larry had occupied. With nothing better to do, I flopped down in the recliner and switched on the lamp. I began flipping pages, and only pausing when I spotted hand written entries.

Too quickly I ascertained that perusing the bible was not my thing. There were too many distractions with all those thee's and thou's and psalms and biblical names. I decided to leave the driving to the expert. I started to close it, when a badly discolored piece of parchment style paper flitted from the binder, and floated like a feather to the floor.

Repositioning the Lazy Boy upright from the recline position; I reached down to pick up the paper. The edges crumbled in my finger tips. Bending down on one knee, I scooped it up, careful not to grab hold of it as before. I turned it to position it on the bible's hard back cover, so that I could safely read it without doing it further damage. Hand written and repeated over and over I read the same phrase.

Heel to toe, hold the line
Heel to toe, hold the line
Heel to toe, hold the line
Heel to toe, hold the line
Heel to toe, hold the line
Heel to toe, hold the line
Heel to toe, hold the line
Heel to toe, hold the line
Heel to toe, hold the line
Heel to toe, hold the line
Heel to toe, hold the line

It made absolutely no sense to me, *heel to toe, hold the line.* Apparently it held some significance for the author. It reminded me of some sort of dance or marching instructions. Rubbing my chin, I stared at it, as if expecting the words to magically transform into something earth shattering. It didn't, not at first but then, bam, right between my eyes; it had been repeated eleven times. Eleven certainly meant something, apparently something very powerful and forbidden.

Lightening struck my soul a second time, when I read that the child Claudette L'ouverture feared for had indeed been her eleventh. She had given birth to the young boy on the eleventh day of November 1862. Eleven this and eleven that, this damned eleven crap was just plain wearing me out, yet, it was so powerful.

Her writing indicated the young lad appeared to have some physical discrepancies, not normal or healthy like her previous ten. Based on her own descriptions, the kid must have been a mongoloid, badly disproportioned. We call folks like that retarded or suffering from Down syndrome. She called him special. Others called him evil, a curse, and an abomination. They had apparently shunned her and her child.

She named him *Domhnall*, an odd name for a slave, but I suppose back then they took on the names of their masters or possibly their lovers. I had a tough time wrapping my lips around a name like Domhnall L'ouverture. It didn't exactly roll off my tongue.

I detected movement in the room, and feared I had conjured up one of those evil voodoo spirits, but instead I saw Larry standing in the door way, rubbing sleep from his eyes and yawning. "Reading the scripture I see," he smiled.

"Doing your work for you, but I'm not spiritual enough to be authentic."

"Do we have any coffee brewing?"

"It's too early for coffee."

"So, my son, have you found a blessing in your bible studies?"

"Blessed be you, if you don't cut the wise cracks. I did find out when she gave birth to her eleventh child. I know his name."

"You have been busy, haven't you?"

"Domhnall L'ouverture, and get this. He entered this world on the eleventh of November, 1862, somewhat messed up though. He might have been a mongoloid. He apparently frightened the hell out of the slave population. They called him evil."

"That's not uncommon when a child suffers from obvious abnormities. Back then superstitions ruled."

"What kind of name is Domhnall?"

"You sure you want to hear this?"

"Don't tell me it means eleven."

He chuckled, "Worse, it is of Scottish origin."

"So the kid's daddy was Scottish. Why would that bother me?"

"The name Domhnall translates Donald. Domhnall means world leader or ruler of the world."

"The kid had the same name as Donnie. Oh crap and the evil spirits were interested in him because he could be the underworld's new world leader."

"I wouldn't jump the gun with that sort of speculation just yet, old friend."

I showed him the piece of paper, and asked him did *heel to toe, hold the line*, mean anything to him. He responded, "It sounds like a line dance to me."

"Count them. It is written eleven times. That means something. We have elevens running out of our butt, and now you tell me we have this Donald connection. We were doomed from the minute we stepped foot in that house, weren't we?"

"Destined," he corrected me, now glancing at the bible open in my lap. "Psalm 11, interesting she would write her passage there."

"Why interesting, it's eleven for heaven's sake."

"Yes, that too..."

"Oh man, what kind of a bomb are you about to drop on me now, Larry?"

He stood there, and began reciting Psalm 11 to me, by heart. I followed it word for word on the bible's page. Larry never missed a beat.

In the LORD I take refuge.

How then can you say to me:
"Flee like a bird to your mountain."
For look, the wicked bend their bows;
they set their arrows against the strings
to shoot from the shadows
at the upright in heart.

When the foundations are being destroyed,
what can the righteous do?"

The LORD is in his holy temple;
the LORD is on his heavenly throne.
He observes the sons of men;
his eyes examine them.
The LORD examines the righteous,
but the wicked and those who love violence
his soul hates.
On the wicked he will rain
fiery coals and burning sulfur;
a scorching wind will be their lot.
For the LORD is righteous,
he loves justice;
upright men will see his face.

Larry had really mastered this preacher vocation, even if I still struggled to visualize old Coke Cock as an actual man of the cloth. I felt his transformation to the Godly side might just be what we would need when we returned to the scene of the crime Friday. I wished to reclaim Halloween, my favorite holiday.

"Okay, my esteemed priest, so what does the eleventh Psalm have to do with us, with her, the house?"

"One interpretation is if the foundation is destroyed, the structure collapses."

"Are you saying we must destroy the house?"

"The house in this case is the foundation of the Christine doctrine. If it is destroyed, then so goes the entire structure."

"I think there must be a simpler interpretation."

"There are countless. It is said it makes people believe in their potential."

"My spin on it is we don't run for the hills, we stand and fight to protect God's temple. We stand together against everything that house can throw at us, and the Lord will make sure wicked is returned to Hell where it belongs. Righteousness served."

"Interesting spin, Payne, even for you. I like it better than any I can quote. We'll go with yours."

"I think I'll slip back in bed for a quick couple of winks.

"I know you Payne. Quickie is more what you have in mind. By the way, I like this Cassandra Blake. You better not do anything to break her heart. I get dips on performing the wedding nuptials."

37

Jimbo Price had not slept, pulling a double shift, and now sitting in a booth at the Dutch Oven Restaurant. He had inhaled his breakfast of three eggs over easy, a generous portion of Tabasco grits and slab of country ham. The Sheriff and coroner stuck to the scenario that the confrontation had exploded, when the officer had attempted to serve the arrest warrants.

Jimbo still didn't buy it. The holstered revolver and the machete would not allow him to believe this theory. Obviously Jimbo was not a detective, but he considered himself an amateur sleuth. Six feet tall, clean shaven, with a boyish face, pudgy physic, wispy blonde hair; he had been a model police officer. He was single, but did have a regular girl friend. They had dated for almost five years. Marriage had never been discussed or mentioned.

Mister Easterly strolled up to Jimbo's booth, and slid into the opposite side. "Good morning, Officer Price," he said in his soothing tone. "It is a long night and a dark day for our little city."

"Yes sir..."

"So what really happened back there tonight?" asked Easterly, luring Jimbo into his web.

"Like the sheriff said, an arrest gone very badly."

"Come on son, you can't possibly believe that. Why would an officer kill four men with a machete? We both know those boys were a force to be reckoned with, and one man with a blade could never have done this. Why didn't he just shoot them? I know you're thinking the same thing. I consider myself an amateur sleuth, and I sense that is something we share."

At the mere mention of sleuth, Jimbo gulped down a swallow of coffee, burning his tongue and the back of his throat. His eyes became blurred with tears. He dabbed them with his napkin, and then finally mustered up a response. "You're very perceptive. I was thinking that very same thing, sir."

Easterly had caught his fly. "If we put our heads together, I believe we could blow the lid off this investigation, don't you? Think of it son. You would be the hero, and my paper would have the exclusive. I bet you would make detective. Hell son, you could be elected Sheriff next term with my backing, you can be assured."

"I would like that, sir." Jimbo smiled, like a kid in a candy store.

"I know it has been a long night, but if you're up to it, we could go back to my office and outline the case and compare notes."

"I'm off duty. Let's do it."

38

Almost 9 AM, Shorty, the last one to stumble into the kitchen, looked like he had been rode hard and put up wet, again. I'm sure the rest of us probably looked no better. I still avoided mirrors.

"All right kiddies," said Shorty. "Today is Thursday. Tomorrow is Halloween. Do we have a plan for tomorrow night, or are you pansies still pondering the meaning of eleven?"

"Tis now the very witching time of night, when churchyards yawn and hell itself breathes out Contagion to this world... William Shakespeare," quoted Larry.

"Impressive," commented Cassandra.

"From ghoulies and ghosties, and long-leggedy beasties, and things that go bump in the night, Good Lord, deliver us!"

"And who said that one?" she asked.

"It is an old Scottish saying," replied Larry.

"Quite appropriate reverend," I replied, "with what we have learned about her full name."

"Hold on, man. We don't go anywhere with scary, spooky, haunted, or forbidden in the title...Scooby-Doo," recited Shorty.

We burst into a chorus of contagious laughter. Stan would have been proud of us. I sorely missed him.

"I keep having these visions of *Michael Myers* in that movie that came out in seventies, the one with the sequels," mumbled Peter.

"*Halloween*, 1978," quipped Larry, photographic memory in high gear. "I had a crush on Jamie Lee Curtis. Her character,

Laurie Strode, so suffered at the hands of *Michael. Dr. Sam Loomis, Donald Pleasence* played his part to the nine."

"You most likely had your crush on *Meyers*," snickered Shorty.

"Sorry I mentioned it," said Peter, putting his face in his hands.

"So do we have a grand plan yet, or what?" asked Shorty again.

"Guess we better come up with one," I said, smiling then taking a sip of Mountain Dew. "Let's catch everyone up to speed with what we know first. You start Larry."

****

The driver looked in the rear view mirror and extreme concern stared back. Five dead, five alive, and tomorrow Halloween, a date with the devil or worse, grew ever so closer. Yes, tomorrow it would be over for everyone. Unfortunately, a joker in the deck had complicated the game.

Stan Bronson's journal held the key that would unlock an important door. Truth came with a price, 19 years worth. While the driver of the 1978 green Buick Electra controlled the game today, tomorrow all bets would be off, when the house came into play.

Uncertainty posed its own set of problems. What would those five actually do once they mustered up the courage to set foot on that property? Actions warranted reactions. The lady, what role would she play? A female stranger in the house, now that presented a gaggle of possibilities. Good ones or bad ones, tomorrow night would reveal that answer.

Feeling naked and exposed, first on the agenda, purchase a new machete. Before *Jason* in those *Friday the 13th* movies ever emerged onto the scene, the driver had made use of a machete. Those owning right's to the story line and its characters would dispute the driver's claim, if truth be known. Who cares, thought the driver. It was only a mere technicality. It meant absolutely nothing.

Flipping the pages of the journal, the driver always stopped at the same entry, and cursed the event. No tears this time, too many had been shed. Tomorrow...one way or the other, it would end tomorrow. Trick or treat?

****

"So how does that sound for a plan?" I asked my audience.

"I guess it will have to do," replied Larry.

"You're putting a lot of faith in me," said Cassandra.

"You're one of us now and our wild card," added Peter, placing his hand on her shoulder. "I'm sounding like Larry now, but all we have is our faith and belief we're going to lick this thing."

"Five little peas in a pod," snickered Shorty.

"I'm going to finish going through that bible," advised Larry. "Maybe there are more clues."

"We should return it to where you found it," advised Cassandra. "It belongs to her, Claudette L'ouverture."

"Stole it you mean," corrected Shorty.

"I sense there is a strong connection between her son, Domhnall and your friend Donald, who died there," she explained.

"Another premonition..."

She nodded to confirm. "We still don't know the name of the child's father. Could he have been Scottish?"

"Not necessarily," answered Larry. "Slaves often took the sir names of their masters."

"But you said the child's name had Scottish origins," she reminded him.

"I did, didn't I?"

"So couldn't all of the eleven children have been sired by the same Scottish man?"

"Makes sense," answered Larry.

"Any luck trying to remember where you stashed that envelope you found, Dude?"

"I have one last place to look. There are some old suitcases in the attic, filled with various belongings of my parents. I've never looked through it since they died. It came out of their attic."

"Payne, your parents have been dead for over five years, and you've not gone through their stuff." Shorty just rolled his eyes.

"Digging in the past is not my thing. I've tried very diligently to keep it there where it belongs."

"Peter and I will drag those suit cases down. We'll do this together," advised Shorty.

"It's the matching blue set of luggage, off to the right of the staircase."

I could hear them in the hallway. The loud squeaking springs from the disappearing stairs and clattering of unfolding steps, provided the visuals. Flashbacks of that very first attic spook house flooded my head. I smiled, envisioning Stephen as the wolf man, Charlie as the Cyclops and our assortment of cheesy special effects. That house on the Cedar Springs Road would have made the perfect spook house. We could have raked in the candy.

Returning to earth, I still had no idea what my folks had packed away in that set of old luggage. I should have cared, but after losing both parents in an automobile accident, I had not completed the grieving process. I dreaded potential set backs. After tomorrow, nothing may matter.

"Payne, I really need to take a quick drive to Due west today, and retrieve some of my clothes. I don't have any suited for haunted house exploration."

"I'll go with you," I quickly volunteered.

"Not so fast, Dude," Shorty stood behind me with the first suitcase. "You've got to go through this stuff."

"He's right, sweetie."

"I'll go with her," spoke up Larry. "I need to stop by the Belmont too."

"Perfect," I said. "The exorcist and the medium, Due West will never be the same."

"We'll be fine," she kissed me on the cheek. I felt like she and I had been forever. In reality it had only been five days. I stood at the door like a little puppy dog, until they had driven out of sight. Their departure did not go unnoticed.

39

Jimbo Price did not like the fact that Mister Easterly had asked him to keep Payne and his friends under surveillance. He had to tip toe around his normal duties, and stay a step ahead of the sheriff. Luckily the sheriff had more than enough to keep him occupied with the news media and the investigation.

He still wasn't convinced Payne or the others had anything to do with those deaths, but Mister Easterly seemed to think a connection existed. He wouldn't explain why he believed this. Mister Easterly had been acting a little too weird for his taste. He wasn't sure how this alliance would pan out.

He certainly never noticed the green Buick, and should have. After all, he was supposed to be a seasoned police officer, in tune to his surroundings. Jimbo, eager to prove himself, also felt overwhelmed. Now faced with a decision, should he watch the house, or follow the two now driving away? Nervously, he chose to tail the car. Just the thought of tailing it, ignited his detective juices.

The Buick Electra never hesitated. It completed the caravan, keeping its distance, to maintain an inconspicuous profile. Following the policeman equated playing with fire, but intrigued by the woman, the driver could not fight the urge to follow.

Still the driver found difficultly shaking the feeling of being watched. An unseen presence had tormented the driver's thoughts. A darker, more evil presence was at work here. Heading into Halloween, it had reached a feverish pitch. One hand on the wheel and the other on Stan's journal, the Buick eased along, abiding by the posted speed limit, flying under the radar with expertise.

Jimbo hadn't determined the owner the car, but figured it must belong to the woman, since she was driving. He could have called it in, but thought better of it. He now followed it up North Main. Soon it would be out of the town's limits, and legally he shouldn't follow it out of his jurisdiction boundaries. Being a city cop, he didn't have the luxury of driving the county. He would stand out like a sore thumb if he did it in his police vehicle.

The car headed out of town towards either Due West or Anderson. Which fork in the road would it take was this question. Sweat beaded on Jimbo's forehead and flooded down his nose, dripping onto his uniform. Two more miles and Jimbo abruptly wheeled it around in the middle of the road. He headed back toward Abbeville.

The driver of the Buick Electra had been taken by surprise with the maneuver, but had no choice but to stay the course, and not do anything stupid. The two vehicles passed without incident. Jimbo Price urgently headed back toward Payne's house. Just as he cruised back inside the city limits, the dispatcher called on his radio. There had been a three car fender bender accident near the hospital. He engaged his siren and light, and then proceeded, cursed to do his duty.

The 78 green Buick Electra picked up the trail, and continued on course up Hwy 28. Larry had noticed the police car whipping around behind him, but it meant nothing. He had not spotted the Buick, lagging almost a quarter of mile behind, just another car, unable to tell much at this distance.

Like a primal shark, the green Buick skimmed below the surface, undetected, following its potential prey. Curious to uncover their destination, the shark kept its distance and did not attack.

Larry and Cassandra chatted endlessly on the drive to Anderson, like two best friends. They drew comfort from each other, the priest and the soon to be medium. Oblivious to anything else, they drove toward their destination, her house.

Approaching the street, just past Lander College, where she resided, she asked Larry to take a slight detour. When questioned why, she only responded that she always avoided passing an old deserted and dilapidated house just ahead, because she received bad vibes from it. She warned bad luck would come to those who passed the house, because a woman with a cold dark heart died there and still reached out to those who could feel her presence. Evil tugged at Cassandra. Larry respected her premonitions, left it at that, and didn't push the issue.

The driver of the Buick oddly sensed an ominous presence near by too, and did not possess her intuition or uncanny ability. The driver shrugged off the feeling and then mimicked the turn by turn detour, keeping their car in sight, while maintaining a safe distance behind.

Larry pulled into the drive of a quant little five room, white house, complete with a white picket fence, neatly maintained lawn, an almost fairy tale quality to it. It definitely suited her personality to a tee. It felt warm and cozy, emitting a love of life. He smiled, thinking how perfect.

The Buick stopped a block away. The driver watched the chubby figure emerge from the driver's side. The red headed pixy looking woman exited the passenger side. Curious, the driver exited the Buick, once both individuals had entered the house. Strolling down the sidewalk, concealment not necessary, a stranger to the neighborhood, no one here posed a threat or so the driver assumed. The watcher lurked behind the Buick's rear bumper, observing the antics of the driver. Halloween marked a collision course for all involved.

40

"You've got to see this one," chuckled Shorty, caught in a bent over belly aching laugh, holding the black and white photo up to Peter's face.

Sprawled on the quilted, flowery bed spread, bottoms up, a naked me, as a mere infant, had my buddies in stitches. The next photo of me sitting in the kitchen sink brought the house down. The box of photos in the largest piece of luggage contained a montage of my youth. My parents had taken plenty of pictures, and now I paid the price.

"Look here, how sweet," mocked Peter. "They're such cute little cowboy boots. Payne you couldn't get your big toe in them now."

"Bite me," I responded, giving them a double birdied gesture.

"All the usual suspects," snickered Shorty. "Stephen, Charlie, Larry, Stan, Lester, you and me in that paddle pool, the one you got for your birthday. How old were we, maybe six or seven?"

"Seven, look on the back," I answered, pointing to the date. "Mom always wrote the dates and occasions on the back of any pictures."

"Here are your bronze plated first little shoes," remarked Peter, finding them stowed away. "And a bib that says *My Little Precious Angel*, so special."

"All right assholes, we don't have to look at every single item."

Opening the second piece of luggage, Peter found some of

Dad's old army stuff and more photos. He skimmed through them, finding no ammunition to rag me about.

I opened the third, the medium sized of the three pieces of luggage. In it I found a small box of baseball cards, an old Atlanta Braves Pennant, a Dale Murphy autographed baseball, a GI Joe action doll, my grand dad's pocket watch, and a Crown Royal draw string bag containing an assortment of silver dollars, mercury dimes, Indian nickels and other odd coins. Much of this could be worth something to collectors.

I was about to discard the luggage when I eyed something protruding from the torn and tattered lining. Running my fingers inside, I removed a badly discolored envelop, the one and only missing envelop. Peter and Shorty froze, watching me fondle it like a ticking time bomb.

"Is that it?" Shorty finally asked, knowing it had to be.

"Yep," I replied, flipping it, still starring at the unbroken seal.

"So are you going to open the damn thing, or not?" asked Shorty.

"Let's wait until Larry and Cassandra return. We should do this together. It only seems fitting to me."

Glancing at his watch, Peter remarked, "Shouldn't they be back by now?"

I had not wanted to express my concern, but I had been worrying for a while that they should be back. "I'll call her house," I announced and did, but received no answer. I became panicked. "Something isn't right."

"Should we ride in that direction?" asked Shorty.

"I'll go," spoke up Peter.

"You don't even know where she lives, Dude."

"I know, but I know how to get to Due West."

"I'll go," I spoke up. "I know exactly where she lives. You two wait in case they return before I do."

"Hold on crime investigators. We said no one goes any where alone. We use the buddy system."

"Shorty, that's going to pose a serious problem for the three of us...too many buddies..."

"Problem solved. We all go."

We heard the side door opening. We assumed defensive positions, fearing an ambush from the unknown. We rushed the kitchen. Shorty had a fire poker in his hand, Peter with one of his boots and me with two clinched fists. Ducking the attack, Larry shoved Cassandra against the wall and shielded her from our pathetic assault.

"Whoa guys. It's just us!"

"What took you so long?" I yelled back.

"Sorry, we had a flat," replied Larry.

"And we think we were being followed," added Cassandra.

"The Buick," I asked.

"No, not this time," answered Larry. "She had a premonition. She thought she sensed a second vehicle, but couldn't dial in on the make."

"I'm certain it wasn't the Buick," she advised. "I sensed hatred, despair and death."

"For who," I asked.

"I don't know. I fear we will have our answers tomorrow."

"We've found the missing envelope," blurted Shorty.

"And," inquired Larry.

"And we'll open it now," I finished.

41

"Hello Sheriff Burdette," greeted the newspaper mogul. "How's that ailing back of yours?"

"Not worth a damn, Easterly, what can I do for you?"

"Like everyone else, just wondering how your case is going?"

"Same answer, not worth a damn," he replied, popping a couple of aspirins. "I wish my chiropractor could fix both."

"Do you still think that officer died in self defense?"

"Unless the coroner or any other evidence points me in another direction, it still stands," answered Sheriff Burdette, grimacing as he stood from his chair and stretched. "Are you looking for something to print? Do you want a quote?"

"If you're up to..."

"All right, print that it is still under investigation. The governor has assigned SLED to the case. Other than that, you have the information I have released to the media. That's it. I can't say much more with SLED taking charge. Now if you will excuse me, I have a doctor's appointment."

Easterly returned to his office and a new bottle of Johnny Walker Red. SLED, that's all he needed. He called Jimbo Price at his home number, but no one answered. He poured a double, downed it in one gulp, and then tried again, no answer. Isolation closed in, and he kept the shots coming, trying to ward it off, but to no avail. Desperate times called for desperate measures.

The local television news segment signaled the six o'clock hour. The lead story continued to be tragedy in small southern town, five dead, and no answers. The town mourns the dead, and then the reporter interviewed the mayor, the sheriff and a few locals.

"You could be in the middle of that, Dude, snapping photos for the Wednesday Weekly. Any regrets?"

"None," I professed, but I did have a few.

"Procrastination doesn't set well with my digestive system," added Larry. "Might we open the mystery envelope now?"

I handed it to him. "You do the honors."

Larry placed the envelope against his forehead and launched into his impression of *Johnny Carson* doing *Carnac the Magnificent*. He murmured the letter's contents in his best *Carson-Carnac* voice. "Trick or Treat," then opened it, just as Johnny would. He removed the pages and pretended to read the question, "What does the perfect spook house have in store for us tomorrow night?"

"Cut the shit, Larry" demanded Shorty. "Just read the damn thing."

"It's a letter dated October 31st, 1863."

"Halloween I bet," whispered Cassandra. "Who is it addressed to?"

"It starts with '*If you have found this I have fulfilled my promise.*'

Larry read on. '*I am sorry I have betrayed your trust and faith in me. What I have done is pure savagery, even for my people. You loved my sister and gave her a roof, food and a home. You educated and protected her. You have done the same for me. She named her children for you and you loved her children, your children. You are a good man, doctor.*'

'*I pathetically fell victim to the bottle. Even you didn't know how the demon brew possessed my soul. November of the year now past, I did the most unspeakable thing and for that I must pay and reconcile my indiscretions.*'

'*I have recently learned that your eleventh child, my sister's Domhnall, my nephew, is actually my very own cursed son. I raped my sister that November night, wild and in a drunken state, after finding her sponging that exquisite body of hers, preparing for your return. I ravished her, even as she begged me off.*'

'*I had always been infatuated by her beauty and often hid, watching her disrobe. The alcohol empowered me to react and take what I had always wanted. Do not hold my sister responsible for she could not stop me, nor tell you what I had done to her.'*

'My bastard inbred son now pays the price for my sins. Domhnall is persecuted by spirits of evil origin. Claudette believes that they have chosen him to do their bidding, that he is the key to a door that must not be opened. She loves the child and would never harm him. The bocar counsels her and I fear leads her down a wrong path.'

'I must right the wrong and to do so, it will destroy the lives of all I love; my sister, my bastard son and most of all, you. Please take care of her, your ten children, my nieces and nephews, as I know you will.'

'Death will knock three times on the cabin door and take what can no longer walk this land. Your house hungers, its appetite grows stronger as the witching hour approaches. Eleven children, the special one now eleven months old, the house and its rooms of elevens, all is too powerful. It must end tonight and will by my hands.'

'You will weep, but you will forget the pain and cherish those precious children. Before midnight I must end the madness. If the clock strikes twelve before I complete the incarnation then God above help us all. Evil will forever devour those who dare seek refuge here. I love you, doctor. Forgive me for my sins.'

"Damn," exclaimed Shorty.

"So what was her brother's name?" asked Cassandra.

"It isn't signed and the doctor's name isn't listed either."

"So he apparently in some sort of voodoo ritual, killed his sister, his nephew son and then himself," I summarized.

"It appears that's what he set out to accomplish, but we don't know if he completed the task before midnight."

"And if he didn't," asked Peter. "Does that mean the house was cursed, and hordes of demonic spirits were released?"

"Well whatever happened," continued Larry, "we do know one thing, for sure. Neither this doctor, he mentioned, nor anyone else, ever did find his confession."

"So the secret of the child's father and the rape by her brother was never revealed," sighed a mournful Cassandra. "That poor man lost his wife, his son and apparently a very good friend, and he never knew why."

"I think the brother may have been more than just a friend, from the way it sounds," advised Larry.

"Takes one to know one," smarted Shorty.

"Some sort of ritual either did or didn't take place, and I bet that heel to toe thing has something to do with it," I added.

"And if it's voodoo, it probably had something to do with a bloody chicken and feathers and snakes," proclaimed Shorty.

"Hollywood make-believe I keep telling you," scoffed Larry.

"I'm convinced more than ever now, that the number eleven is the key to our success, but we're six people short," commented Cassandra.

"Well, for damn sure, we won't round up six volunteers before tomorrow night," mumbled Peter.

"I agree. So we go with what we have. We've got to figure this thing out before midnight tomorrow, if we have any hope of ending this hold it has over us," I told them. "We'll go there just after dark. That should give us sufficient time to prepare and possibly solve what has forever dogged us."

"Why not go tonight?" asked Peter.

"It has to be Halloween I'm afraid, to undo what has been done," I explained.

"Payne is right," said Larry. "We have to wait."

"What's another twenty three hours?" shrugged Shorty.

42

The green Buick Electra idled and sputtered on the roadway in front of the old house. The driver tensed up when movement was detected in a third floor window. Someone or something had passed in front of it. Tonight wasn't a night for the curious. Tomorrow, yes, tomorrow would be better. The shadow darted pass a second time.

Having witnessed too much already, the Buick kicked up gravel as the driver sped away. The watcher from the window nodded and waved sarcastically. Tomorrow would come soon enough and all the eggs would be in one basket, come home to roost one last time.

Officer Jimbo Price pulled into his drive, off duty and craving a little shut eye. He had Halloween night off. He dreaded it. He did not like being home for the Trick or Treating. He didn't plan to be here when the doorbell began ringing. Parking his patrol car in the back, he approached the door stoop.

"It's about time you got here," a voice spoke from the shadows, causing Jimbo to un-holster his pistol. "Shoot first and ask questions later, officer," said a calm Easterly.

"Sorry, sir," he apologized in an irritated tone. "I'm not accustomed to anyone being behind my house."

"So," paused Easterly, "what has transpired today?"

"I watched Payne's house this AM. I observed Larry McCurry and that woman depart mid morning. I followed until they breached the city limits on Hwy 28."

"So you don't know their final destination. Is that what you are telling me?"

"Sorry, sir. I'm not authorized to take a city vehicle into the county unless in pursuit of a chase that commenced inside the city limits. Even then, I must alert the dispatcher, and call for county back-up."

"Just great, we have no idea what they were up to. So did you return to Payne's house and keep them under surveillance?"

"Sir, I was on duty. I warned you yesterday that my ability to conduct surveillance was contingent of my obligations to the police department. Unfortunately it was a very busy day around town. There were three vehicular accidents, one domestic dispute, one aggravated assault; two drug related arrests and three investigations of shop lifting. Not to mention old maid Myra Wynn complained someone had been walking through her flower garden again."

"That's not the report I expected to hear," snapped the agitated newspaperman.

"If we're finished, sir, I really need some shut eye."

"So, no one will be watching them tonight then?"

"Unless you're pulling the graveyard shift," replied Jimbo, displaying a little agitation of his own.

"What about tomorrow," asked Easterly.

"It's my day off, sir."

"So..."

"So, it is my day off," he repeated.

"I thought you were in this with me," he inquired, having no control over this officer. "I'll pay you for your detective work."

"Then I guess I'm working," Jimbo smiled. "Cash up front and I report to duty at 9 AM."

"Will this be enough to secure your services?" asked Easterly, handing Jimbo Price three, one hundred dollar bills.

"A good start, sir," he replied, shoving the money in his pant's pocket. "This really has nothing to do with those five dead men, does it, sir?"

"Here's another fifty, no questions, you just keep an eye on Payne and that assortment of misfits. You report to me what they are up to, understood?"

"Mums the word, your business...now if you will excuse me,

I'm going to bed."

"Eight o'clock," Easterly reminded him, not accepting nine.

Standing at attention and saluting, Jimbo confirmed the orders, and then disappeared inside his home. He trusted the newspaper man even less now, but the benefits were good. Moonlighting was not a crime.

Easterly returned to his automobile and sat under the wheel, thinking how he had originally hoped to extinguish Payne's digging up of old bones. The incident and his son's death loomed large. Now he had worse publicity tarnishing the town's reputation, and he still had not squashed Payne's efforts to mettle where he had no business.

Taking a sip from his flask, he decided to simply take his revenge out for the nineteen year cloud that had darkened his life. He no longer thought rationally. He had become hopelessly pushed over the edge, in too deep and nothing to lose. He figured SLED would connect the dots sooner or later, and implicate him somehow in the murders. He saw this clearly now.

He ceased to care for the town or his own reputation. He had transformed into a very dangerous and desperate human being, rivaled only by the house and its dark secrets. A collision course was inevitable and unavoidable.

43

I watched the minute hand on the den's wall clock tick down to eleven PM, as if expecting something magical. No magic, no surprises, just the passing of another minute occurred. I glanced over at Peter, nodding on the sofa. Larry was reading his bible in the Easy Boy. All seemed so tranquil and peaceful, but it was anything but.

Cassandra had just pitter pattered down the hardwood floored hallway to take a shower, encouraging me to join her. I had reluctantly waved off her invite, choosing to pass on sex tonight, as if I were preparing for the big game tomorrow. Many jocks thought sexual escapades would diminish their ability to deliver a winning performance. I had never turned down sex before, and I was certainly no jock, but it felt like the wrong thing to do, so I didn't.

I heard Shorty clinking ice cubes in a glass, mixing another drink. I would have joined him, but I had no dill pickle juice. I opted to stay sober tonight. What the hell was I thinking? No sex and no alcohol, who the hell had I become?

Did I really think we could somehow reconcile the past? I'm not sure I bought into it hook, line and sinker, but what could it hurt? Now that was a stupid assessment, even for me. Being dead wasn't a good alternative, if the house truly had that much power. I couldn't deny its power, because it had undeniably ruined my life, and still had its claws planted in my psyche.

The looming question remained. Could we actually reverse

this, or just make it much worse? Would five have the same power as eleven? I had my doubts, but what else could we do. You can't get blood from a turnip. Did we really believe that the house was haunted? Do we want to believe the house is haunted? We should know these answers in less than 24 hours, figuring if we survived from dusk to midnight.

Shorty flopped down beside me, smelling strongly of Jack and Coke, but I could tell he wasn't drunk. His eyes were clear, alert and concerned. "So tell me, Payne. Do you believe in spooks and goblins and those things that go bump in the night?"

"You know me. I've always wanted to believe. That's why I insisted on visiting those old houses and cemeteries. Why you're at it, you may as well add Big Foot, UFO's and the Loch Ness Monster to the list."

"So which one of your legendary creatures do you think we'll find tomorrow night?"

"Well, I think we can only rule out Nessie, unless you think there's a possibility she exists in Little Mountain Lake."

"You missed your calling. You should have been one of those scientists that investigate that crap."

"I'm not so sure the pay would have been that great."

"All it would have required, one discovery, and you would have been set for life."

"Well, maybe tomorrow will be my day, Shorty."

"I hope not. I don't need a close encounter to fulfill any of my top ten wishes. Curses I can handle. Evil spirits, I'm not so sure. What do you really think happened to Donnie that night?"

"I personally don't think he jumped from that window or accidentally fell. I'm convinced he was helped. I don't think it was me." I stuck by my convictions on this one.

"One of those voodoo spirits, you think?"

"I don't have the answers, but you know as well as I do, Donnie was not suicidal. He was tough as nails."

"But when he got really messed up on that PJ he did weird out on us. It's like the dark side came out, and he was just plain pissed off at the world or something. He sure targeted poor Stan, didn't he?"

"And we did very little to stop him. What a bunch of pussies we were back then."

"And we basically still are."

Larry asked, "Mind if I weigh in on this conversation?"

"Might as well tip the scales big boy, and you shouldn't find that too difficult," added Shorty.

"I have prayed for guidance, but unfortunately my faith will not allow me to support or participate in this séance you are proposing. I will be there for moral and spiritual support, but I can't join the circle or attempt to contact any of those from the beyond."

"But you Catholics do exorcisms, so how far fetched can spook phoning be for a priest," asked Shorty, as only Shorty could ask.

"We can only perform or be involved in exorcisms with the church's approval, as I've already told you. I do agree with Cassandra. We should return Claudette L'ouverture's bible. I believe her brother's confession is instrumental in making this work too. She should do fine as your medium."

"Are you going to bring plenty of holly water and crosses and rosary beads?" I asked him.

"Only if you bring the garlic, mallet and stakes and the silver bullets," he laughed.

"Deal..."

"You boys are having way too much fun," snorted Peter. "A man can't rest his eyes in peace around here."

"Can you believe we're back together again? It's just like old times."

"Well, Shorty, almost half of us are here," corrected Peter.

"That just makes us a bunch of half asses then," I slipped back into my sarcastic persona.

"Do any of you own a gun?" asked Peter.

"Why in the hell would we need a gun?" blurted Shorty. "Ghosts are already dead!"

"Call it my premonition," replied Peter, not cracking a smile. "I have a double barrel shotgun, a 45, and 30-06 in the trunk, and they'll be coming with us."

"I agree," added Larry. "Why should we take fire arms to a ghost fight?"

"We still have that green 79 Buick Electra out there some where," Peter reminded us. "That's not Casper at the wheel."

"I'm in, bring the guns," advised Larry.

"Dibs on the double barrel," added Shorty.

"79 Buick, eleven year newer model than 1968, coincidence, I don't think so," I professed. "We should get some shut eye."

"Something tells me there won't be much sleeping in the house tonight. See you dudes in the morning."

There wasn't much sleep going on outside the house either. Webb Easterly poured another cup of coffee from his thermos and observed each room darkening, the occupants retiring for the night. His wrist watch indicated the time, eleven past 2 AM. Tomorrow would be the 19th anniversary of Donald's death. He toasted his dead son with coffee, spiked with a tad of brandy.

The driver of the Buick silently approached the Caddy, parked a block from the house, occupied by the five survivors. The smell of warm brandy drifted from the Caddy's driver's side window. The driver recognized the brandy drinker. He could have been taken easily, but there was no reason to do so. Making not a sound, the Buick's driver slipped back into the shadows, and continued the vigil from a safe distance.

The watcher eyed both people, and could have taken them down with ease too. Instead, the watcher decided to let the scene play out. Tomorrow, the watcher would not be so complacent. Any intruders would be dealt with swiftly. The truth of that eventful night must never be exposed.

Easterly decided to call it quits, finally sensing Payne and the others were in for the night. He headed home, but sleep would not be his friend tonight.

The driver of the Buick sensed the watcher's presence and smiled. "I will see you soon;" came the whisper, "evil comes home to roost. It does take one to know one, indeed."

44

Dawn made its presence known when a single ray of light burned its mark in my left eye from that damn crack in the curtain again. Rubbing the crusty sleep from my eyes, I stretched then turned to face Cassandra. Lying on her back, still deep in sleep, her lips sputtered almost in mechanical rhythm. She had that very sexy little purring snore going again. I was a lucky man. I prayed luck would be with all of us.

I didn't know what the future held for her and me, any more than I could fathom what tonight had in store for us. I did know what I had with her felt better than anything I had experienced before with any woman, including my ex-wife. The past nineteen years had been such a blur and a waste.

Thirty five years old, divorced, no children, unemployed and about to embark on a potential suicide mission with my best friends, who are as crazy as me, now how inspiring is that? I had so much to offer the potential new woman in my life. Was she crazy or what?

But, if I didn't see this through, the next nineteen years would probably be a repeat of the first nineteen. That would be a pathetic existence for both of us. She deserved better. Hell, I deserved better. We all deserved better. Damn that house.

Oh I could have so easily nudged her from her slumber, and made wild passionate love, but I resisted the temptation, allowing her an escape from reality. I briefly thought how stupid of me.

This could be our last chance, if things went tragically wrong tonight. Not one known to make the best of decisions, I slipped out of bed, showered and made my way down the hallway to the kitchen.

I smelled fresh brewed coffee and found Larry sitting in the Easy Boy, lamp on and reading his bible. I still had a tough time wrapping my mind around my chubby friend being an ordained minister, but drew comfort from his faith, devotion and conviction. He had done well for himself, much better than the rest of us.

Normally I opt for a cold beverage in the morning, but I uncharacteristically poured myself a cup of coffee and joined Larry in the den. He looked up from his morning devotion and smiled. I could almost envision the halo hovering above his angelical face. The extra weight did enhance the stereotype of a fatherly priest.

"So Payne, I guess today is the day."

"It would seem so. Strictly speaking from a biblical stance, do you believe the house is haunted with evil spirits?"

"I've shared with you what I experienced there. It wasn't from an overactive imagination, or induced from Boone's Farm wine. I'll just keep the church out of it, if you don't mind. For me, this is personal."

"It is for all of us. What do you really think we'll find this time?"

"Answers I hope. More misery I fear, but we really have no other choice that I can see."

"I know I harp on this eleven thing. I have beaten the dead horse until no blood remains, but I can't help but believe it holds the missing piece of the puzzle. I am both excited and terrified about our return. A part of me craves the opportunity to actually see an entity, but another part of me hopes they don't exist in that house."

"Something is there or at least it was in 1968. By night's end we should know if it still is, and if we can send it back to where it belongs."

"I'm glad you're a priest."

"It doesn't matter whether I am or not, Payne, if you don't believe? My faith alone will not get us through this. So, tell me, are you a believer in the Lord?"

"Well Larry, you are aware of my religious upbringing or lack of. The Pentecostal church is a far cry from the Catholic. I'm not one of those church goers. I haven't really attended church since I was a kid. It just hasn't been a priority for me."

"You're not answering my question. Do you believe in God?"

Taking a long deep breath I pondered that question. I had never really given it much thought, one way or the other. Do I believe there is a God? I'm certainly not an atheist, so I suppose I did believe in something. Strange, I couldn't remember the last time I had actually said a little prayer, or I had asked forgiveness for my numerous sins. I did not speak the Lord's name in vain, so I guess that sort of counted for something. I had probably broken most of the commandments, but really wasn't sure I could quote all ten. I had never killed anyone, but I had certainly done my fare share of coveting and adulterating.

"Yeah," I finally answered. "I suppose I do believe there is a God, even if I don't follow the righteous path myself. I don't think I have done the sort of crap that should condemn me to burn in hell for eternity, but I haven't exactly done much repenting or asking forgiveness either."

"As a priest, I could listen to your confessions before we embark on our journey."

"Thanks Larry, but I'm not into to that. I don't envision me and you in the confessional booth with me spilling my guts, and you splashing me with holy water. I don't think I could convincingly spout ten thousand Hail Mary's to atone for my long list of sins. Sorry it's just not me. I'll take my chances without repenting."

Larry smiled and asked, "How about we meet somewhere in the middle, and you join me in a little prayer?"

I got nervous and squirmy, just thinking about doing this too. Praying wasn't my bag. I might get struck by lightning or something, if I tried to fake my way through it. To pacify him,

I finally conceded, "I'll close my eyes and you give it your best shot."

"Fair enough," he replied, and as my mom would say, he said the sweetest little prayer. He finished with amen at the end. I remained silent.

"Now that wasn't so bad was it?"

I just mustered up a smile, and decided to refill our coffee cups, anything to avoid further biblical conversation, and in the immortal words of *Snaggle-Puss*, I blurted *"exit stage right."*

45

Jimbo, now on his third cup of coffee, sat in his usual booth at the Dutch Oven Restaurant. He had just inhaled three eggs over easy, a generous portion of bacon and sausage, a bowl of grits, a stack of silver dollar pancakes and four buttered biscuits with grape jelly. He loosened his belt by one hole notch to compensate for his expanding waist line.

The *Felix the Cat* clock with the wagging tail and bobbling eyes told him Webb Easterly should be here by now. It was quarter past eight. He picked up *The State Paper* he had purchased on the way, and the front page still mentioned the tragedy in Abbeville, but very few new details. It listed the rap sheet for the four good old boys, and the impressive law enforcement history of the fallen officer.

A hand clutched the top of his newspaper and pulled it down. Coming into view, Easterly now sat across from him, looking like death warmed over. He wasn't well suited for the graveyard shift apparently. When he spoke, Jimbo detected the faint smell of liquor on his breath.

"I assume you rested well."

"Better than you it appears, sir. Did you stake out the place all night?"

"Only until just past two, and that's when they retired for the night. I should have just stayed there. I didn't sleep."

"So I can tell. Well boss man, what's first on the agenda for today? I'm on your clock, remember."

"Just watch them and contact me if they do anything out of the ordinary."

"And what do you define as out of the ordinary, sir?"

Webb Easterly thought about Jimbo's question, obviously understanding what out of the ordinary meant, and decided what the hell. "They will, without a doubt, visit the Frazier-Pressley House, located down the Cedar Springs Road. You call me when you have confirmed they are on the move and heading in that direction."

"How can you be so sure they will go there?"

"Trust me. I know exactly where they are going."

"Then why not just go there and wait on them. I can bust them for trespassing."

"First of all, I don't won't them arrested, just followed. Secondly, I'm not sure when they will make their move, and what else they might try to pull before then; hence, you will watch them. Thirdly, whatever happens today, you keep your mouth shut."

"Sir, if they venture onto that property or enter that house, they're breaking the law. Must I remind you? I'm an officer of the law."

"In case you have forgotten. You're on my payroll today, no uniform, no police cruiser, no badge and no laws to enforce."

"The sheriff will have my ass, if he finds out what I'm doing, sir."

"Then it is best he doesn't find out, right?"

"You still haven't explained to me what they're up to and why you care."

"Very perceptive, no I haven't. It better protects you and your reputation, by not knowing the full story, don't you think?"

"Now that you put it that way, I see your point, sir. Just one question...we're not going to do anything illegal, are we?"

"Just trespassing, but tell you what Officer Price, to protect you, I'll follow them when they do go inside and they will. You remain in surveillance mode outside the property's perimeter. That way, you'll be free and clear of any wrong doing."

"Except that I will have stood by and watched the crime being committed, and that makes me an accessory."

"Only if we get caught or blab what happened," warned

Easterly.

"I don't like it, but I already know too much, so I either help, or report it."

"So which is it then?"

"One more question...was that dead patrolman on your payroll too?"

"Absolutely not," lied Webb Easterly, looking Jimbo Price straight in the eyes, always having been taught that a liar never makes direct eye contact, will look away.

"Okay, just as long as we don't go too far out on a limb, that it breaks," cautioned Jimbo. "I'm still confused. I thought you wanted to solve that case."

"And we will, but first things first."

46

Peter and Shorty had joined Larry and me in the den. Each looked as if they were headed to the gallows. Too bad they had missed the prayer meeting. They could have probably used it more than me.

"So this is it, D-day" exclaimed Shorty.

"Why the gloom and doom?" asked Larry.

"Because that's how it feels. I know we've got to do it, but I remember how something unnatural chased me across that lawn the last time we were there. I didn't actually see it, but I know it was behind me."

"I saw it," Larry reminded him. "I didn't know you could run so fast."

"Well at least I didn't hide under the floor mats like you did."

"Come on fellers," coached Peter. "This is going nowhere. I saw that bright light on the second floor. I admit it. It scares the crap out of me thinking I might encounter something like that again."

"You better take an extra pair of underwear this time," I advised him.

"I knew I should have never admitted that in front of this crowd."

"Admitted what?" asked Cassandra, standing barefooted in the doorway, her erect nipples greeting us through her Betty Boop night shirt.

Realizing four lusty men...well three lusty men, had zeroed

in on her perky head lights; she crossed her arms over her bosom to conceal the chill in the morning air. For the record, men will look at a pair of tits no matter what shape, size or age they are. We can't help ourselves. Well, there's always an exception, Larry, gay man of the cloth.

"Man stuff," I side stepped the question. "So, did you sleep well?"

"Like a bug in a rug..."

"Have you had any new premonitions?"

She shook her head no, and then headed to the kitchen for her own cup of java. As she twirled, I caught sight that she wasn't wearing any underwear. The others had been just as perceptive. I was a lucky man indeed to have her in my life.

I quickly joined her in the kitchen. The others gave us some breathing room. She poured a cup, then eased onto a bar stool. Crossing her legs she made sure I saw what lies beneath, teasing me and enjoying it immensely.

I placed one hand on her knee and the other behind her neck, leaned over a kissed her deeply. "You're such a naughty little girl this morning."

"Not naughty," she corrected me. "I just need you. Today we need each other, before we go to that house. Take me here, right now." And I did. It was the quickest quickie I had ever had, over in about thirty seconds, but she had been right. We had needed this.

I returned to the den a completely satisfied man, my buddies never knowing any better, except for Larry. He smiled and winked then asked, "How do we spend our last day?"

"Boy that sounds so final," Peter remarked.

"Sorry, I didn't mean for it to sound quite like that. If we don't have anything to do right now, we could visit some of the old hangouts. We could set the mood like we did back in 68."

"Does that mean you're going to want to stick your pecker in a coke bottle or run naked somewhere?" asked Shorty.

"I don't believe so," snickered Larry. "And Peter, we can do with out your door knob trick."

"Furthest thing from my mind, I assure you."

"So tell us Larry. Just what do you have in mind?"

"Yeah Dude, Cream-Land is gone. The Bantam Chef is now

Lee's Fried Chicken and we've already visited Little Mountain. We've already cut the square so what's left? It's too cold to jump off the Secession Dam spillway."

"I'm sorry. I'm just feeling a little nostalgic. I've been living in Conway for a while, and this has been my first time back in eons."

"Stan's funeral is this afternoon at 2," I reminded everyone.

"Why don't we visit Leroy's gravesite in Lauren. Then we can swing by the Ranch in Greenwood for a burger and fries before going to his funeral," suggested Shorty.

"Guys, we haven't done anything with Stephen's body yet," said Larry, making the sign of the cross. "I still can't believe I allowed you to talk me into putting his body in his freezer chest."

"At least it's not rotting somewhere," Shorty defended the decision. "We all agreed. Steven would want us to finish this."

"We'll make sure he gets a proper burial soon enough," I promised. "I'll see if Cassandra would like to come."

Larry gave me that silly grin and wink again. "I'm sure she would love to...again."

Ten minutes later we had piled into Peter's Town Car and were heading to Laurens. I looked forward to paying my respects to Leroy. I had been cheated from doing that because Shorty and Webb Easterly had kept this from me. I couldn't really blame them though, because I hadn't kept up with any of the guys since we graduated. I planned to reconcile my past short comings, and embrace our friendship from this point forward. I had learned my lesson, a life lesson at that.

"I wish we had time to drive to Columbia and visit Brody," I suggested to Shorty.

"Thank you Payne for the thought, but it's probably best we don't right now. I'm not sure he's up for it. Maybe after this is all over, we can take the time, if his doctor says it's all right."

Larry, changing the subject, asked Cassandra, "Have you actually performed a real séance? I'm not talking about those make believe ones you did with your sisters."

"I guess I haven't really done one by the book, if that's what you're asking. Are there rules for conducting one?"

"I'm sure there is a method to the madness to ensure optimum success."

"I thought you knew all and told all, fat boy," exclaimed Shorty.

"I've never had a reason to research séances. I suggest let's take a little detour to the Greenwood Library after we visit Leroy's gravesite, and before we attend Stan's funeral."

"I have noted the itinerary change," saluted Peter from the driver's seat.

"Wonder if we can summon Donnie or Stan or any of the other guys?" asked Shorty.

I suggested, "Before we go open line, why don't we make sure we can make contact with our resident spirits first."

"I think we better do that research before we do anything," cautioned our medium in the wings "I'm no seasoned veteran at communicating with dead people."

"You're a notch above the rest of us with those premonitions of yours," I advised her.

"That's just it. I haven't had a premonition in awhile. I'm not sure if that's a good thing or a bad thing. I mean, I don't have any control over when they come or don't, so I'm not really trying to read anything into the lack of them."

"Don't beat your self up about it," I told her. "What happens, happens."

I'm not sure why we all shushed up, but the Town Car became almost tomb like silent. Maybe it was an omen of things to come. Regardless, an eerie hush shrouded the remainder of our drive, a regular one car funeral precession. Other vehicles followed, monitoring our jaunt through the county's back roads.

"That's right, sir, they've left Abbeville County," reported Jimbo Price to Webb Easterly. "Lucky for me they stopped at this little hole in the wall gas station. There was a payphone here I could use. No, they didn't see me, sir. The phone was on the opposite side of the station from where they parked. No, I have no clue where they are headed, sir. We're in Greenwood County and driving toward Laurens."

Jimbo paused for a second then answered "Could be sir, I don't know this Leroy Hanks gentlemen, but they could be heading to his gravesite I suppose. Hold on, two of them are returning to their vehicle and they're pulling out. I've got to go, sir. Yes sir, I will report to you next opportunity I have."

Jimbo eased out of the gas station, now driving his personal car. He gave them sufficient breathing room. The tail didn't stop with his automobile. The 79 green Buick Electra kept its distance, but fell in line. A fourth vehicle tailed the Buick. The watcher, much more agitated than those being followed, pounded a clenched fist against the dashboard, fully aware of the lead car's intended final destination.

It hit me like a ton of bricks, while I stood overlooking Leroy Hanks' gravestone. There lay the gentle giant. I had been cheated from attending his funeral service. I knelt on one knee. I touched the marker, but still drew little comfort from it. Dead is dead.

I thought about Stan Bronson. I still struggled with the notion that a house or evil sprits could have impacted our future, and had influenced our lives. It didn't really seem possible, even for a connoisseur of the unknown like me, but then again, I had never encountered the supernatural yet. I had only skirted the edges of the phenomena in 1968.

I'm not saying I'm a non believer, because I truly wish to believe, but I still have no first hand evidence to substantiate their existence. Stephen, Larry, Shorty, Peter and even Brody have had encounters, so who am I to argue with their testimonials. I believe they saw and experienced something out of the ordinary, something beyond explanation, and it forever impacted their perception of the unknown.

I stand here; dry of any tears, mournful just the same of our fallen comrade. I dread laying Stan to rest. I'm guilt ridden about Stephen still packaged like a slab of meat in his freezer. What had we become? Surely we faced criminal charges for concealing Stephen's body, but only if we got caught. How many times had we used that excuse when trespassing? The odds of not getting caught this time were probably not skewed in our favor.

I finally exclaimed, "I'm toast, I'm done, I can't do this any more. He's dead and we can't undo it. Let's head to Greenwood."

Receiving no questions to my outburst or opposition to my request, we piled back into the Town Car and sped off toward our destiny. Sometimes friends just get it. The county library would be our first stop, and then to the Ranch for burgers and fries. I had done all I could do to pay my final respects. I would salute Leroy with a chocolate shake. My mission would then be complete.

Jimbo Price, now on high alert, had seen the late model Buick too many times to be just mere coincidence. He had decisions to make. Continue to tail the Town Car as Easterly expected him to do, or double back and determine the identity of driver following in that Buick. He didn't appreciate being on the receiving end of a tail, but figured it best to do what he had been paid to do for now. Never the less, he would keep a close eye on the car that now followed him.

The Buick had problems of its own. The driver had seen the same car lagging behind too often through these back roads. It should have caught and passed the old 79 by now, but seemed to replicate its speed instead, always maintaining a safe distance behind. The Buick's driver, feeling almost claustrophobic, didn't appreciate being sandwiched like this. The trailing auto had never gotten close enough to identify the make or model, but the color was obviously black with a streamline body.

The black car sensed being made, and decided to peel off to the right at the next intersection. Curiosity satisfied, its driver no longer needed to be part of this traveling road circus, opting to return to Abbeville instead.

"Hey Peter, why don't you swing by the library and drop me off before going to the Ranch," spoke up Larry. "I'll research séances."

"I thought you weren't going to participate in the séance?"

"Payne, I'm not, but that doesn't mean Cassandra doesn't need the best possible information to prepare for her role."

"And I can't believe you're passing up a cheeseburger at the Ranch," added a bewildered Shorty.

"I'm not. You can grab a take out order for me. Make it a half and half, fries and onion rings too."

"And me too," added Cassandra. "I'll go with Larry."

"All right girls," added Shorty, "you have a wonderful time at the library."

"Give us about an hour," advised Larry.

"You got it," answered Peter.

I took her meal order before we arrived at the county library, located on the west side of downtown Greenwood. I stepped outside the car, and gave her one last kiss and hug before she and Larry entered. I didn't like splitting up the group like this, but at least she and Larry would be in a public place, so they should be safe.

Jimbo Price decided to follow the Town Car, after observing the two passengers enter the Greenwood County Library. He checked his mirror for any signs of the Buick, but couldn't ID it. Satisfied it had either ceased trailing him, or it had possibly been his over active imagination, he kept a save distance and now backtracked, following the other three northbound Hwy 25.

The Buick's driver pulled from behind the service station, after both cars had driven out of sight, and parked near the back of the library. The driver consumed by curiosity did the unthinkable, and decided to venture inside.

Head down, hat pulled low, the driver cautiously slipped through the entrance, scanning the perimeter for the chunky male and alluring female. Strolling past the endless aisles of books, the driver abruptly slammed face to face into the female. He turned immediately, and then slinked out of sight, down the next row.

"Well excuse you too," exclaimed Cassandra, rather loudly.

Larry stepped from around the opposite aisle, "Are you okay?"

"I'm fine. I have a low tolerance for rudeness. That's all."

"Down here," motioned Larry, squatting and peering on a bottom shelf. "I think I've found what we're looking for."

Exiting and returning quickly to the Buick, the driver flopped down under the steering wheel with the woman's scent still lingering on his clothing. That had been too close, but most enjoyable. Because they were strangers, the female would have no idea how close she had come to solving part of the mystery.

"I think this book will serve our purpose."

"I don't have a library card. Do you?"

"We don't need one."

"You're not going to steal, it are you?"

"Indeed not," grinned Larry. "Remember, I have a photographic memory. Just give me about fifteen minutes and we'll be good to go."

Cassandra stared out the window while Larry skimmed the

book. She glimpsed the green 79 Buick Electra, backing out of the parking place. The tinted glass prevented her from identifying the driver. She motioned for Larry, but the car had driven around the corner before he saw it. They decided to remain in the safety of the library until the others returned.

Jimbo Price opted to employ a different strategy. He parked next to the Town Car, pretending not to pay any attention to the occupants. Curb service had just taken their order, and now the young lady approached his window. He spoke deliberately, loudly to attract the attention of the passengers.

"Jimbo, what are you doing here?" I yelled from the backseat.

"Day off and I craved the best onion rings around," he yelled back. "What you guys up to?"

"We had the same thought, except I have a weakness for the cheeseburgers. I'm sorry to hear about that slain patrolman. It sounded like he had his hands full with that wild bunch of drug peddlers."

"Yep, just trying to do his duty and got caught up in a bad one. Did you know any of those bad asses?"

"I've seen a couple of them around town, but I really didn't know any of them personally. Why did the patrolman take it to them with a machete?"

"That's what SLED is trying to figure out. Who are you friends?"

"This is Peter Woods and Wayne Henderson. Guys this is one of Abbeville's finest, Officer Jimbo Price."

"Shorty Henderson, I didn't recognize you from here. And Peter, are you from the Abbeville area?"

"Originally but I've been over in Georgia for a while."

"Well just listen to me. Sometimes I just kick into interrogation mode. It's just habit. I do apologize. You boys have any Halloween plans? There I go again. I don't mean any harm."

"Well we're way too old to go trick or treating," spoke up Shorty. "I reckon we're too old to help Payne build one of his famous spook houses too. I guess we'll just sip a few cold ones, and hand out candy to the kiddies."

"Yeah, I do believe I've heard a thing or two about those legendary spook houses of Payne's from the Sheriff. He said his daughter told him years later how some of you boys had wondering hairy hands at her expense."

So she did tell on us. "We were inquisitive boys back then, pushing the envelope I suppose. She was a little honey, built like a brick shit house for sure and older than us. We're sure glad she didn't spill her guts on us that night or our butts would still be throbbing from the licking we would have received from our parents."

"Which one of you was that infamous wolf man?"

"That would have been me," lied Shorty. He had never been part of that night. He pulled a smart move, keeping Stephen's name and corpse out of it.

Jimbo caught the lie. The Sheriff had told him she had said a Stephen Poole had put the feels on her. Jimbo tried to rationalize why Shorty Henderson would lie about something that happened, when he was just a mere kid. He didn't like being left in the dark. It seemed the deeper he got, the darker it got. Where was Poole?

We finished our burgers and shakes. We then ordered the take out for Larry and Cassandra. I liked Jimbo, but I wasn't so happy about being this close to an inquisitive off duty policeman.

"You boys sure are hungry."

"It saves us a return trip later," answered Peter. "Glad to have made your acquaintance, officer. Will you be protecting the town from the new generation of vandals?"

"Lucky me, I have the night off. It's just as well. I really hate Halloween. You boys keep your noses clean tonight, and stock up on the candy treats for the ghost and goblins that come knocking. Oh yeah, and don't stomp that burning bag on the porch."

We smiled and waved good bye. Peter backed out, and we headed toward the library to retrieve our other two passengers. "He seems like one of the good guys," remarked Peter.

"Yeah, old Jimbo is pretty harmless as cops go. He plays it by the book, most of the time, but he can be bought though, usually very cheaply. He's been my deep throat in the police department for over a year, but I am confident he would never cross any major lines. He likes policing too much to ever jeopardize ruining his career."

"Mister Easterly, this is Officer Price. I'm in Greenwood near the county library. Payne and the others are now picking up the chunky guy and female. They appear to be heading back toward Abbeville."

A pause, "No sir, I didn't witness them do anything out of the ordinary. They grabbed a bite at the Ranch after dropping the other two off at the library, all just normal stuff. No sir, I don't know why they visited the library. Yes sir, I'll ask the librarian if they checked out any books and call you back. What do you want me to do now? Yes sir, will do, sir."

Jimbo didn't mention the Buick he thought had been following him, nor did he tell Webb Easterly about the little white lie from Shorty Henderson. He could keep secrets too. He just wasn't really sure what one had to do with the other, or what it had to do with why he was following Payne and his friends.

After watching Jimbo Price enter the library, the driver of the Buick made a hasty retreat toward Hwy 72 West, towards Abbeville. The driver had already quizzed the librarian while the undercover officer had been preoccupied on the pay phone. No books had been checked out, nor did the librarian recall what books the two had been researching. She had apparently bought the driver's story about a scavenger hunt.

Jimbo asked the librarian the same questions, and she smiled, saying this must be a very hot spot for the scavenger hunt. Clueless, Jimbo pried and got a description of the other person, but didn't recognize the enquirer. He didn't like what was transpiring. He didn't know what to make of it and headed to Abbeville, still on Easterly's clock.

"So did you find everything you ever wanted to know about séances, but were afraid to ask?"

"Indeed I did Payne. I have it filed away up here," answered Larry, pointing to his head. "She'll do just fine with my divine coaching."

"Dialing up spooks and things that go bump in the night," commented Shorty. "This should be priceless."

"Like Larry said, we'll do just fine," repeated Cassandra.

"I'm sure it'll go perfectly," I added, not believing a word of what I had just said.

"I saw the Buick," she blurted out.

"You saw the Buick," I repeated. "Where?"

"It was parked outside the library."

"Did you see the driver?"

"It was parked near the back. I couldn't see the driver but it was definitely following us."

"We can't really fear the driver," surmised Larry. "After all, if not for his or her intervention, those hooded freaks would have surely clobbered me or worse."

"I just wish we knew what that stranger was up to. That vehicle isn't shadowing us for the hell of it."

"I tell you, Payne, it's our guardian angel.

"Or an avenging angel," clarified Shorty.

"Guys, can we change the subject?" asked Peter. "We have a funeral ahead of us. Let's focus and devote the afternoon to Stan Bronson, if you don't mind.'

"Thanks for reeling us back in loggerhead and Shorty, smart thinking with that Stephen thing back at the Ranch."

"No sweat, Payne, but next we honor Stephen. It's so not right, him being stuffed in that freezer."

"Regardless to what happens tonight, we clean the slate tomorrow."

"You don't sound too confident about tonight, sweetie?"

"I'm still not sure why we are going back, and what we expect to gain, but I know we've got to do it." I told them with absolutely no confidence or high expectations at all.

"Just like old times," chuckled Peter, inspiring all of us to bust a gut, just like Stan would have expected us to do.

47

Stan's funeral was pathetic at best. No immediate family attended, not even his brother from Texas, but his absence had been anticipated. The five of us stood shoulder to shoulder at the grave side, sending him off like the friend he had been. There had been no receiving of friends as is customary for these parts, but if there had been, it would have been the same five. Besides the Pentecostal Preacher, the undertaker and the grave diggers, Sheldon, the owner of the Rough House and us, no one else from town attended the modest little burial, except for the driver of the Buick and the Watcher, but we weren't aware of their presence.

We saw neither of them, and they didn't see each other. Both were secluded from view in separate corners of the old cemetery. Easterly sat in his office, sipping Scotch, avoiding the news cameras still lurking the streets. Newshounds were sniffing out any leads about the five deaths. No new trails had developed.

Preliminary reports coming in from SLED indicated they didn't believe the patrolman had killed the hooligans, or that they had killed him. They had no suspects. This transformed a somber mood into a panic stricken one for Webb Easterly. The revelation reinforced his suspicions. The link, Payne and his gang, they were the likely culprits. He was damned certain of it now.

Tonight, it all must end tonight. Donald's death, the death of these five men, someone must pay for these crimes, and he had no intentions of it being him. The integrity of this town must be restored, if possible, but it wasn't his first priority. Contrary to his original inclinations, old bones would have to be excavated before the past could be buried for good.

The phone rang. "Officer Price, what do you have to report? So they're back at Payne's home...all of them? It's almost five. They'll be on the move soon, and so will we. No, sit tight. Call me when they leave."

Hanging up the phone, Webb Easterly began cracking his knuckles, slowly and deliberately, something he rarely did unless he had reached a crossroad, a decisive moment, or maybe just a point of no return. He had given his all for this town, forever, putting it ahead of his life, his bastard son's life, too many secrets and too many lies. He must first learn the truth of that Halloween night of 1968, before he could decide on the path forward.

I advised my cohorts, "Let's get out of here, before the trick or treating begins."

"We're ready to rock and roll," commented Shorty. "Guns are in the trunk, fresh batteries in all the flash lights. This time I made sure we all have one. I have a video camera, a tripod and have double checked every thing. Just to add a little nostalgic flavor to it, I purchased these." He tossed an assortment of Halloween masks and hats onto the kitchen table.

"Nice touch," I told him, picking up an over the head mask of an obviously deranged mad scientist, "Perfect for me."

"We have the wolf man mask with hairy gloves, a Cyclops mask, and Merlin's magician hat, a snake charmer with flute, complete with basket and a pop-up cobra, and a gypsy costume with a black wig, head scarf, earrings and a crystal ball. I'll be the werewolf, since I sort confessed to that part to Officer Barney Fife."

"Well obviously I'm the gypsy woman," chuckled Cassandra, holding up the large looped earrings to her ear lobes. "Accessorizing is my game."

"Merlin, I want to be Merlin," giggled Larry, placing the pointy hat on his round head. "Abracadabra..."

Peter groped his crotch and pointed to the snake charmer outfit. "Appropriate don't you think?"

"Just keep the real spitting cobra in your britches," advised Shorty.

"It seems we have an extra one, the Cyclops mask." Picking it up, I stared at it, turning it in my hands.

"They were sort of on sale, reduced anyway, and I couldn't pass up that one for some reason."

"I always said that place would make the perfect spook house," I reiterated. "I guess tonight it's ours to own. It seems rather fitting I must admit. Great idea you came up with, Shorty."

"I've got her bible and the letter from her brother," advised Larry. "We should plan on using these during the séance."

"We?" I asked for confirmation.

"Well, ya'll is who I meant."

"Are you still sitting on the sidelines, monsignor?" asked Shorty.

"Bless you my child for being so intuitive," he snickered, dipping his fingers in his glass of white wine in a mock display of holy water, splashing it on Shorty's face, then signing the cross.

"Messing with fire aren't you fat boy?" asked Shorty. "I don't think God would appreciate you pulling stunts like that."

"Lighten up Shorty. Even God has a sense of humor," rebutted Larry. "He created you didn't he? Plus, you guys bring it out of me."

"Just promise me you won't streak through the house tonight wearing nothing but that pointy hat," winked Shorty.

"I promise you will not see this fat ass of mine, uncut and raw or other wise."

"Let's make like horse shit and hit the trail buckaroos," I yelled. "A haunting we will go."

"A house is never still in darkness to those who listen intently; there is a whispering in distant chambers, an unearthly hand presses the snib of the window, the latch rises. Ghosts were created when the first man awoke in the night; *J.M. Barrie*," quoted Larry.

"Thank you for sharing," added Cassandra.

Darkness paced us on the fifteen minute drive down the winding old Cedar Springs Road. We passed the turn off to Little Mountain Lake. I suddenly became anxious, almost hyperventilating. I wasn't sure if I was overly excited or just plan scared to death or a mixture of both.

Peter drove by the house first, getting the lay of the land. All entrances had been chained to prevent entry. Even as twilight approached we could see the place had not been maintained. High weeds had overtaken the front lawn. Bushes were in need of trimming and trees required pruning. Numerous windows had been boarded over, most likely having been broken by the younger generation of trespassers.

Miraculously the old log house still stood off to the right of the three story structure. The roofs on both buildings were still in tact. *No Trespassing* signs were posted about every twenty yards. Those were intended for law abiding folks, just like restraining papers. You got a least one shot at ignoring them before being busted.

Peter found a turn around spot about a mile past, and we rode by the house a second time, now only barely able to make it out against the dark background. We had spotted an old overgrown pulpwood road three hundred yards from the house. It wasn't the same access road we had used in 1968, but it would have to do.

Peter maneuvered through a ditch, the tail end of the Town Car dragging as it bottomed out. With one wheel on the embankment and the other bouncing over a small log, the undercarriage dragged, digging up dirt like a farm furrow. Finally we made it forty yards down the road where the overgrown path made it unsafe to venture any further.

Just as we stepped out of the car, headlights whipped in behind us. A much larger vehicle leaped over the obstacles, lights blinding us as it approached. The guns were still in the trunk. We had allowed ourselves to be caught with our britches down around our ankles, so to speak.

The vehicle now parked less than fifteen yards behind us. From the driver's side, someone spotlighted us one by one, sizing us up, as if deciding which of us would be taken first. For once, I hoped we were staring at a game warden or some other law official, and not a horde of hooded banditos. Trespassing sure beat dead or painfully mangled.

Still blinded by the headlights and spot light, we heard the passenger side door open, but could not see our potential worst nightmare. Silence, the person said nothing. The driver's side door opened, and the spot light adjusted, but still blinded us. We now knew there were at least two of them. Spot lighting, how many times had we done this very thing to unexpected deer? I now we knew how they must feel.

I was conflicted between screaming to everyone to run or defy the unseen, and ask just what the hell they wanted. I finally decided running would just prompt a potential deadly reaction, if they were not law enforcement, so keeping my hands by my side, I asked, "Who are you? What do you want?" These seemed reasonable questions under the circumstances, if these were reasonable individuals. No answer, that ruled out the law. I thought about poor Stephen and expected we could be next on their menu.

In a voice that I almost thought I recognized, the passenger ordered, "Remove your clothes, all of them, now!"

"Now hold on," I pleaded.

"Don't make me ask a second time," boomed the voice through some sort of speaker.

Larry peeled out of his in record time, standing buck naked in the brightness, sweat glistening off him, as if he had been submersed in oil. Between the overhang of his belly and the cool October night, it was difficult to tell if he was male or female. Everything was thankfully drawn up like a turtle in a shell.

The rest of us took our good time, unsure what these ambushers had in mind. I thought about how Stephen had been raped, and almost decided to refuse to go any further. I was never cut out for that hero stuff, so I just continued to undress.

"You too, runt," the voice commanded Shorty.

"Screw you," Shorty yelled back. "You want my clothes. Come get them, if you have any balls at all."

I closed my eyes, dreading what was coming next. Rape was better than murder, wasn't it? I was down to my underwear. Cassandra was taking things slower. Peter had only removed his shirt.

"How did you get here, you little fart?" asked Shorty.

Our tormentors doused the spot light and dimmed the headlights. Laughter irrupted from both sides of the truck. At the driver's side stood a short, rollie-pollie, bearded black man in a red and yellow plaid shirt, faded jeans, red suspenders, with a shaved head and toothless grin. At the passenger door stood

Brody Henderson, splitting a gut laughing.

"You boys and girl didn't think I would sit there all locked up and straight jacketed, letting you have all the fun without me, did you?"

"Damn you Brody," exclaimed Shorty, rushing toward his little brother to embrace him in a bear hug. "I thought you were too messed up to come."

"Sometimes it takes a while for the meds to kick in," Brody explained. "And this little plan of yours did catch me off guard."

"How did you get out?"

He pointed over to the driver. "Thank Ezek Patterson, facility custodian and fellow ghost believer. He's seen an apparition or two, so he says."

He nodded, continued to grin his toothless smile, then finally spoke, "I sho have. I seen me one of them Big Foot coming out of a flying saucer before too."

"Bro, you sure can pick them," said Shorty, shaking his head in disbelief. "Welcome to our merry little band of misfits, Ezek."

"Hey Larry," shouted Brody. "I know you're a full fledged exhibitionist, but you could save our appetites by getting dressed. I'm screwed up enough without these prolonged images."

Cassandra glanced over at him. I could almost see her glowing in the dark, red faced and all. "A man in need of the cloth right now," she giggled.

"And you promised you wouldn't do this to us," Peter reminded him.

"He ordered us to, so don't blame me."

"So what's the plan?" asked Brody.

"You're not afraid to go back in there, are you?" I asked Shorty.

He held up a prescription bottle. "Wonder drugs; the more you take, the more you wonder where the hell you are, and often who the hell you are. Good stuff, taken in mass quantities."

"We'll fill you in as we go, Bro," said Shorty, slapping him on the back, and then grabbing him in a head lock.

Walking the path toward the house I began to recite the introduction for one of my favorite horror shows. Every Friday night at 11:30, I huddled in front of my little seventeen inch black and white TV to watch Inferno, with its old horror flick reruns.

In a deepened voice, and with a glowing flashlight resting under my chin, I cut loose.

"Come in, I've been waiting for you.
Venture with me into a world of strangeness,
A world where reality slips past you
like sand in an hour glass,
Inferno!
The meeting place of the supernatural,
and the unknown!"

Ezek howled, "I loved that show. It was like real life stuff."

"Yeah, real life," I nodded, smiling at the newest addition to our little band of trespassers.

48

Cedar Springs certainly buzzed with covert activity. The Buick had parked a quarter mile back in an overgrown pasture. The driver had been camped out inside the house, waiting the arrival of the others. Equipped only with a pen light and a brand new machete, the intruder patiently watched the approaching parade of flash lights.

The Watcher had not entered the house, but instead stood in the seclusion of pines long ago engulfed by the menacing Kudzu. A canopy of the grayish, frostbitten, crawling plants, formed the perfect hiding place, less than fifty yards from the house's northern corner, an ideal location for observing the returning visitors.

Webb Easterly had caught a ride with Jimbo Price, the officer parking behind the nearby church, and both walking through the woods. They were now hiding behind the old log cabin. Easterly passed his flask to Jimbo, but Jimbo waved him off. He would be back on duty tomorrow afternoon and besides, he wasn't much of a drinker. This situation called for a clear head, whatever this situation was supposed to be. He wasn't sure he had made the best of decisions, joining Easterly on this property.

Eleven unsuspecting souls had merged on the house, some searching for answers, others closure, a few possibly seeking revenge, while a handful would rather just keep the past where it belonged. Only Jimbo Price and Ezek Patterson questioned their purpose for being there, but both were intrigued never the less, caught up in the unfolding saga.

The house lay dormant, deathly quite, almost non-threatening. No evil spirits whirled around seeking out victims to possess or haunt. Creepiness permeated just the same. The octagon shape lured and captivated all of the intruders, lulling them into a false sense of tranquility. The door could slam shut in an instant. Once caught in its web, very few escaped unscathed, or so spread the rumor by the locals. Plain and simple, the house had to be haunted.

We had only ventured inside that one time. It had proven the town's folks theory to be dead on. Our lives had certainly been impacted for the worst. We now searched for retribution for our past intrusion on a house that we should have never awakened.

I so wanted to believe in the paranormal phenomena, but at what cost would I be willing to pay for the price for knowing. I had others to think about, friends who didn't share my convictions. Some had already witnessed and experienced enough to last them a life time. I hadn't. Yes, I had been impacted by the event, the curse or whatever you want to call it, but I didn't experience the essence of that night, like most of my pals had.

One thing for sure, I had to remain focused. We returned to undo what had been done, and not to confirm a spiritual existence. But to successfully undo it, we had to believe it existed in the first place, didn't we? The others had already experienced it, so that just left me from our original troupe, the only one who had not actually encountered something unexplainable in 1968.

Sure, Cassandra believed in this sort of stuff, but even she had not experienced it up close and personal. Hers were more clairvoyant. Premonitions are one thing, eye witness experiences take it to a whole new level. Can it really be fair to take her down this path? Look at the damage this house had already inflicted on us. A second visit might undo it for us, but what impact would it have on the first time visitors? There were too many questions and absolutely no valid answers.

I can see the house clearly now, silhouetted against the stand of great oaks. I don't feel any tugs on my soul right this minute. It just looks like an old house, harmless and empty. For the first time I admire the uniqueness of the house's design. I had not noticed the architecture during our 68 encounter. Those sorts of things didn't interest a kid looking for spooks in a house allegedly haunted.

We stopped for a quick huddle. I wanted to make sure everyone was still gung ho. They seemed to be or at least were putting on a good front.

"I think we should make a piece offering first," proclaimed Larry. "Let's deposit the bible and the letter in the log home."

"Any volunteers?" I asked.

"I'll go with Larry," replied Peter. "Let's get this ball rolling."

"We'll wait on the front porch until you guys get back," I told them. "Yell, if you see anything."

"Don't worry. You'll hear my screams, and will see my fat ass stampeding like a rampaging rogue elephant," confirmed Larry.

"And me," added Peter, "all I've got to do is out run you and I don't think that will be a problem."

"Be careful and don't trip over that trunk of yours," chuckled Shorty.

"Five minutes," I said, holding up five fingers. "Then we come looking for you."

Larry held up two fingers, indicating don't wait for five to expire. We watched as their flash lights disappeared behind the cabin. A tinkling of glass indicated they had to force an entry, something I normally oppose. These weren't normal circumstances.

Easterly and Price backed around the opposite side of the cabin, spotting the flash lights approaching. Peeping in a window, they observed Larry McCurry and Peter Woods climbing through another window they had just broken.

Jimbo Price didn't take kindly to first watching trespassers, and now witnessing them breaking and entering. He reluctantly stood down. He followed Easterly's instructions to let it run its course, but he didn't like it. Worst case, these guys were building their own list of felonies that could and would be used against them in a court of law, eventually.

Larry pointed towards the shelf. "That's where we first spotted the bible."

"Do you think she is here right now?"

"Claudette L'ouverture," confirmed Larry. "I suppose she could be, unless her soul has found its final resting place. It has been 19 years."

"If she has gone on then, what happens if we try to contact her in the séance?"

"If she still has an opinion, I guess she'll answer."

"Can you sense anything, her presence I mean?" asked Peter.

"Get real Peter. I'm a priest, not a medium or liaison to the spiritual world. I'm no different than you or any of the other fellers. I put my collar on one neck at a time."

"Let's get the hell out of here then," said Peter, just as the cabin's entrance door squeaked open.

"I do believe the mistress of the house has accepted our token, and is honoring our request," gulped Larry, both stumbling over one another, fleeing the cabin.

Well sure enough, I spotted the stampede heading in our direction. Larry was pacing Peter's every step. They came sliding onto the porch like a duo of Seinfeld Kramers, making their grand entrance. Both were sort of pale and wild eyed.

"So what happened?" asked Shorty.

"Apologies accepted," stuttered Peter, followed by a nod from a winded Larry.

"What do you suppose that was all about?" asked Jimbo Price. "Did you see that door just open?"

"Must have been the wind," answered Webb Easterly.

"The night is still. There's no hint of a breeze."

He shrugged. "Let's see what they placed on that shelf," replied Easterly, ignoring the officer's observations.

Easterly jiggled the cabin's door knob, but the door would not budge. "Damn old houses have a mind of their own. Keep an eye on the rest, while I retrieve what they left inside."

Jimbo slunk along the edge of the cabin, moving cautiously within the shadows, until he could see the congregation of flashlights gathered on the front porch. Easterly climbed through the broken window, suddenly overtaken by a chill that sent shivers down his spine.

The Watcher had moved closer to the house, along the exterior wall at one end of the porch, and opposite from where Jimbo kept the seven under surveillance. Detecting movement through a window, the Watcher attempted to zero in on a shadow moving toward the stair case. Someone or something had taken up residence. The Watcher cursed and balled both fists, before then placing a hand on an equalizer, and restoring calm to an irritated disposition.

Gaining entry from an already shattered window, the Watcher silently breeched the room, eyes adjusting to the darkness before moving toward the second stairway. Overcome by dizziness, the Watcher applied pressure to both sides of an aching head. Time once endless now ticked against the Watcher. There would be but one opportunity to preserve the past. There would be no second chances.

The Buick's driver advanced to the second story. The aged wooden steps creaked with almost every other footfall. Not sure where the others planned to go, the driver decided to stay one floor ahead of them. As if not having enough to worry about, the driver of the Buick had to wonder if the other had already arrived, and might be in the house.

Webb Easterly, using his oversized flash light, eyed the old bible on the shelf. He reached for it. He heard something shuffle along the floor directly behind him. Expecting to see Jimbo, he twirled and saw no one. Aiming the light toward the floor to minimize deflection, he searched the single room cabin, but saw no one and no place for anyone to hide. Scratching his ear, he turned his attention back to the bible. Picking it up, he began flipping through a few pages.

He heard the same sound again, only louder. He turned quickly, but still saw no one. The room felt colder. Webb Easterly slipped the bible inside his shirt for safe keeping, until he had better lighting to examine it closer. He heard the creaking of the door opening as it had done before. "Just the wind," he whispered, walking toward the exit.

The cabin door slammed abruptly, when he had gotten within a couple of feet of it. Falling backwards, he stumbled over an old cane back chair, which he swore had not been there. A pungent odor invaded his nostrils. He inhaled the scent of perspiration, but it wasn't the offensive kind found in a locker room, but instead a feminine smell, but not perfumery.

Webb Easterly quickly made his way to the window and half fell, half tumbled through it. He heard a crash inside, just behind him. It sounded like kitchen wear, something made of glass or porcelain, shattering against the wall. Cutting the corner and still looking over his shoulder, he crashed into the backside of Jimbo Price, both taking a spill onto the ground in a loud thud.

"You hear that?" asked Ezek. "Spooks are arising!"

Like search beams, a half dozen flash lights scanned the yard and the cabin, but detected no movement, no intruders, no rising spooks. "Let's go inside and get this thing over with," I advised everyone.

The front door was locked like a fortress. Most of the first floor windows were boarded up partially or completely. This wasn't the way it had been last time.

"Look up there," pointed Brody. "I can climb that trellis to the second floor window. It's not boarded. I can break the glass, work my way back down, and then open the door from the inside."

I dreaded the thoughts of breaking another window, but it had to be done. We had to finish what we had started. I looked over at Cassandra, and she smiled.

"You sure about this little brother?" asked Shorty. "That's the second floor where it happened."

"I am the youngest and best climber. I know what floor it is, big brother. I'm prepared to face my fears."

"Go to it then. The trellis looks fairly new but be careful just the same." Shorty propped on the tripod, camera posed to photograph the house's spirits this time.

Brody scampered up the trellis like a spider monkey. He shattered the window with his flashlight. He then unlatched it and disappeared inside. He flicked on his light and realized to reach the stairs; he had to pass through the room where he had been held captive in that trunk. He suddenly broke into a cold sweat, and began to tremble. A single tear ran down his cheek. He stood frozen. It was time to man up, he thought, if he could just get his feet moving.

He then heard what sounded like footsteps directly above him on the third floor. Shinning his light toward the ceiling, dust particles floated in the light's ray, disturbed by whatever walked the floor above. He swallowed deeply; thinking ghost shouldn't have such heavy footfalls, but what the hell did?

Brody mustered up a sudden surge of courage. He broke for

the steps, throwing caution to the wind. He cleared the stairs in three single bounds, missing the landing and falling belly first across the hardwood floor, rattling the front window panes.

Shorty screamed, dropping the tripod and camera, "Are you okay in there, Brody?"

Up righting himself to his knees, he answered, "Just took a little clumsy spill, I'll get that door open for you." And he did, after unlatching a series of dead bolts, luckily none required a key.

We filed inside. "Where do we want to hold the séance?" asked Peter.

"Third floor," I answered. "Where Donnie plunged from that window, but we don't do it until eleven o'clock."

Shorty glanced at his watch. "That's almost two hours from now! Just what in the hell are we going to do in here for two hours? I don't like this plan. We're here. We should just finish it." He then reached for the tripod and realized the camera's lens had been shattered in the fall. "Damn it," he fumed.

"The house doesn't want to be in your movie," spoke up Ezek.

The camera was the least of my concerns. "It's got to be eleven tonight, I know it."

"You're still hung up on the eleven thing, aren't you, Payne?" asked Peter.

I shrugged. It just seemed appropriate to me, the power of number eleven. Why wasn't it obvious to the rest of them?

"Payne, I'm not so sure it's that important we wait until eleven," commented Larry. "But if you insist, we can stay busy for a while setting it up. We need to see if we can locate a table, a round one preferably."

"You heard the man, spread out and see if you can find a big old round table," ordered Shorty. "I'll look on the third floor first."

"Me and Ezek will go with you," replied Brody.

"Cassandra and I will search the second floor," I told them.

"Then that leaves this floor for Peter and me," chimed in Larry, as he donned his Wizard hat.

"Good idea, Larry," I grinned. "It's Halloween. We may as well make the best of it." I slipped on my Mad Scientist mask.

Cassandra was already dressed in her gypsy attire, black wig and all.

"How do I look?" asked Peter, as the snake charmer.

"Just keep that spitting cobra in your britches and we'll be just fine," I laughed.

"Do you mind telling me what we're really doing here, sir?" asked Jimbo, losing his patience.

"Like I've told you numerous times," snapped Easterly, also short on patience, and still rattled from what had or hadn't happened in that cabin. "I want to see what these derelicts are up to."

"Trespassing, unlawful entry, what else do you expect them to do, sir?" I say we nail them, and haul their asses to jail."

"A boy died here in 1968 under peculiar circumstances. Ten others got off Scott free. Five of them are in that house right now, and are up to something, maybe even hiding or destroying evidence of their crime," explained Easterly. "My intent is to make them pay for that boy's murder."

"Sir, they were cleared almost twenty years ago. What can be gained here? This is not that Unsolved Mystery show."

"I want to expose them for what they are, common murderers," he responded, elevating his voice.

"You might want to hold it down, sir. They almost caught us when you stumbled over me. Let's not give them more opportunities."

Easterly crept closer to the house. He peered in a window. He saw no one in the room. He moved to the next window. He repeated his Peeping Tom routine two more times before finally spying flashlights moving about. Payne and his woman friend came into view. Payne was the root of this evil. Webb Easterly wanted to punish him in the worst way.

"Sir, I saw lights on the two upper floors moving about. They have split up, and appear to be searching for something. Do you have any idea what that might be?"

Easterly said nothing. He focused on Payne and the female, clinching his jaw and balling a fist. "My son would be alive if not for you."

"Son?" asked Jimbo Price. "I never knew you had a son."

Easterly turned to face the officer. The cat was now out of the bag. This was quite unfortunate for him and the officer. It made this situation a bit too awkward.

"The murdered boy was your son?" asked Jimbo.

"This is beginning to make some sense. You're out for revenge, aren't you? I didn't sign up for this." Tormented souls can be driven to the brink, over the edge and forced to do things normally uncharacteristic of their nature. Jimbo Price stared into the eyes of a much tormented soul, and never saw the blow coming. Using the almost foot long metal flash light like a club, Webb Easterly planted a severe whack to the side of Jimbo's temple. The officer fell like a tree, crashing onto the porch violently, rattling the windows, and alerting Payne and the woman.

Easterly quickly dragged Jimbo Price's lifeless body off the porch and around the corner just as the flash light illuminated the porch below the window.

"What was that?" asked Cassandra.

"I have no idea but it almost sounded like someone fell."

"But isn't everyone above us?"

"Yep, everyone but the driver of that Buick or those hooded thugs," I replied.

"Do you think we're being watched?"

"I've been feeling that way for a while now. Do you have any premonitions?"

"I'm afraid not. My senses appear to be on radio silence."

"Stay close and alert. I don't like this."

Outside, Easterly checked Jimbo Price for any sign of a pulse. He found only a very weak one. Blood trickled from an ear and the corner of his mouth. What had he done? He had to think. If the officer gained consciousness, he would be arrested for assault, plus his secret would be out. If Jimbo Price died, he now became a murderer.

Taking a deep breath, Webb Easterly removed a handkerchief from his back pocket and stuffed it into Jimbo Price's mouth, and then he pinched his nose. He watched the man suffocate. Webb Easterly just continued to dig his hole deeper. He decided he would somehow make this look as if the Payne Lewis gang had stuck again.

Taking the officer's pistol, and slipping it in his belt, he tried to locate Payne's whereabouts in the house. Spotting light several windows away, he picked up the trail like a bloodhound. Pausing to peek in, he retrieved the flask. He took a long swig of courage.

"No tables on this floor," said Cassandra.

"Not much furniture here at all," I confirmed. "Let's go up to the next floor."

"We shouldn't have come here tonight."

"Premonition?"

"Fear..."

"I regret getting you involved."

"I regret none of this, especially the time I've spent with you."

"I don't think I can let the house take credit for us."

"Destiny is my bet."

"I can deal with destiny." I pulled her close and kissed her, and then wished we weren't here.

Larry and Peter had found a couple of raggedy end tables, one coffee table and several miscellaneous chairs. The second floor offered no table suitable for the séance.

The Watcher had side stepped the two men, and had circled around behind them as they completed their sweep room by room. Why did they need a table, and why were they costumed like a couple of trick or treaters, grown men, how ridiculously silly? Just what were they up to?

On the third floor, Shorty, Brody and Ezek had found one table but two of its legs were broken off. Ezek had located the severed wooden legs, and with some creative ingenuity and duct tape from his overall pocket, had reattached them. It wasn't round and was extremely wobbly, but it should work for their purposes, if they took care not to prop heavily on the table's top.

They had located only one chair and a stool. Luckily they had found no empty trunks this time, so Brody breathed a sigh of relief. Ezek had been quite the chatter box, spewing psycho babble about ghosts, Big Foot, UFO's, werewolves, vampires and zombies. He claimed to have seen them all. He professed to be an expert on the subject.

Shorty elbowed Brody in the ribs, "This boy is severely brain damaged, isn't he? But lucky for you, he's a custodian with a driver's license and a truck?"

"He's harmless," shouldered Brody back. "Just play along with him like we used to do with our screwy Uncle Joe with that Old Timer's disease. What's that tucked in your jacket?" asked Brody, seeing an exposed clump of hair.

"Oh this," Shorty pulled it from his pocket. "It's a wolf man get up, mask and hairy gloves."

"Go in that room," pointed Brody "And put it on, then let's have a little fun with Ezek."

"It shouldn't bother him. Didn't you just say he said he had seen a werewolf before?" asked Shorty.

"Just do it," egged on Brody.

Shorty slipped into the adjoining room, removed his jacket and slipped on the mask and gloves. At the opportune moment he charged from the room, heading directly toward Ezek. Ezek calmly turned around, grabbed the rickety bar stool, and cold cocked Shorty on the head. Lights out and down for the count, Shorty crashed face first onto the floor.

"You don't happen to have a silver bullet handy do you, Brody? We really need to shoot this critter before it gets back up. It's going to be some kind of pissed when it shakes the cobwebs free."

Brody knelt down beside Shorty, rolled him over and removed the mask. Shorty had a bloody skull and lay motionless, but he was still breathing.

"You never told me your brother was a werewolf," commented Ezek, with a surprised look on his face. "Are you one, too? I'm going to need to make me some silver bullets if you both are."

The Buick's driver could not believe what idiots these three were. Watching from the far closet, amazed by their antics, there slap stick was tailor made for a Three Stooges episode. Moe, Larry and Curley Joe, they had it covered.

Brody slapped Shorty several times on his cheeks, attempting to revive him. Shorty opened his eyes and came up swinging. An uppercut caught Brody just under his left arm pit, sending him backwards into Ezek, squatted behind him.

"Well, I see you're just fine, big brother," coughed a stunned Brody.

"I knew we should have used a silver bullet," said Ezek,

standing up, and nonchalantly brushing himself off. "Only way to kill one of them is a silver bullet. I would really hate killing your brother though."

Shorty felt his scalp, and then examined the blood on his palm. "Harmless you said! Have some fun you said. Bullshit..."

Ezek picked up the wolf man mask and examined it. "Good news, Brody, your brother is not a real werewolf. He was just make believing to fool us. This is just too funny. Does your brother always kid around like this?"

The Buick's driver almost chuckled out loud. What a bunch of morons? The black guy is a riot.

Cassandra and I had caught up with Larry and Peter. We heard the loud thud above us, and bolted for the stairs, expecting the worst. I feared I would find another one of my friends had somehow crashed through a third story window.

The Watcher listened to the stampede, until it faded at the top of the stairs. Now emerging from the hiding place, hands resting on hips and head cocked, the Watcher decided to take the second stairway to the third floor.

Webb Easterly had concealed Jimbo Price's corpse and had entered the first floor. He listened, trying to determine the whereabouts of the others. His hand felt the pistol resting in his belt. He knew what he would eventually have to do to end this madness. The newspaper man had totally lost it and was extremely dangerous now.

49

I stood there, stopped in my tracks, when I spotted Shorty's bloody head. Ezek and Brody appeared fine. Larry scrambled to reach them first, the priestly thing to do. I didn't see anyone that appeared to require their last rites. Neither Brody nor Shorty was Catholic, but I didn't know about Ezek Patterson.

Ezek spoke up first, "He's not really a werewolf you know. It's just a mask. We would have needed a silver bullet, if he would have been a real one."

"No shit, dip shit!" snapped Shorty. "I owe you one Brody."

"He's all right," yelled Larry.

"Do I look all right? I'm bleeding. Bleeding isn't exactly all right."

"What in the hell happened here?" I finally asked them.

"Practical jokes, sometimes they just damn backfire," cursed Shorty, unleashing a tirade of four letter words, un-werewolf like language.

"Cover your ears," I warned our female spook house adventurer.

"Too late," she answered. "Sadly, I think I'm becoming used to this behavior.

"We did find this here table for your séance missy," advised Ezek, sporting his toothless grin.

"Thank you, Ezek," she replied, nodding to the child like black man. "It will do just fine I'm sure."

After doctoring on Shorty's head to ensure the bleeding had

been halted, we began preparing the stage for the pending séance. Candles were set in place and even the fake crystal ball had been centered on the rectangular table. Larry recalled that the rule of thumb for optimum size for a séance should be divisible by three. Six would work just fine, with him coaching from the side lines. We were eventually able to round up an assortment of chairs, stools, and boxes for the six participants.

"Ideally we should have an oval or round table," advised Larry. "It's supposed to create the symbolic circle for the ritual."

"Now you tell us, Mister Photographic Memory!" grunted Shorty, rubbing his head.

"I just remembered. There's a round table in that cabin," said Peter.

"Can it be hauled up here?" I asked.

"I think so. Ezek, Brody, and Shorty, if you're up to it, let's go get our séance table."

"Hold on a minute, gentlemen," spoke up Cassandra. "If we're going to try to contact her, wouldn't the obvious place to do so be in that cabin? After all, the bible and letter are there."

All eyes diverted to me, since I was the one damned and determined to have it on the third floor, and at eleven o'clock. I shrugged. "All right, what the heck. We'll go to the cabin then. I suppose that's her hang out."

"Grab a chair, stool or box and let's move this circus to the other building," shouted Peter.

The Watcher and the Buick driver were displeased with this development, but neither could assert their opinions. They could only watch as the seven single filed and descended the stairs.

Webb Easterly scrambled for a hiding place, hearing the bunch of misfits coming down the stairway. He fondled Jimbo's pistol in his belt. He watched as the precession passed his location and ventured outside. He recognized everyone but the bald headed Negro. Now where had he come from, and what was his role tonight, wondered Easterly.

Arriving at the cabin, we discovered the door standing wide open. Larry assured us, he and Peter had closed it after they deposited the bible and letter. A large round table was centered in the room. A couple of cane back chairs were located near by, flipped on their sides. Upending the chairs, we positioned four of the various chairs and stools we had brought, to round out the seating for six.

Larry arranged six candles in a circle on the table's center. "I wish we had something eatable. It is recommended, placing some sort of aromatic food in the center of the table. Experts believe the food attracts spirits, seeking physical nourishment. We should have bought an extra cheeseburger from the Ranch."

Ezek reached into his pocket and withdrew something wrapped in tin foil. "Will this here do?" He produced a very pungent tuna salad sandwich. "I was saving this for later, but you can use it for them ghosts, if you want to. I reckon they get hungry just like us."

"I think this will do nicely," said Larry, figuring he was rescuing Ezek from a most probable case of food poisoning. "I do believe our spirits will catch a whiff of this puppy with no problem."

Peter yelled from the other side of the room, "Larry, the bible is gone."

The Watcher observed Webb Easterly crawling on all fours, towards a window at the cabin. The old man displayed agility. Another figure countered on the opposite side of the cabin. Shadows concealed that person's identity.

After ensuring both individuals had taken up their posts at windows on either side, the Watcher crept up to the remaining window at the back of the cabin. Closed raggedy curtains offered only a small opening for observing the proceedings inside.

Mystery solved, they were planning to conduct a séance. What could they possibly know about having a séance, wondered the Watcher. Fools, all were such damned fools.

Easterly overheard Peter Woods saying the bible was gone. He placed his hand on it, still concealed inside his shirt. When he did so, a breeze kicked up, sending dust particles into his eyes. Wiping his tearing eyes, he refocused on the scene inside. It took him a few minutes longer to ascertain what they were planning. He shook his head in disbelief. They're idiots. Glancing at his watch, it displayed ten forty five. Where had the time gone?

The driver of the Buick glanced behind him, sensing a presence, but unable to zero in on its origin and then finally shrugged it off. Peering back in the window, it became all too obvious what they were up to, but so called priests don't do séances. This was very odd indeed.

"Could a spirit have taken the bible?" asked Cassandra.

"A Big Foot stole my red moped one time when my truck was in the shop," stated a serious looking Ezek. "He was hairy and at least ten feet tall. Police wouldn't believe me and he got away with it."

"I doubt that really happened," replied Larry. "I wonder if our Buick owner is amongst us."

"Should we check outside just in case?" asked Peter.

"Buick?" asked Brody.

"I'll fill you in later, Bro."

"I had a cousin that drove a Buick Skylark, a fine riding machine," commented Ezek. "I still like my truck better though."

"It wouldn't hurt to take a quick look," I advised them. "Brody, how about taking Ezek, and you two do a walk around the cabin."

"Consider it done," replied Brody, motioning to Ezek to follow. When he reached the door, it would not open. He yanked on the knob, but the door held firm.

"She doesn't want us to leave," whispered our soon to be medium.

"Premonition?" I asked.

She nodded yes. "I think it's for our own protection."

"I do not like this," commented Shorty. "Who is out there?"

"I'm not sure, but I feel we are not alone."

"Ten more minutes and we get this thing started and on time, the eleventh hour," I notified everyone. "Let's take our places."

I sat to the right of Cassandra and Peter to her left. Closing out the circle to Peter's left was Shorty, Brody then Ezek. After lighting the candles in the center of the table, everyone prepared to cross over into the dark side. Larry perched on a stool, just behind us, and advised us to turn off all flash lights.

"Begin," instructed Larry. "Please join hands."

We did as he said. Cassandra's hand felt cool to the touch, while Ezek's hand was sweaty. I took a deep breath. I waited for Larry's next instructions.

"Okay everybody, you must speak these words together," stated Larry. "Repeat after me. My beloved Claudette

L'ouverture, we bring you gifts from life into death. Commune with us, Claudette L'ouverture, and move among us."

In unison we spoke, "My beloved Claudette L'ouverture, we bring you gifts from life into death. Commune with us, Claudette L'ouverture, and move among us." We paused but nothing happened.

"Again," Larry commanded.

"My beloved Claudette L'ouverture, we bring you gifts from life into death. Commune with us, Claudette L'ouverture, and move among us."

Still, there was no response. "Keep repeating the welcome," Larry encouraged us.

"My beloved Claudette L'ouverture, we bring you gifts from life into death. Commune with us, Claudette L'ouverture, and move among us," we chanted eight more times, and then on the eleventh, the table trembled ever so slightly.

Larry noticed candle movement in the center of the table. "I believe we have company. Ask the spirit a question, Cassandra. Tell it to rap once for no and twice for yes.

After delivering those instructions, she asked, "Are you Claudette L'ouverture?"

Two raps almost caused me to break hands. I swallowed deeply, and eyed the others. I could see fear on their faces. I'm sure I mirrored the same look.

Larry stood up now, overwhelmed by the spiritual contact. He made the sign of the cross, and then sat heavily back on the stool. "Lord be with us," he whispered.

"Are there any others with you?"

One rap

I was relieved to hear we had no others to contend with right now. One spirit at a time was plenty. I was having my moment.

"So your children are no longer with you?"

One rap

"Can any of us ask her a question?" I directed my question to Larry.

Two raps communicated the response, before Larry could answer.

My mouth was a dust pit. "Did your brother harm you and your eleventh child, Domhnall?"

One rap confused me. If no, then he did not make good on his promise, as specified in his letter.

"Was anyone harmed on that Halloween night, October 31st, 1863?" I followed up.

Two raps

"Did your brother harm anyone?" I was on a roll.

Two raps

"Did anyone die that night in 1863?"

Two raps

"Did Domhnall die?"

Two raps

"Did you?" I asked.

Two raps

"Did your brother?" asked Cassandra.

Two raps

Totally perplexed, I had no follow up questions, requiring a yes or no answer. I glanced over at Larry for guidance.

Cassandra Blake, resident medium, suddenly stood up. Her hand locked like a vice in mind, she dragged me along. The others followed and we began walking around the table, still holding hands. She began chanting, "Heel to toe, hold the line, heel to toe, hold the line, heel to toe, hold the line, heel to toe, hold the line, heel to toe, hold the line, heel to toe, hold the line, heel to toe, hold the line, heel to toe, hold the line, heel to toe, hold the line, heel to toe, hold the line."

On the eleventh repeat of the lyric, "I killed my bother after he murdered my child, his son," spoke Cassandra in a most peculiar accent, continuing to lead us in a counter clock wise circle.

"Double damn," exclaimed Larry, standing back up. "Claudette L'ouverture is speaking through her."

"Will this harm her?" I asked.

"I don't think so. She has chosen to communicate in this matter. I'm not sure Cassandra will even remember it happened, but better keep circling the table, until she decides to stop."

"Ask your questions, the one called Payne."

"So you're telling us that your brother stayed true to his threat and killed his son, your child."

"He did," replied Claudette L'ouverture, Cassandra's eyes

wide open.

"Did you take his life?"

"The bokor, I confided in him. He wanted my son for his evil doings."

"What did you do, Claudette L'ouverture?"

"My brother would not hear of it. I trusted my brother to protect Donhnall," replied our medium in a nervous broken voice.

"This is just all too weird," commented Shorty.

"Shush," warned Larry.

"Your brother misled you, didn't he?"

"Yes, the bokor warned me. My brother came to take Domhnall's life."

"So what did you do?"

"I was too late. He strangled his nephew, his son...my son."

I took a deep breath and shook my head in disbelief. I repeated my question. "What did you do?"

She sounded so grief stricken, using Cassandra as the conduit; she spoke in a heart broken tone. "I stabbed my brother in the heart."

"Just like that, you decided to kill your own brother for killing Donhnall?" She had killed her brother, after he had just murdered his bastard son, one born of incest.

"The bokor promised a good life for Donhnall, if I took his life."

"So spirits were playing a human chest game with us that night," spoke up Larry. "Ask her why us?"

Before I could ask the question, she took a deep breath, as if to compose her self. She looked around like she was sizing us up. A chill ran the length of my spine.

She spoke. "I knew I could not live with it. I took my own life. My soul can not rest on the other side. I am now the evil one. I can never leave this place, not until I make it all right, atone for my past sins."

"Be careful," warned Larry. "This could be a trick, the bocor's trick."

I nodded but continued. "Do you remember us from a time before now?"

"You were but children. I tried to scare you away. You were

in danger here."

"We were in danger of what, from whom, the bocor?"

"Evil, yes, other spirits were here, summoned by the bocor."

"You tried to save us from these other evil spirits threatening our lives."

"Evil, yes," was the reply.

"Did you attack my brother in that trunk?"

"No, I did not attack your brother."

"Who did?" demanded Shorty, as Brody nervously stood his ground.

"The evil ones, Kalfu or Bacalou," she answered.

"Why did they want to harm us?"

"Evil feeds on the fears of human's in the dark. That night, the elevens made strong magic. The house invited the uninvited."

"Crap," spat out Brody.

"What about Donnie Ray Clark?" I asked. "Did you see what happened to him? Did the Kalfu or Bacalou cause his death?"

"No," the voice paused, "not directly."

"Then was it an accident that he fell from that window?" I asked. My sanity hung by a thread.

"It was no accident."

"Was he murdered?"

"Yes."

I looked at the others one by one, and then asked, "Who murdered Donnie Ray Clark?"

"They are here," the voice replied, in an almost panicky frenzy.

Five classmates holding hands now exchanged glances, wondering which one had done the unthinkable. Ezek smiled, enjoying the adventure.

"Don't look at me," exclaimed Brody. "I was the one in that trunk, being attacked by those things!"

"I was eating dirt on the floor board of Lester's car," spoke up Larry.

"Claudette L'ouverture was busy chasing my sorry ass across that yard. I'm the one that had found Peter and Brody at that trunk, remember. You were on the third floor with him, Dude." stated Shorty, making his own accusations.

"What about Stan or Stephen?" asked Larry, not liking where

this was headed.

"Stephen was hiding in my car like you, remember," said Larry.

"Stan would have had the best motive? Donnie always like picking fights with him." I reminded everyone, unintentionally throwing Stan under the bus.

All of them slowly turned and looked at me. "Are you guys really siding with the town and holding me accountable?"

"Of course not," spoke up Larry. "Come on guys. Let's stop turning on one another. Pointing fingers, that's not us."

"Which one of us was it, then?" I demanded of Claudette L'ouverture.

"Cassandra's eyes rolled back in their sockets and she began mouthing something. I leaned closer, as did everyone else.

The window pane exploded. Shorty broke rank. The séance ceased. Cassandra collapsed in my arms. A figure rolled across the floor, partially concealed by the shadows on that side of the room.

When the figure stood, we found ourselves staring down the barrel of a pump action sawed off twelve gauge shotgun. "Son of a bitch!" exclaimed Shorty.

I could not believe it. I would have run over and hugged him, if not for the shotgun aimed at us and no display of encouragement on his face. I saw nothing but hatred in those eyes. It suddenly dawned on me why.

"You killed Donnie Ray Clark, didn't you?" I asked. I saw my answer in those cold brown eyes. I saw his finger tighten on the trigger. He intended to kill us...all of us.

A thunderous shot rang out. We scrambled and ducked for our lives. The old wooden slat floor shook from the thud. The shotgun waving intruder lay face down on the floor, the back of his head missing. The Watcher was dead.

Silhouetted, just outside the window and holding a revolver, stood my former boss, Webb Easterly. He stepped through the window and yelled, "I knew you sorry bastards were responsible for Donald's death! I knew it! I always knew it!"

"Hold on just one minute," cautioned Larry McCurry, now on his feet, hands up and taking a step toward Easterly. "Mister Easterly, please think about what you're doing. Drop the gun.

There is no need for more bloodshed. We all came here for the same reason, to find the truth. Surely you are a man of faith. Donnie would have never intentionally wished harm on any of us," Larry stepped towards my ex-boss.

"What do you know about Donald? You're responsible for his death. Payne said it. The one laying on the floor killed Donald and the rest of you covered it up."

"I assure you we did not do what you think. Please, do not take more blood in the name of blind justice. Do it for Donnie Ray Clark." Larry smiled, made the sign of the cross and took another step towards Webb Easterly, arms extended and his hands open, palms up. "It's over. The truth shall set us free… all of us."

A thunderous shot sent Larry tumbling backwards to the floor, blood gushing from an open hole blown into his chest cavity. The priest, our buddy rolled over on his side. A puddle of blood formed underneath his lifeless body. Cassandra, knelt by his side. I cringed, expecting another shot.

"I think Larry is dead," she sobbed, blood now smeared on her hands. "You just murdered a man of God and our friend." She stood and started towards Easterly. I grabbed her by the arm and pulled her to my side. I held her firmly to prevent her from collapsing, shock most likely overcoming her.

"Why in the hell did you do that?" I screamed, knowing he intended to pick us off one by one.

"He was my son! And you suckered him into your little worthless inner circle of criminals. He was a good boy with a promising future, my only son! And eye for an eye..."

I had to stall and try to talk some sense in to him. "Donnie Ray Clark was your son. He would have never condoned you murdering us. Larry was right. This has gone too far; enough is enough."

"So what are you going to do, kill the rest of us?" asked Shorty, madder now than a wet hen. I was convinced Shorty would surely be next if he didn't calm down.

"As a matter of fact, I am," he answered, in his smooth, deliberate tone.

"And how do you think you will possibly get away with killing eight people?" I asked.

"Fourteen," he mumbled, with no remorse in his tone.

"What is that supposed to mean?" asked Shorty.

"Officer Jimbo Price is dead just outside and guess what? You little shits murdered him," answered Easterly, with a smug grin on his face. "Then there's that dead highway patrolman and those other four derelicts. Surprise, you killed them too. Payne will write a confession to confirm this. He always wanted to be a writer."

"You're crazy. Just what motive would I have for going on a killing spry?"

"Well, I don't see Stephen Poole here with you, so I am assuming he is either badly injured or already dead. You see, you were out for revenge on those four good old boys for what they did to your friends, Poole and McCurry. The patrolman showed up to serve warrants, and you had no choice but to kill him too. Payne, take note. I don't want you to leave any of these details out in your confession."

"You sent those hooded assholes after Stephen and Larry, didn't you" fumed Shorty, taking a step toward Easterly.

"Difficult situations require extreme solutions."

"Why did you kill Jimbo?" I asked, both curious and trying to buy us some precious time, or at least an opportunity to jump him.

"I had hired him to help me keep a watch on you. Unfortunately, he figured out Donald was my son. He was putting too many of the puzzle pieces together. He smelled something fishy in that bloodbath with the other five too. There are always casualties in every war."

"So now you're going to murder fourteen people to justify Donnie's death. He would have hated you for that."

"An eye for an eye, your fallen reverend there would have understood that concept. Larry McCurry, a man of God, how hypocritical is that?"

"You bastard," spoke up Brody.

"Do your friends act like this all the time," asked Ezek.

"You can't possibly stage something as enormous as this," exclaimed Peter.

"It really won't matter," he smiled. "There will be no witnesses for the investigators to question. It will take law enforcement years to figure it out, if they ever do at all. Good crime stories for the city I suppose. They can milk and draw in the tourists, just like the secession by the South. I really hate for our town to be known for such a tragedy, but we'll survive. We always have."

"You never wanted bad PR for this town. That's why you covered up Donnie's death," I told him.

Webb Easterly didn't respond. I was getting to him, I hoped. I had to defuse this mess.

"They'll catch you sooner or later," yelled Brody. "They always get their man."

"But that's where you're wrong. I'll be dead too. Payne, I'll save you for last, just before I set it a blaze. After I kill you, I'll take mine. It is only fitting that you watch them die first. To really complicate their investigation, we'll all be in the smoldering ashes of this godforsaken place. They will find only Payne's confession to confuse matters."

"You're plain loony," shouted Peter.

"I've never been saner. I've dreamed about this moment every single year since Donald's death, seeing you pay."

"Look," shouted Ezek, pointing toward the window behind Easterly. "A Cyclops! I've never seen a real one before."

I whispered to Shorty, "Your mask?"

"Nope, I left the mask I bought at your house. I can't take credit for this one."

"Oldest trick in the book," replied Easterly, shaking his head in disbelief. "I look, then you over take me. I don't think so. Wayne Henderson, your turn, come on down and meet your maker!"

Suddenly the door whooshed open. A chair hurdled across the room, tossed by unseen hands, just missing a side stepping Easterly.

"Claudctte L'ouverture," whispered Cassandra. "She's still righting the wrongs, her ticket to the ever after."

The buttons ripped from Easterly's shirt, plucked by an invisible entity's hand. The bible floated effortlessly from where he had it hidden. It came to rest some twenty feet away on the shelf, where it belonged.

"Enough of this smoke and mirrors, spook house staged, bull

crap of yours, Payne," shouted Easterly, aiming the pistol at Shorty. "It's time to tidy things up."

A machete tumbled through the air, tossed from the shattered window. It penetrated Easterly's left shoulder. He spun and fired three shots. The Cyclops framed in the window, dressed in army fatigues, fell backwards into the darkness.

Before Webb Easterly could recover, we rushed him, overpowered and disarmed him. Shorty had to be restrained from beating him to a pulp. I pulled the machete from his bleeding shoulder and tossed it to the floor.

Regaining my composure, I leaned down and rolled over Lester Coburn's dead body and bided him farewell. The mystery had been solved. He was no longer missing. I retrieved his sawed off shot gun. While I felt certain he had been Donnie Ray Clark's killer, I still agonized over an explanation. What could have really prompted him to kill one of us? Possession came to mine. The evil spirits had been inside him.

My friend, our beloved friend, Larry also lay dead. I collapsed back on my ass, face in my hands and cried. This wasn't how I had expected tonight to turn out. What had I really expected?

"Hey fellers, you better come over here," waved Ezek, standing by the shattered window. "I think the Cyclops is still alive. You want me to finish him off? I don't think it takes a silver bullet for a Cyclops."

We rushed to the window and sure enough, the figure donning the Cyclops mask and army uniform, lay on his back. His chest was heaving for breath, blood spurting from two holes, one in his upper left shoulder and the other, a gut shot.

With flash lights illuminating its face, I removed the mask. "Charley Moody! I'll be damned!" Even with his mangled and obviously useless right eye, he still resembled the Charley I remembered.

"One in the same," he answered weakly. "Good to see you, Payne. I suppose I'm a real Cyclops now, compliments of Nam, lost that eye in the copter crash."

"We thought you were dead."

"Dead is a relevant thing, Shorty. You know how you boys always accused me of stretching the truth. It served me well."

"This is way too much crap for an insane man like me to have to endure," commented Brody, sitting down on the windowsill, popping one of his magical pills from the bottle before tossing it and the bottle to the floor.

"You're the driver of that Buick, aren't you?" I asked.

He just smiled, and then coughed up blood.

"What made Lester do this? Why have you been pretending to be dead? Why has he stayed hidden all these years?" I asked, craving closure.

"Stan's journal," he said, retrieving it from inside his jacket and handing it to me, "I got it from Stan the night he died. Good man, sorry he got caught up in this mess. I've filled in the missing parts. It's all there now. It makes for good reading. It would be one hell of a book and a blockbuster movie," he coughed, blood pouring from his mouth now. "Don't forget about Stephen, he deserves a good send off too. And Donnie, he knew Webb Easterly was his dad. That's why he had that chip on his shoulder."

"Save your strength until we can get you to the hospital," I encouraged him, knowing he didn't buy it any more than I did.

He held up the mask. "It's the original one we used in that first spook house, you remember, the one in your attic."

"I just recently watched The Night of the Monsters," I told him, holding his hand. "You were our star attraction, shared billing with the wolf man."

"I was beheaded in that one. I loved making those spook houses," he smiled, and then he just closed his eye and died.

One by one, seven candles, in the cabin were extinguished by the lips of Claudette L'ouverture, paying her last respects to our fallen brothers, Donnie Ray Clark, Leroy Hanks, Stan Bronson, Stephen Poole, Lester Coburn, Larry McCurry and now Charley Moody. Only four of our original eleven remained. Four candles still burned brightly. Seven smoldered. Funny, I had not remembered seeing eleven candles before now. We had only brought six.

Peter Woods stood watch over Webb Easterly. He shook his head, thinking about all the fire power we had brought with us, only to leave it in the trunk of his Lincoln Town Car. Wayne and Brody Henderson stood shoulder to shoulder, two brothers now at peace, hopefully no longer in need of a head doctor.

I had found my possible soul mate in Cassandra Blake. And there was Ezek, our new friend. He was a piece of work.

"She's gone," whispered our medium.

"Premonition," I asked her.

"No, fact," she answered. "Returning the bible with that letter from her brother enclosed, paved her way to the other side. I don't think her helping us here hurt either. She brought peace to the house and your lives."

"But at what cost," I answered. "Five of my best friends have died in less than a week. Let's get to a phone and call the sheriff. I hope we can convince him we had nothing to do with this."

"He'll never believe you as long as I'm alive," shouted Webb Easterly.

"Just say the word, Payne," spoke up Peter, aiming Jimbo Price's pistol at Easterly's head.

"Don't waste a bullet. He's not worth it. Hopefully, this journal holds all the answers."

"This is the best Halloween I've ever had," bragged a toothless Ezek. "Can we do this every year?"

The Journal

Stan Bronson had begun scribbling in his journal the summer of 1969, after we had graduated, a few months shy of the first year anniversary of that Halloween night. He displayed excellent penmanship, and articulated his feelings masterfully in the earlier entries, but as the years whizzed by, the journal took on a darker content. The entries were fewer and far between. I attributed this to a combination of his heavier drinking and troubled soul.

August 31ˢᵗ, 1969

I'm writing this for me right now. Maybe some day it will help straighten this mess out, but now's not the time for that. I feel so alone.

It's been almost ten months since that night that Donnie Ray Clark died, and I still have awful nightmares about it. It was wrong for Payne to take so much of the blame. None of us did anything, including me and I'm pretty sure I know exactly what happened. Lester, Leroy and Charlie had planned to let me take the fall, but somehow I gathered my senses. I sobered up enough to make it down those stairs. It's taken me a while to piece everything together, because so much of that night is a blur. It sort of came back to me in spurts. I'm still not sure how much of it is real.

Lester kept coming around for the longest time, asking me what I remembered. I haven't told him everything. I don't trust him anymore. He scares the you know what out of me. I think I could end up like Donnie, if I told him everything I remember. That's why I decided to just not say any more, and I pray to God that it will soon just blow over. I reckon what I find most troubling is how all us friends seemed to have gone our separate ways. I thought we would be inseparable. Things changed last Halloween.

I've been drinking more than just on weekends, but it sure is hard for an eighteen year old to afford it. I need to find a job. I've managed to sneak a bottle or two of wine from Five Points under my coat. I hate stealing. I hate those nightmares even worse. I haven't seen the others too much since we graduated. I guess I've seen them, but we don't hang out or talk any more. I wish I had a time machine, and could go back before that night and make things turn out differently, but I can't. I wish I could tell somebody what I think happened, but nobody is talking about it, except all the town people, and they hate our guts, especially Payne's. We could have won the state football championship in 68 if Donnie would have been around, I bet. That's why they hate us so much, I suppose, because he didn't make it.

October 1969, Halloween

Lester showed up out of the blue and really scared me today. He was acting crazier than usual. He outright threatened to do me physical harm, if I ever said anything to anybody about that night. I think he knows I saw more than I have admitted to him, and being Halloween he's thinking about it a lot. We probably all are. I just keep pretending like I was too drunk. I really was, but something real bad happened. I think that old creepy house had something to do with it. People would really think I was crazy as a bat if, I told them what I really think happened. Nope, I'm staying alive and keeping my mouth shut. I started to put it in here, but sure if I did, that Lester would get a hold of it and I don't know what he might do. The people are still acting mean to us, even the kids. They act like it's our entire fault, even a year later. It's just not fair. Charlie Moody shooting his mouth off with all his lies sure didn't help. For the life of me, I don't know why anybody believed him in the first place. He's such a liar. Lester doesn't bother him though, because he isn't telling what really happened. I hate the way I'm still picked on all the time. It is just worse than ever. I miss my pals. I miss how it used to be.

Charlie Moody, before he died, had said our answers were here. So far all I have read are the babblings of a tormented soul.

I skipped over page after page of his entries; many just repeated what he had already said. Sometimes he would scribble out his feelings daily, then skip weeks, even months before another entry. I could tell he had been troubled, just as badly as the rest of us; probably worse than most of us.

None of his entries were explaining what really happened, even though he hinted about it continuously. He really feared putting it down on paper. Maybe he thought it would be too final, too real. His so called diary over the first few years seemed to more or less be his way of keeping tabs on us, and how he perceived our lives were going. Then abruptly his entries ceased, skipping seventeen years until October of 1987, eleven days before that night we would return to the scene of the crime.

October 20th 1987

I found my journal after all these years. I forgot I had it, and don't know why I hadn't tossed it. I'm not thinking too clearly. I really ought to stop drinking. I think about stopping a lot, but then I don't. Drinking, no; passing out makes me forget until the nightmares wake me up. They've gotten bad again. Drinking is not helping anymore. I saw myself in the mirror the other day. I didn't recognize me. I stopped looking at me too many years ago. I didn't like what I saw then, and what I remembered. I decided I should tell somebody. Funny, I can't remember who I should tell what, but I know it is important. Maybe I'll remember tomorrow. Right now I need a drink, and have to take a leak.

Another entry (no date)

The chickens have come back to roost. The chickens have finally come back to roost. I need to clear my head. I need to be ready. Something tells me we're going to set it right. We need to make it right. I saw Donnie Ray Clarks' daddy today. He knows the time is near too. I could tell. I don't like him. He's a bad man, just like Lester turned out to be. I'm glad Lester went away, but I don't think he's gone for good. He probably knows it's starting again too. Payne shouldn't be working for Donnie's daddy. He doesn't care much for Payne. He still hates him and blames him. He blames all of us, but he especially blames Payne

I saw the one eyed one last night. The Cyclops is back. I think that means something, but I can't will my brain right now to know why. I always see a lot of things. I know it's caused from the drinking sometimes. I think this was real, but real isn't always real. I should have ended it long ago. I think I knew the truth, so how could I take the cowards way out, without telling my friends what really happened. I really don't have the guts to take my own life, even with the booze. Just what do I think happened that night up on the third floor of that evil place? I do owe it to them. I owe it to Payne. I owe it to Donnie. I owe it to Leroy. I still don't think Leroy's accident was an accident. I hope it can't read my mind. I think

The sentence just ended. I just feel so bad about what he went through alone. We all fought it alone. That was our biggest mistake.

Another entry without a date

My pen ran out of ink the other day. I forgot where I left my binder. I thought it got stolen. I was afraid it got read. I think that was two days ago, but I'm not sure. I'm not drinking right now. I don't know why I've lost track of time. I don't think so well when I'm drinking. I don't think clearly when I'm not. I think I just wrote the same thing, two different ways. I was at Payne's house today. I saw Shorty and Larry and Stephen and Peter and Payne. Leroy is dead. Charlie is too and I hope Lester is. Poor Brody, he's gone crazier than the rest of us. I like Cassandra Blake. I think she likes Payne. I'm supposed to meet all of them like old times at the Belmont Hotel. It's just a block away. I had my binder hidden behind the Roughhouse.

I'm going to finish this before I meet them. It helps me to think better by writing everything out. I wanted to tell them at Payne's house, but I couldn't make myself take my turn at telling. I'll write it here, and let them read it tonight. They need to know what I know. I feel good, lot better than I've felt in along time.

I sort of remember going up those stairs, then everything was fuzzy. I came to a little. Donnie was beating on me. He liked beating on me. Leroy and Charlie and Lester were there too. Donnie was in a bad place and kept pounding on me. Then he stopped. Lester had him by the arm, yelling at him to quit. His eyes, Lester's eyes didn't look right, evil, almost glowing red in the dark. He flung Donnie across the room like he was nothing. Lester never ever did anything like that before.

That really pissed off Donnie. He forgot about me. I was glad. I propped up against the wall and puked down my shirt. Donnie yelled something and ran at Lester, like a wild man. I puked some more, but I think I saw Lester close line Donnie, and he laughed about it. Lester hardly ever laughed out loud about anything. He jumped on top of Donnie and just kept hitting him. I think Leroy and Charlie tried to stop him.

I must of sort of passed out a little. I heard glass breaking, and heard a bunch of yelling. All of them were looking out that window. I heard Leroy ask why did you do that. He said it again, and was talking to Lester. Charlie was saying something too, but I couldn't understand him. Lester threw him out the window. Lester killed Donnie, but what I saw in those eyes wasn't Lester. I closed my eyes and hoped they would leave me alone. They did, but I heard Lester tell Leroy and Charlie to stick with him, and say I did it. He wanted to say I killed Donnie. I couldn't kill anybody. They must have not agreed with Lester, because they left the room.

I took my chance. I went down those stairs. I passed Payne on the way up. I don't know what happened after that, but Payne didn't kill anybody either. Donnie was already dead. I hid and kept my mouth shut. I shouldn't have done that, but back then I couldn't exactly remember everything so good. I thought maybe what I thought might have happened, might not have. I'm sorry for that. I've done stopped drinking. I'm going to do better, because we're all back together now. I don't want to really go back like everybody else though, but I will, if that's what everybody wants to do.

I got this book off a wino. I saw him steal it from Stan. Stan is dead. I reckon his heart or something just give plum out. He's better off than the rest of us, I suspect. That wino shouldn't have stripped off Stan's clothes like that. I put on the Cyclops mask, and really scared the crap out of him. He'll think twice next time.

I read what Stan wrote. I'm not as good at writing as him, but he had it right. I lied and covered up for Lester. I didn't want Payne to catch so much blame, but he didn't get stuck with the killing, not by the law any way.

I never ever saw Lester act like he did that night He was Lester and he wasn't, is best I can tell it. Me and Leroy shouldn't have sided with him after he threw Donnie through that window. We did and I can't take none of it back. Lester, after all them years, went and killed Leroy, because he feared he was going to tell what was true. Me, I just took the coward's way out. I pretended to be dead. I haven't seen Lester since he went out there to find his kids and wife. I don't know if he's dead or alive, and really don't much care. It would be best if he's dead. I think that house did something to him that night, but Payne's the expert on this stuff, not me.

Like everybody else, I was drawn to come back this year. I kept watching everybody. I knew something was fishy. I wish I could have saved Stephen, but those four assholes took me by surprise. I fixed that. I killed all of four for what they done and kept trying to do. That sneaky cop tried to plant those drugs at Payne's house to frame all of you and especially Payne. I fixed that too.

Strange stuff is still going on. I keep riding by that house. I can tell it wants us back. All of us. That Jimbo Price has been following yawl. I've been following him, but there's somebody else out there. That other car was following me or maybe all of us.

I saw Webb Easterly meeting with Jimbo. They've got to be in this together. Easterly must be the one who has been following me. Like Stan, I wanted to say my part to make things right too. I'm sorry for how I lied. I promise I'm not going to let nothing happen to you boys. I know you got to go back to that house. I'm going too. We started it together and we'll end it together. Nineteen years was way too long to wait. We'll fix this thing, if that old house will let us. Nobody is going to stand in our way. I don't know the woman hanging out with yawl, but if she's a friend to yawl, she's a friend of mine too.

Payne, I'm sorry for throwing you under that bus and know this won't make us all square, but I'll try hard the rest of the way to make it right. I reckon that's all I got to say until I see everybody at that house. God bless Stan, Steven, Leroy and Donnie. They didn't do nothing wrong.

The journal clearly absolved us, the survivors, from any wrong doing, other than trespassing, breaking and entering, which the sheriff waved off with a mere hand slap. We concealed Stephen's death, hampered an investigation, but charges were eventually dropped, once the truth was told. Webb Easterly was in the center ring. We had been forgiven.

Lester had been implicated in Donnie's murder, but how do you prosecute a dead man? Same goes for Charley. He had committed five murders, but what can you do? I say let them rest in peace. Donnie, the bastard son of Easterly, ended up being the conduit for the other bastard son, Claudette L'ouverture's Donhnall. Everything perfectly aligned that night in the octagon universe.

Webb Easterly had been accused of murdering Jimbo Price, Lester, Larry, had been implicated in Stephen's death, and for killing Charley, charges of attempted murder and conspiracy to commit murder. A trial would have to be delayed, because he now occupied Brody Henderson's padded cell in Columbia. Somehow that's a fitting ending for one so obsessed.

I am presently preparing for a local book signing at the Radio station, my first signing in Abbeville. Night Train and DABO-DOO invited me to appear. It should be a hoot with those two boys. My novel, The Perfect Spook House, has been number one on the New York Times Best Sellers List for the eleventh consecutive week. It's my new lucky number.

Go figure. I am an accomplished author with ink flowing through my veins. Royalties have enabled me to place a down payment of that house on the Cedar Springs Road. My fiancée, Cassandra Blake, and I plan to restore and convert it into a bed and breakfast. It will be the perfect haunted house experience.

Peter Woods, investor and primary caretaker, will maintain the house and its acreage. He'll be assisted by Ezek Paterson, who now resides in the restored cabin. Ezek, with no fear of the unknown, seems so at home there.

My old pals, Shorty and Brody Henderson, no longer require psychiatric assistance, even after the new trauma they had endured at the house. Both plan to work a couple of weekends a month at the octagon house, recapping their encounters for the tourist.

I so look forward to those upcoming Halloween nights, when we will unveil The Perfect Spook House Experience to those paying the price for a night's stay. Werewolf and Cyclops sightings will surely be a part of the adventure, providing I can prevent Ezek from going monster slayer on them. He believes, you know.

This is the best I can do for a happy ending, considering how much we have lost. I miss every single one of them, and how they touched my life. I just finished watching Night of the Monsters again for the zillionth time. A copy of our cheesy three minute movie is included with every novel purchase. I was no Spielberg back then. I could be one now.

Larry would be proud of me. Cassandra and I have been attending my old church. That's where we plan to be married. Shorty will be my best man. The other boys will be there too. We'll have our reception at the Rough House, in memory of Stan. I convinced Sheldon, the owner, to add Gin and Pickle Juice Shooters to his drink menu.

We sure did give Stephen one heck of a send off. He was buried with the wolf man mask, no silver bullets. Peter is serious with Katherine, his ex-doctor. I'm pulling for them. Brody is living a normal life. Shorty, well, he and Kim worked things out, marital bliss is alive and well. God bless my friends, my old ones and my new ones. The town has forgiven us. I'm here to stay. It is where I belong, where all of us belong, where we've always belonged, The Perfect Home, in the Perfect Town, why would anyone ever want to live any other place. Halloween returns in eleven days, our first as a bed and breakfast. I can't wait to see what happens next. Can you?

"Nature is a haunted house--
but Art--is a house that tries to be haunted."
— Emily Dickinson

www.ingramcontent.com/pod-product-compliance
Lightning Source LLC
Chambersburg PA
CBHW051257210726
48287CB00002B/542